THE HARDY BOYS

UNDERCOVER BROTHERS™

PAPERCUTZ™

THE **HARDY BOYS** ®

Graphic Novels
Available from Papercutz
#1 The Ocean of Osyria
#2 Identity Theft
#3 Mad House
#4 Malled
#5 See You, Sea Me (Coming May 2006)
$7.95 each in paperback
$12.95 each in hardcover

Please add $3.00 for postage and handling for the
first book, add $1.00 for each additional book.
Send for our catalog:
Papercutz
555 Eighth Avenue, Suite 1202
New York, NY 10018
www.papercutz.com

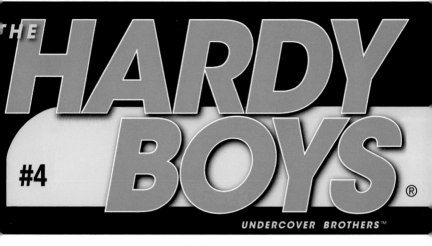

THE HARDY BOYS

#4

BOYS ®

UNDERCOVER BROTHERS™

Malled

SCOTT LOBDELL • Writer

DANIEL RENDON • Artist

Based on the series by
FRANKLIN W. DIXON

PAPERCUTZ™

New York

J-GN
HARDY BOYS
369-9249

Malled
SCOTT LOBDELL – Writer
DANIEL RENDON — Artist
BRYAN SENKA – Letterer
LAURIE E. SMITH — Colorist
JIM SALICRUP
Editor-in-Chief

ISBN-10: 1-59707-014-9 paperback edition
ISBN-13: 978-1-59707-014-0 paperback edition
ISBN-10: 1-59707-015-7 hardcover edition
ISBN-13: 978-1-59707-015-7 hardcover edition

10   9   8   7   6   5   4   3   2   1

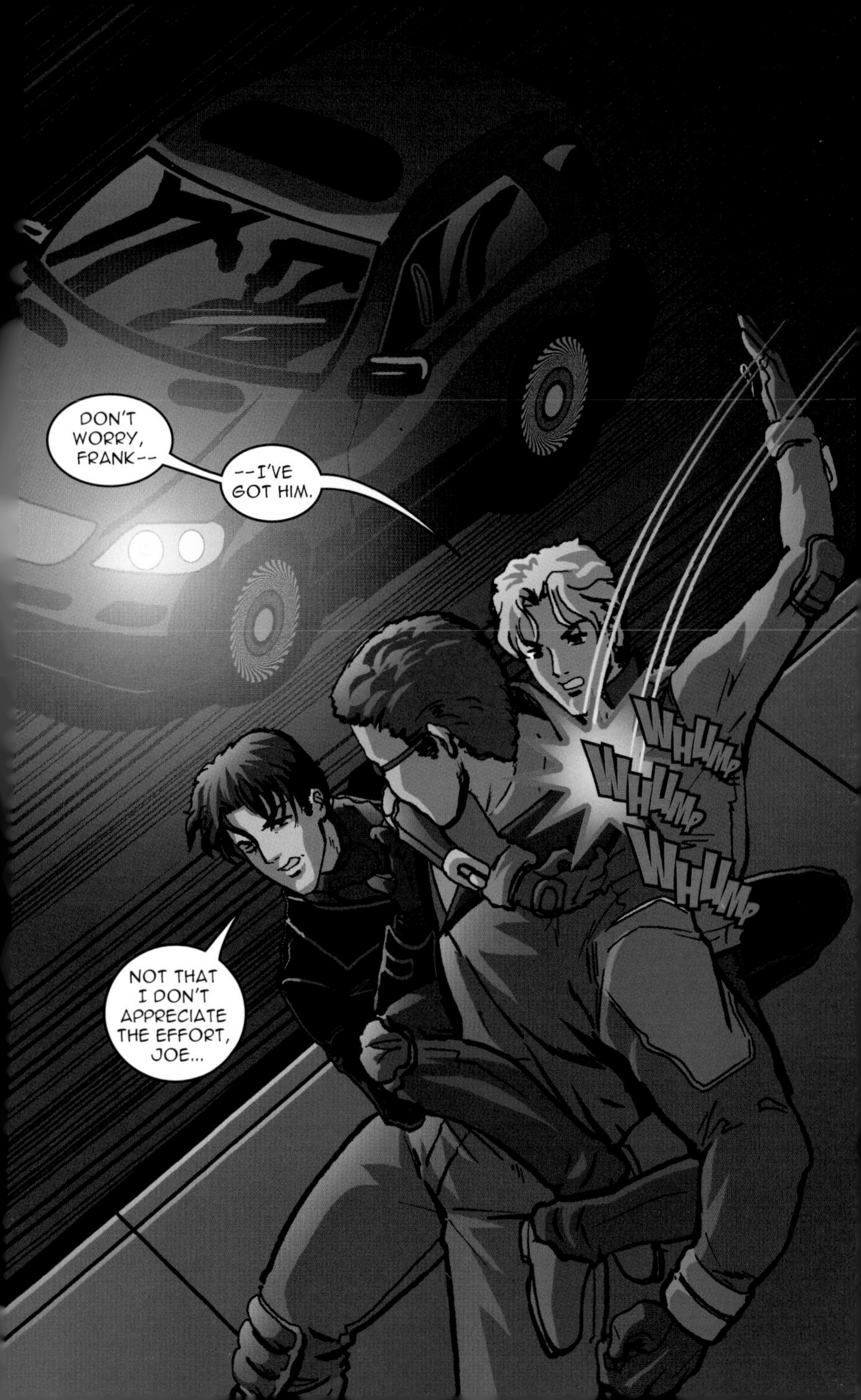
DON'T WORRY, FRANK--
--I'VE GOT HIM.
WHUMP
WHUMP
WHUMP
NOT THAT I DON'T APPRECIATE THE EFFORT, JOE...

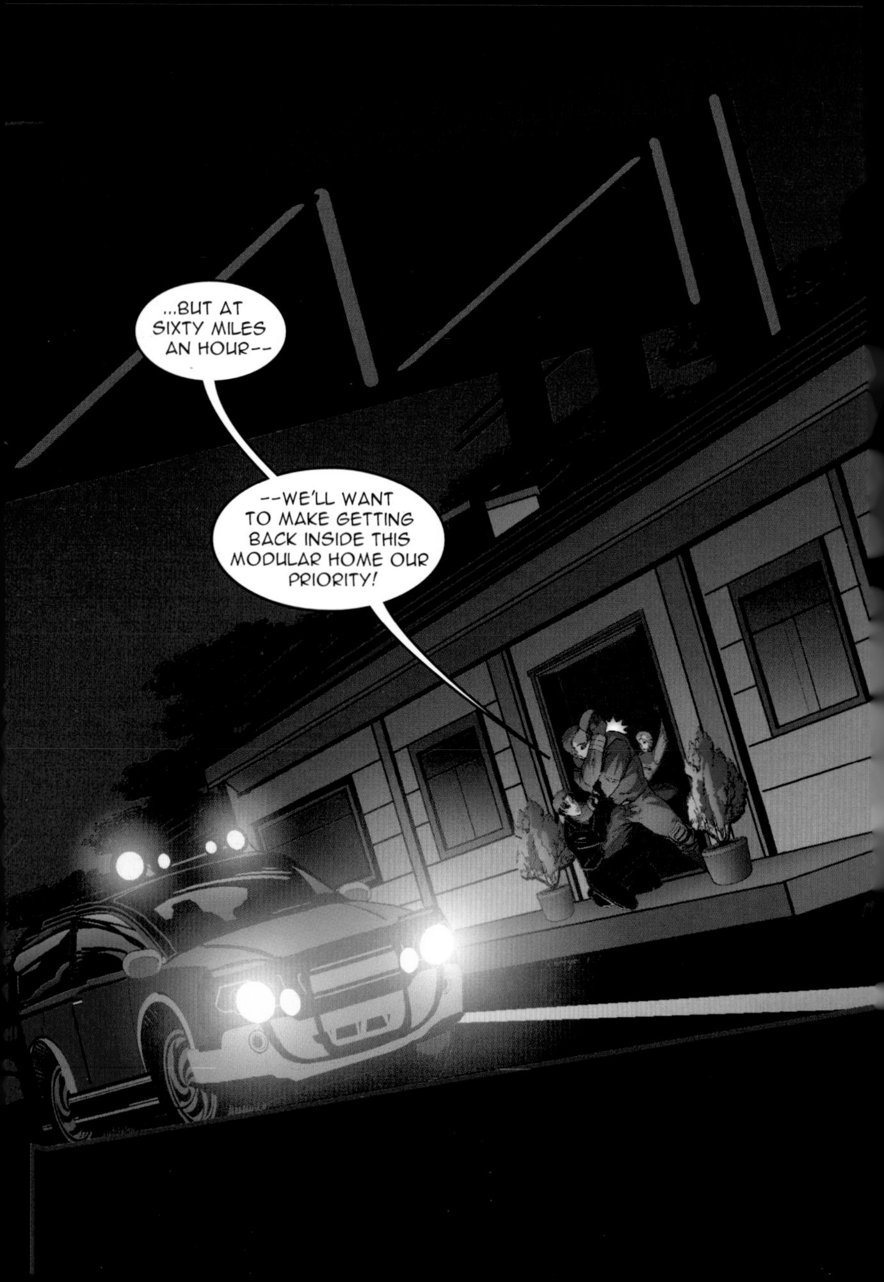
...BUT AT SIXTY MILES AN HOUR--
--WE'LL WANT TO MAKE GETTING BACK INSIDE THIS MODULAR HOME OUR PRIORITY!

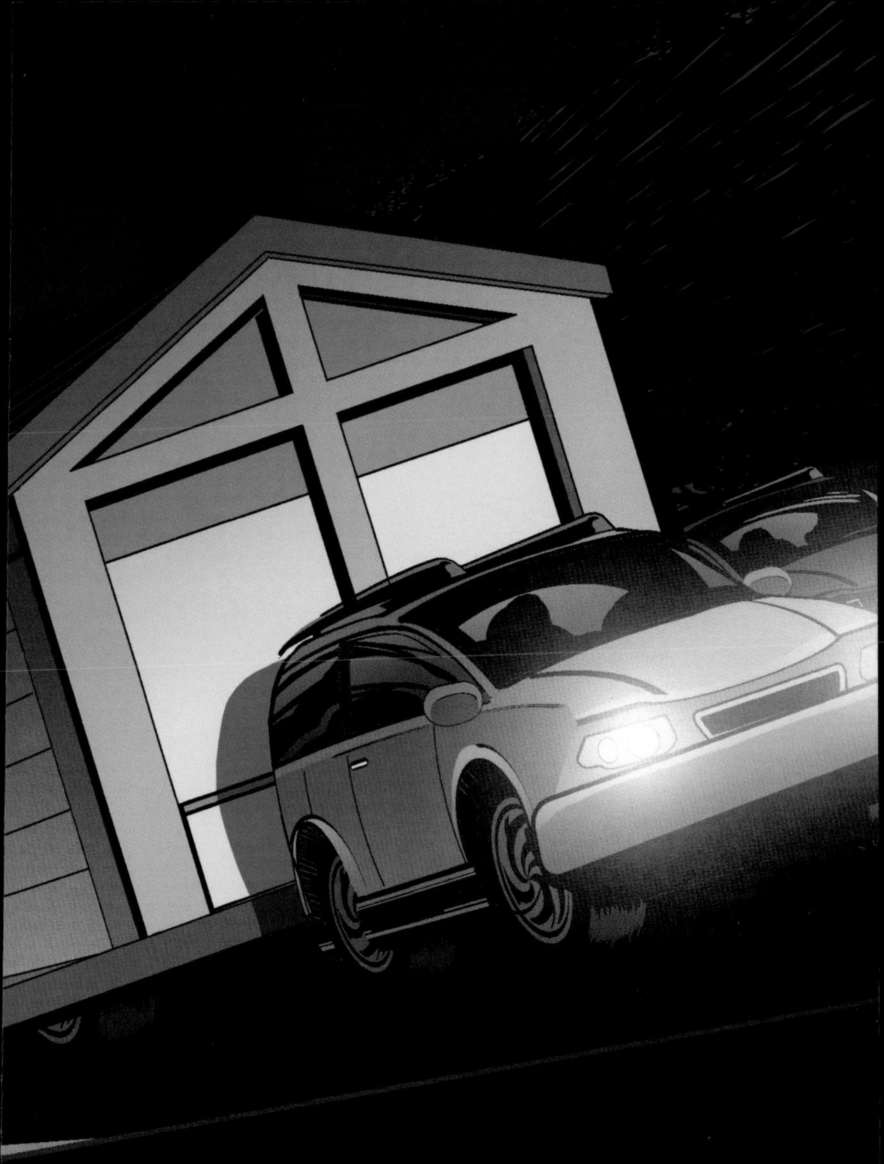

CHAPTER ONE:
“What A Long Strange Drive It’s Been”

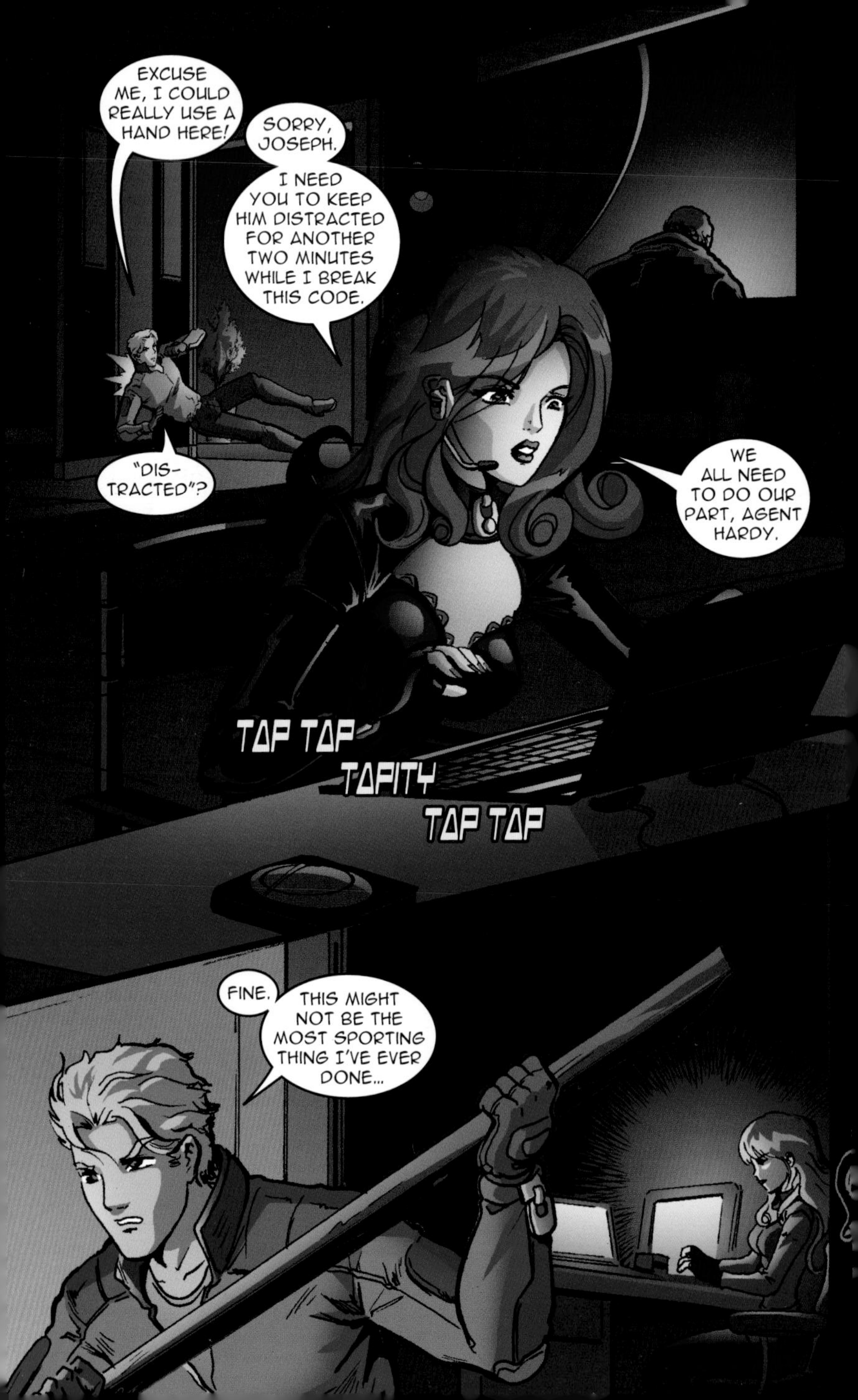
EXCUSE ME, I COULD REALLY USE A HAND HERE!
SORRY, JOSEPH.
I NEED YOU TO KEEP HIM DISTRACTED FOR ANOTHER TWO MINUTES WHILE I BREAK THIS CODE.
"DIS-TRACTED"?
WE ALL NEED TO DO OUR PART, AGENT HARDY.
TAP TAP TAPITY TAP TAP
FINE.
THIS MIGHT NOT BE THE MOST SPORTING THING I'VE EVER DONE...

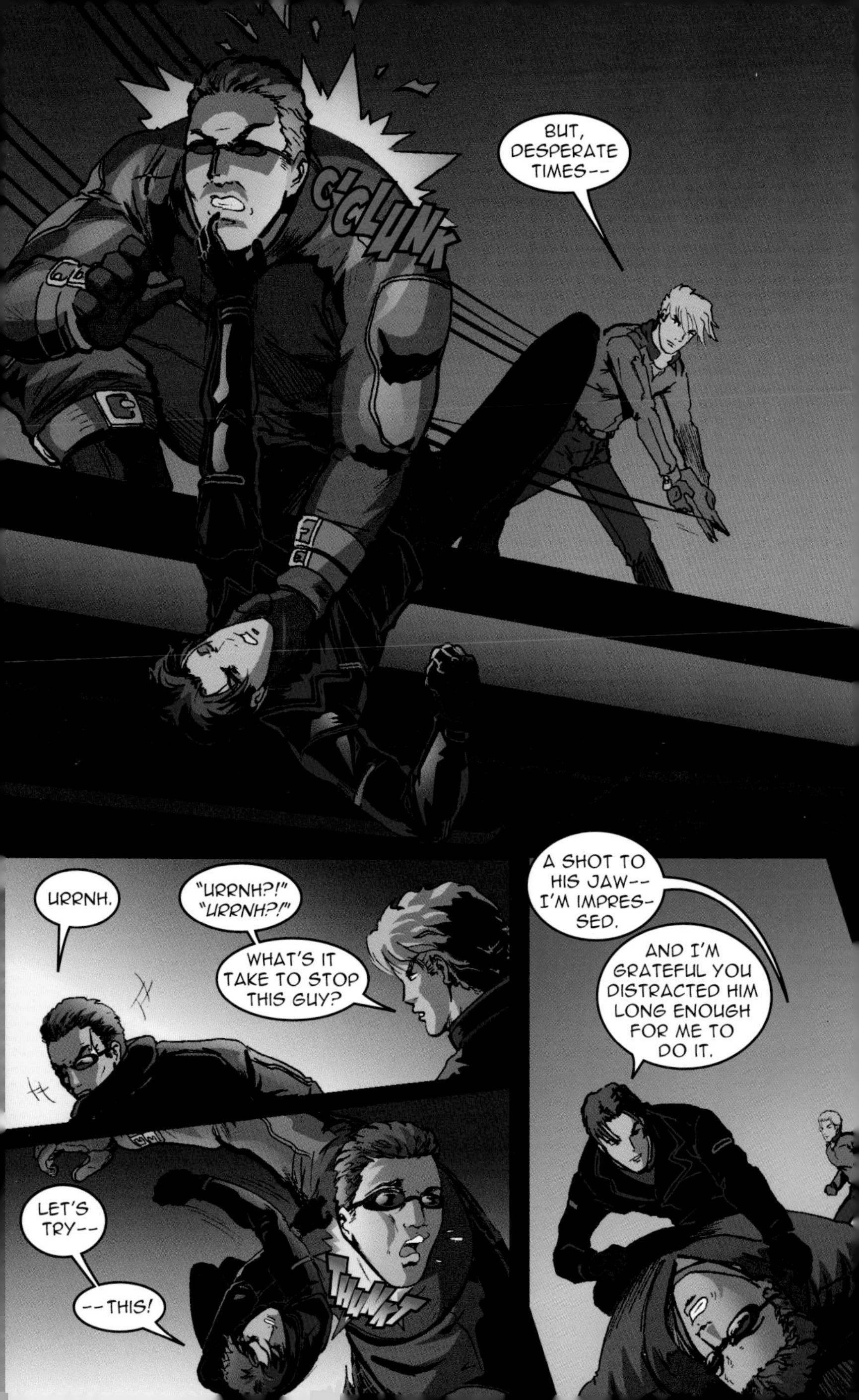
C-CLUNK
BUT, DESPERATE TIMES--
URRNH.
"URRNH?!" "URRNH?!"
WHAT'S IT TAKE TO STOP THIS GUY?
LET'S TRY--
--THIS!
THUNK
A SHOT TO HIS JAW-- I'M IMPRESSED.
AND I'M GRATEFUL YOU DISTRACTED HIM LONG ENOUGH FOR ME TO DO IT.

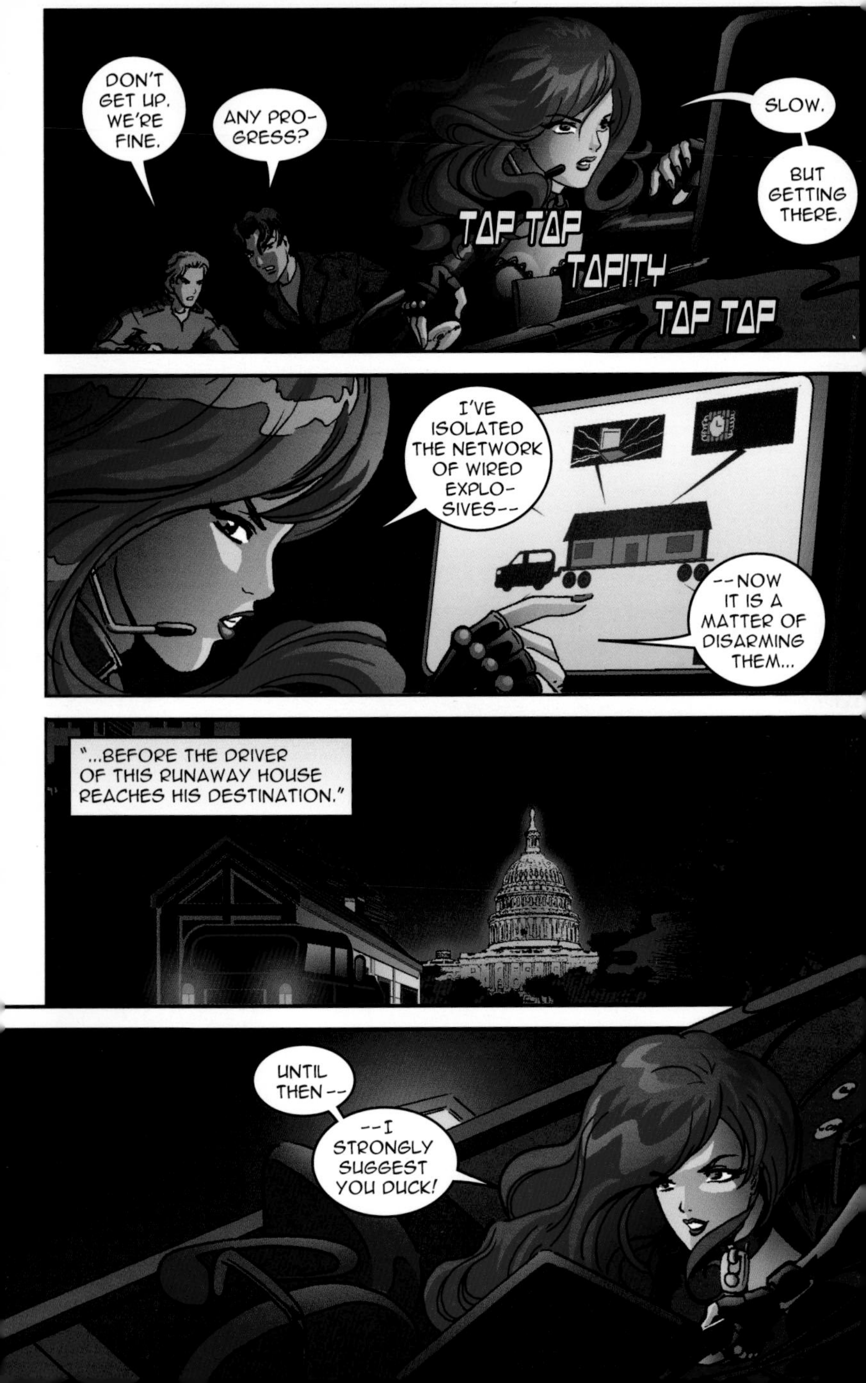
DON'T GET UP. WE'RE FINE.
ANY PRO-GRESS?
SLOW.
BUT GETTING THERE.
TAP TAP
TAPITY
TAP TAP
I'VE ISOLATED THE NETWORK OF WIRED EXPLO-SIVES--
--NOW IT IS A MATTER OF DISARMING THEM...
"...BEFORE THE DRIVER OF THIS RUNAWAY HOUSE REACHES HIS DESTINATION."
UNTIL THEN--
--I STRONGLY SUGGEST YOU DUCK!

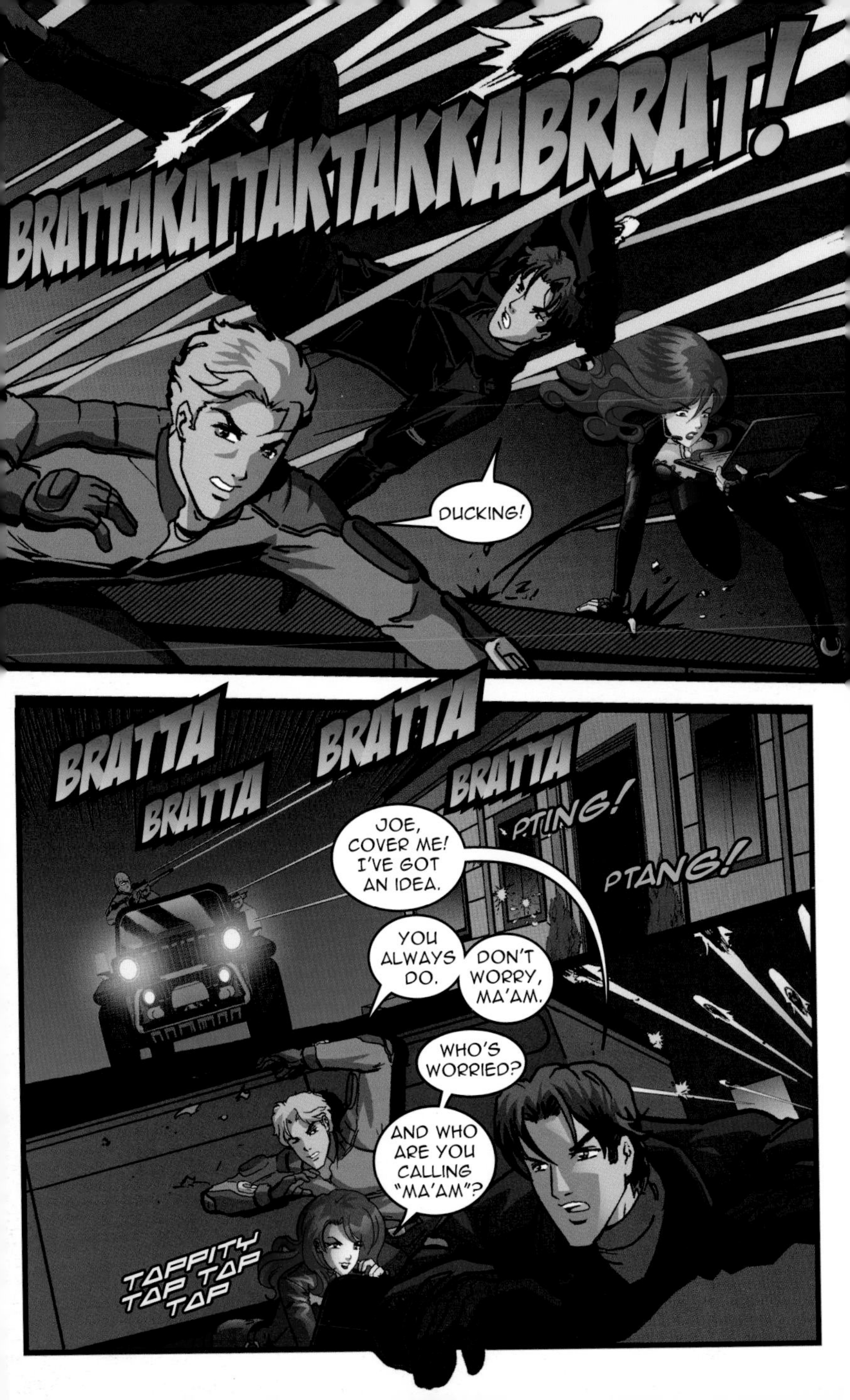
BRATTAKATTAKTAKKABRRAT!
DUCKING!
BRATTA
BRATTA
BRATTA
BRATTA
PTING!
PTANG!
JOE, COVER ME! I'VE GOT AN IDEA.
YOU ALWAYS DO.
DON'T WORRY, MA'AM.
WHO'S WORRIED?
AND WHO ARE YOU CALLING "MA'AM"?
TAPPITY TAP TAP TAP

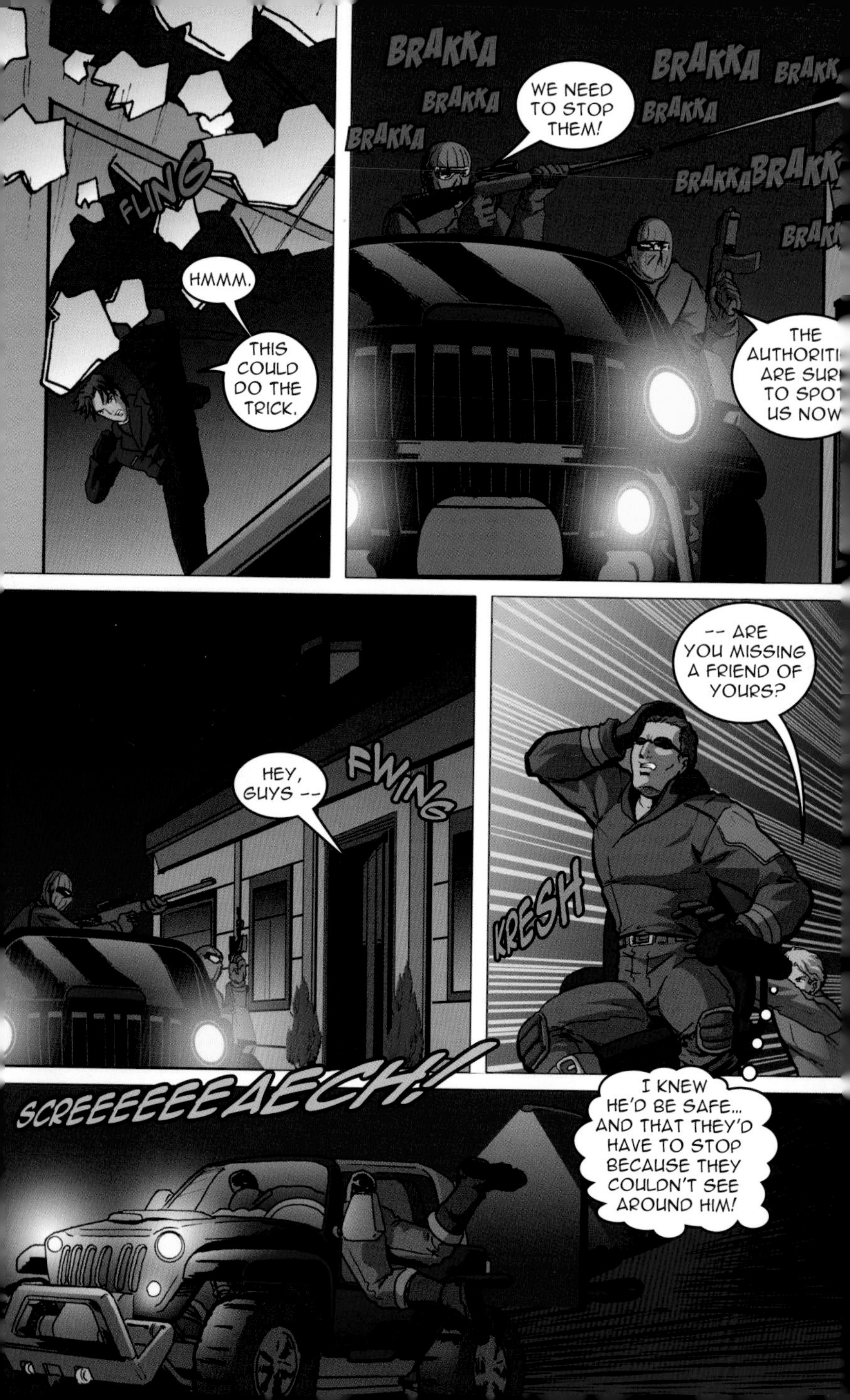
FLING
HMMM.
THIS COULD DO THE TRICK.
BRAKKA
BRAKKA
BRAKKA
WE NEED TO STOP THEM!
BRAKKA
BRAKKA
BRAKKA
BRAKKABRAKK
THE AUTHORITI ARE SUR TO SPOT US NOW
HEY, GUYS --
FWING
-- ARE YOU MISSING A FRIEND OF YOURS?
KRESH
SCREEEEEEEAECH!!
I KNEW HE'D BE SAFE... AND THAT THEY'D HAVE TO STOP BECAUSE THEY COULDN'T SEE AROUND HIM!

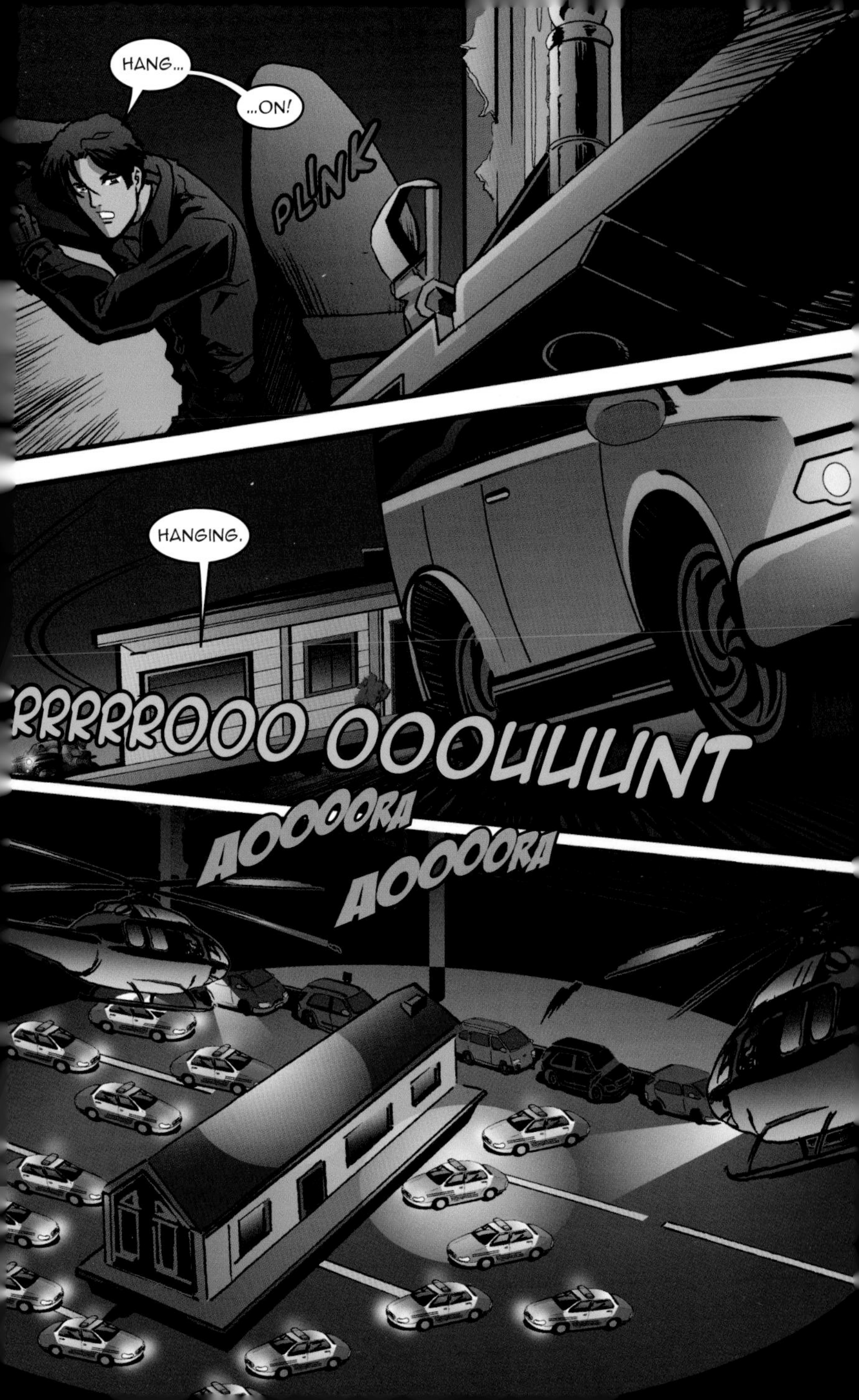
HANG...
...ON!
PLINK
HANGING.
RRRRROOO OOOUUUNT
AOOOORA
AOOOORA

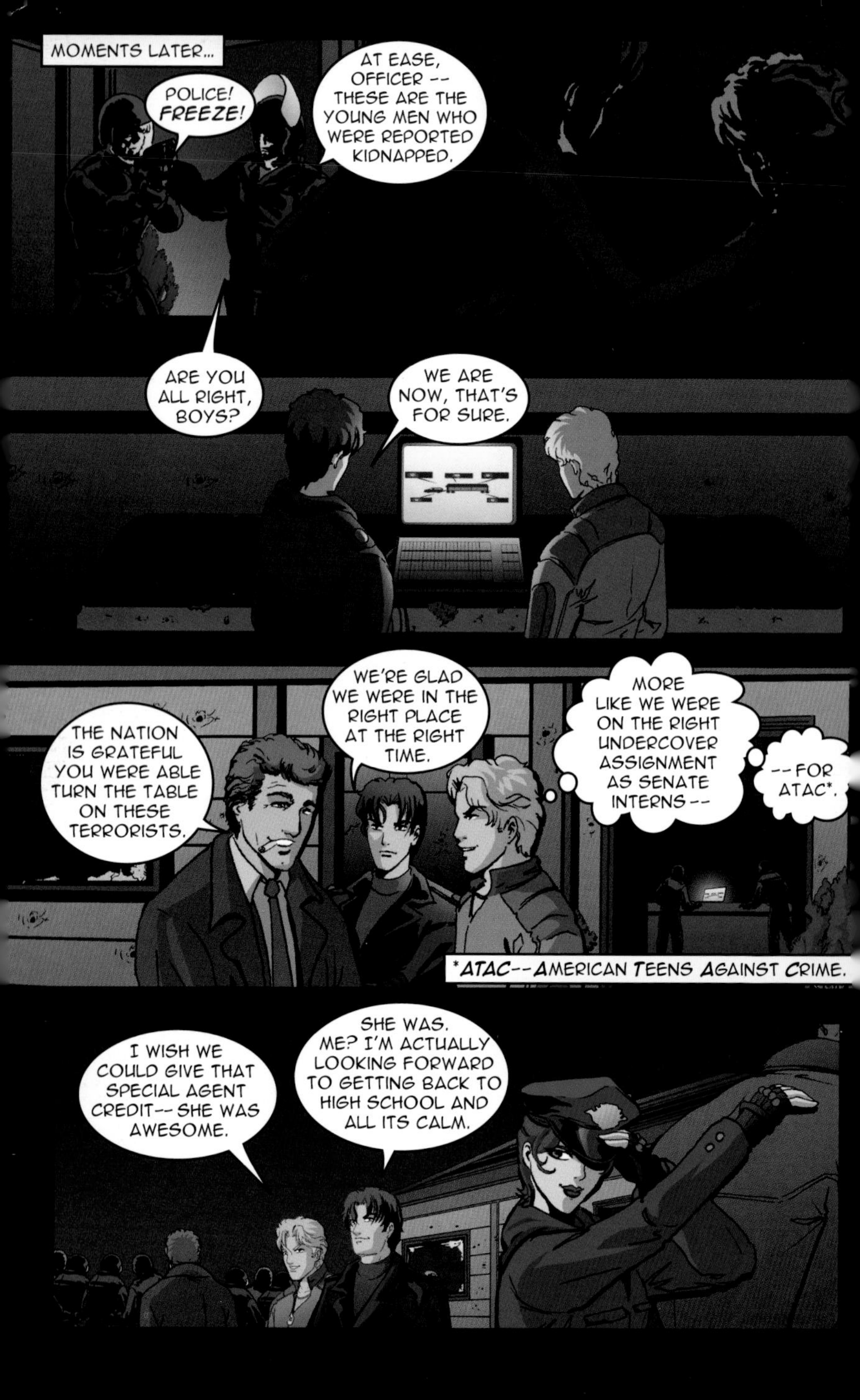
MOMENTS LATER...
POLICE! FREEZE!
AT EASE, OFFICER -- THESE ARE THE YOUNG MEN WHO WERE REPORTED KIDNAPPED.
ARE YOU ALL RIGHT, BOYS?
WE ARE NOW, THAT'S FOR SURE.
THE NATION IS GRATEFUL YOU WERE ABLE TURN THE TABLE ON THESE TERRORISTS.
WE'RE GLAD WE WERE IN THE RIGHT PLACE AT THE RIGHT TIME.
MORE LIKE WE WERE ON THE RIGHT UNDERCOVER ASSIGNMENT AS SENATE INTERNS --
-- FOR ATAC*.
*ATAC--AMERICAN TEENS AGAINST CRIME.
I WISH WE COULD GIVE THAT SPECIAL AGENT CREDIT-- SHE WAS AWESOME.
SHE WAS. ME? I'M ACTUALLY LOOKING FORWARD TO GETTING BACK TO HIGH SCHOOL AND ALL ITS CALM.

CHAPTER TWO: "First and Ten!"

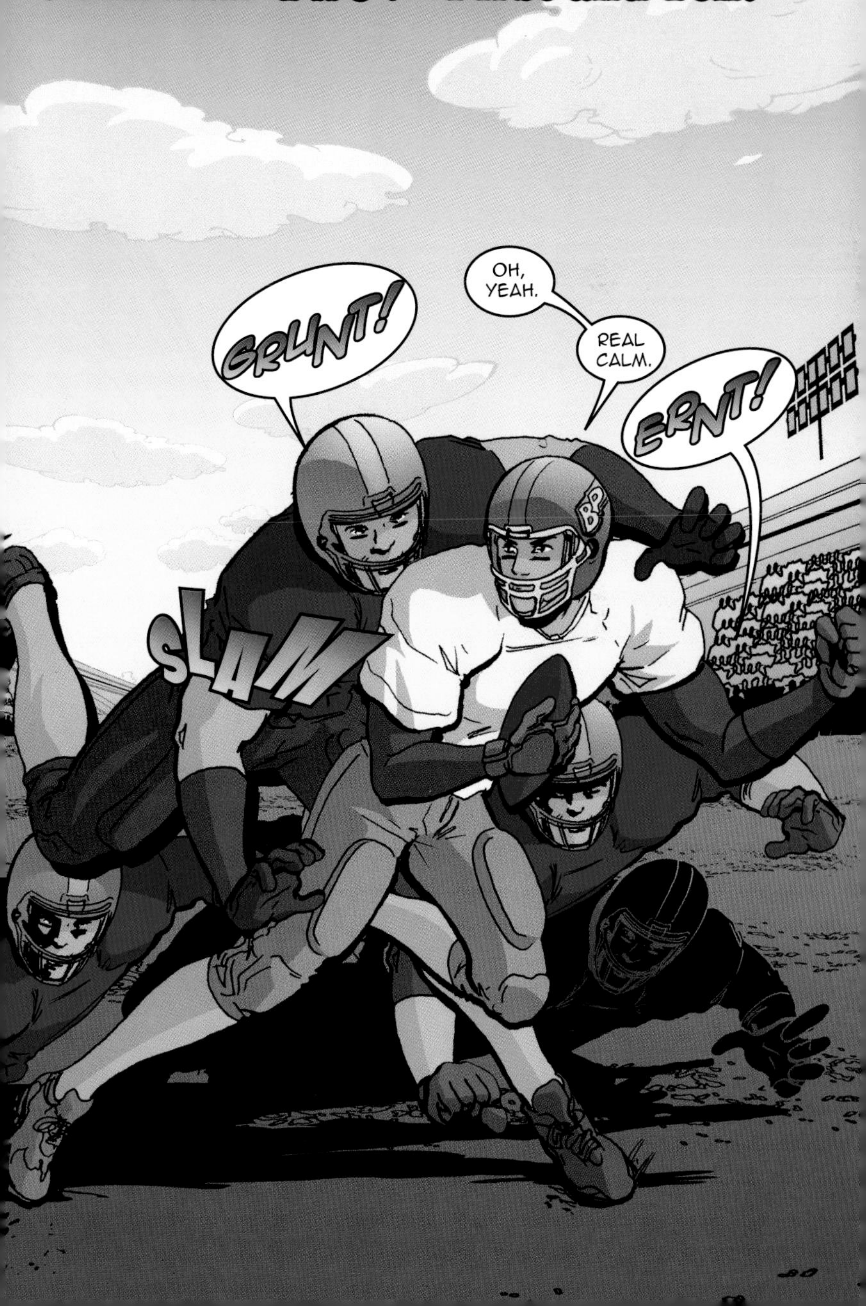

GRUNT!
OH, YEAH.
REAL CALM.
ERNT!
SLAM

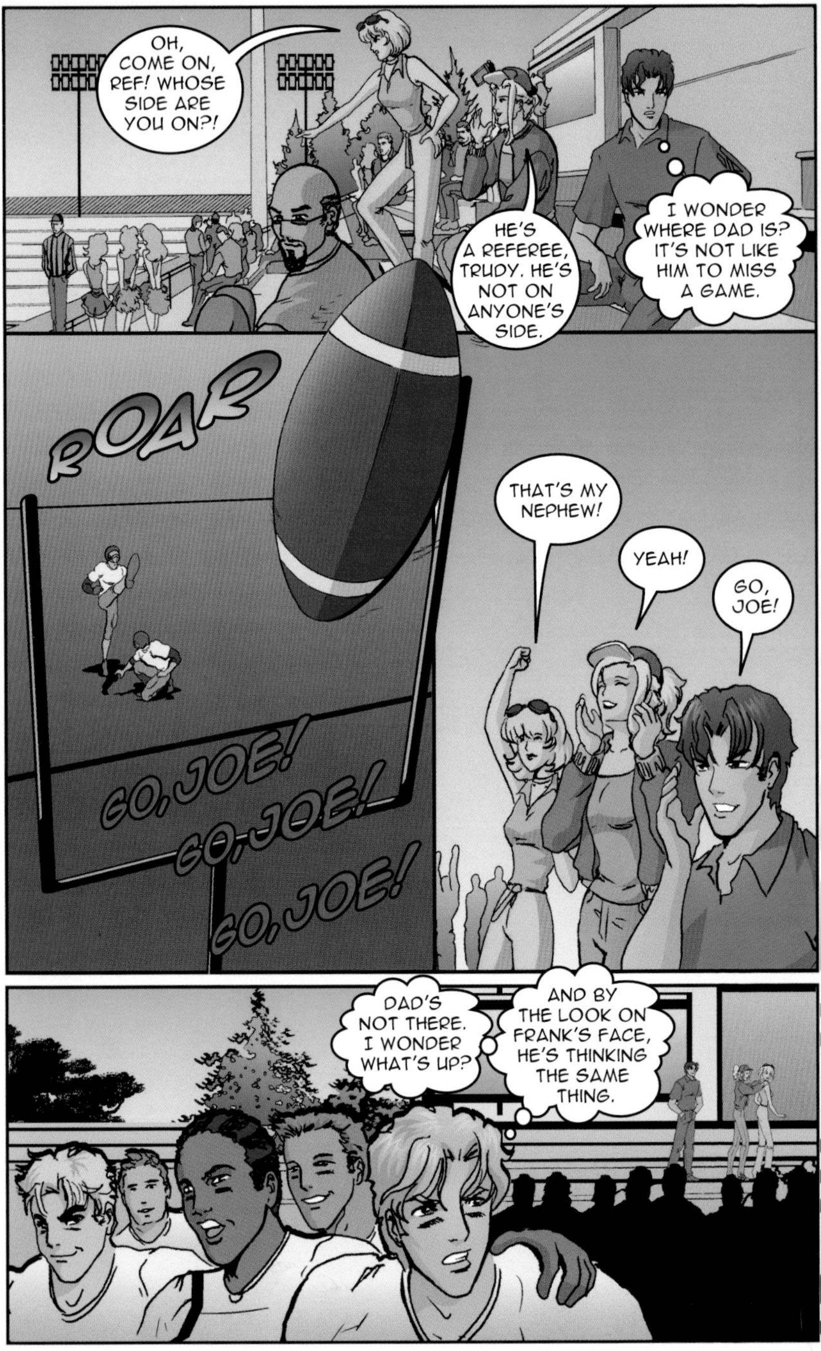
OH, COME ON, REF! WHOSE SIDE ARE YOU ON?!
HE'S A REFEREE, TRUDY. HE'S NOT ON ANYONE'S SIDE.
I WONDER WHERE DAD IS? IT'S NOT LIKE HIM TO MISS A GAME.
ROAR
GO, JOE! GO, JOE! GO, JOE!
THAT'S MY NEPHEW!
YEAH!
GO, JOE!
DAD'S NOT THERE. I WONDER WHAT'S UP?
AND BY THE LOOK ON FRANK'S FACE, HE'S THINKING THE SAME THING.

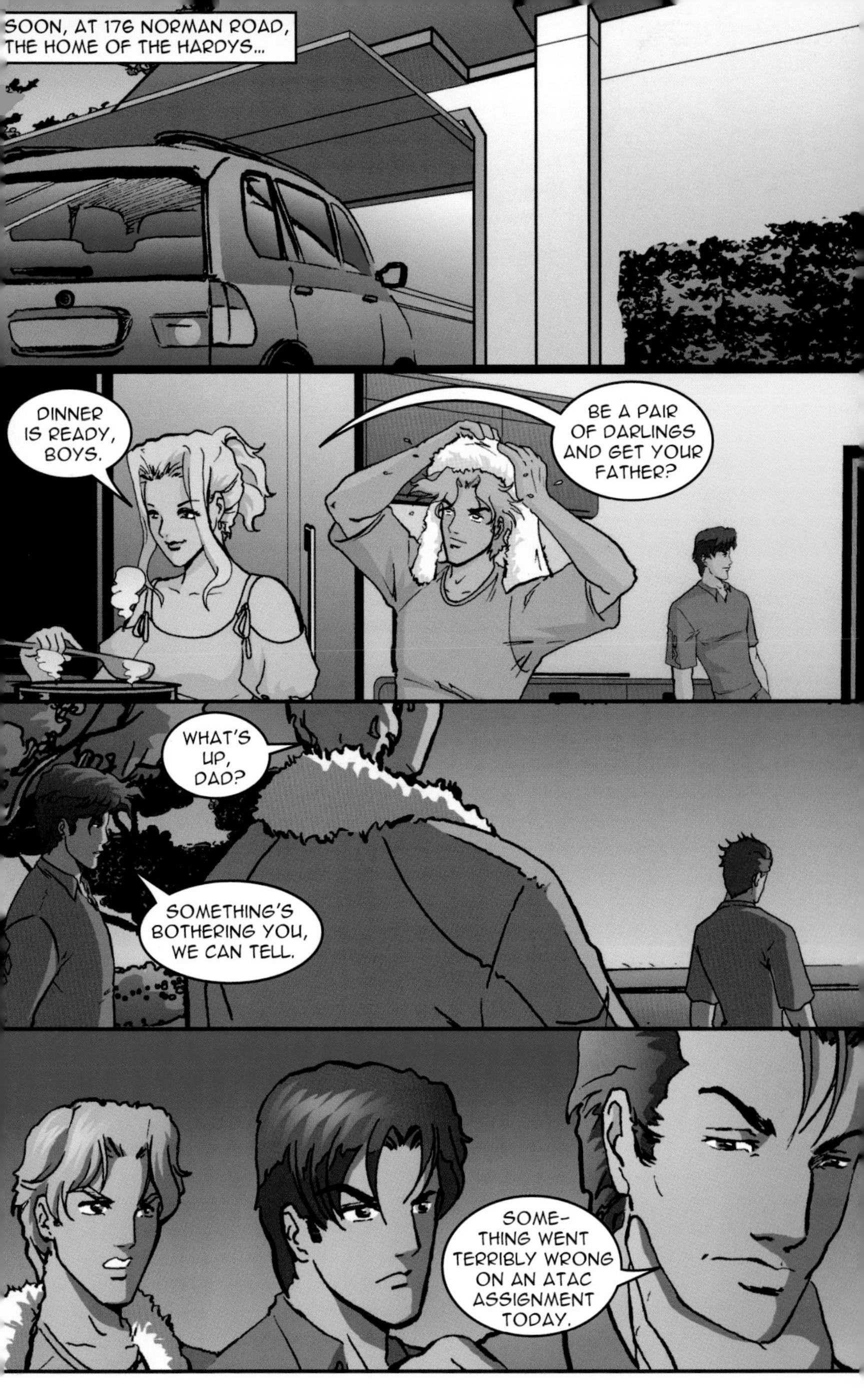
SOON, AT 176 NORMAN ROAD, THE HOME OF THE HARDYS...
DINNER IS READY, BOYS.
BE A PAIR OF DARLINGS AND GET YOUR FATHER?
WHAT'S UP, DAD?
SOMETHING'S BOTHERING YOU, WE CAN TELL.
SOME-THING WENT TERRIBLY WRONG ON AN ATAC ASSIGNMENT TODAY.

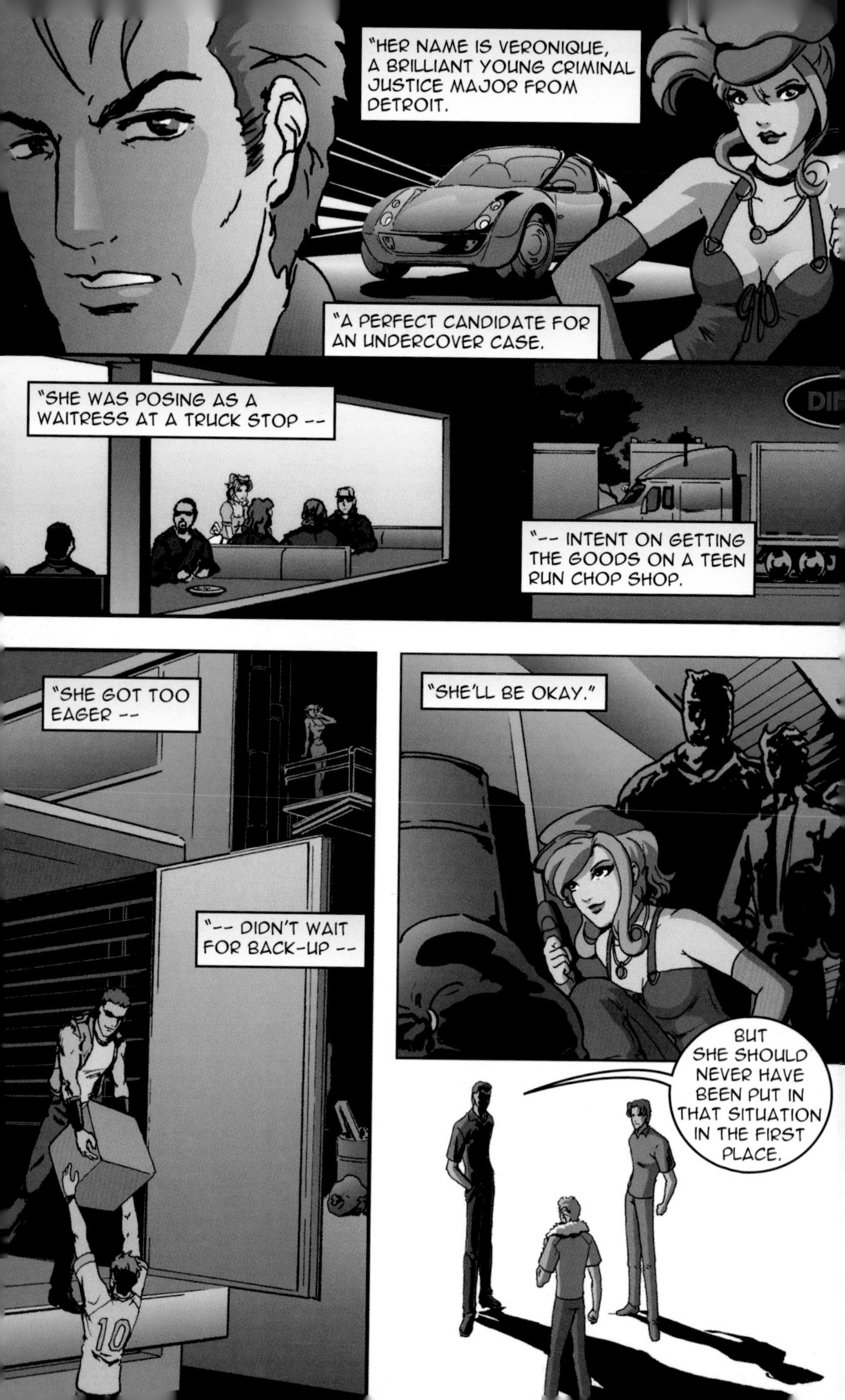
"HER NAME IS VERONIQUE, A BRILLIANT YOUNG CRIMINAL JUSTICE MAJOR FROM DETROIT.
"A PERFECT CANDIDATE FOR AN UNDERCOVER CASE.
"SHE WAS POSING AS A WAITRESS AT A TRUCK STOP --
"-- INTENT ON GETTING THE GOODS ON A TEEN RUN CHOP SHOP.
"SHE GOT TOO EAGER --
"-- DIDN'T WAIT FOR BACK-UP --
"SHE'LL BE OKAY."
BUT SHE SHOULD NEVER HAVE BEEN PUT IN THAT SITUATION IN THE FIRST PLACE.
10

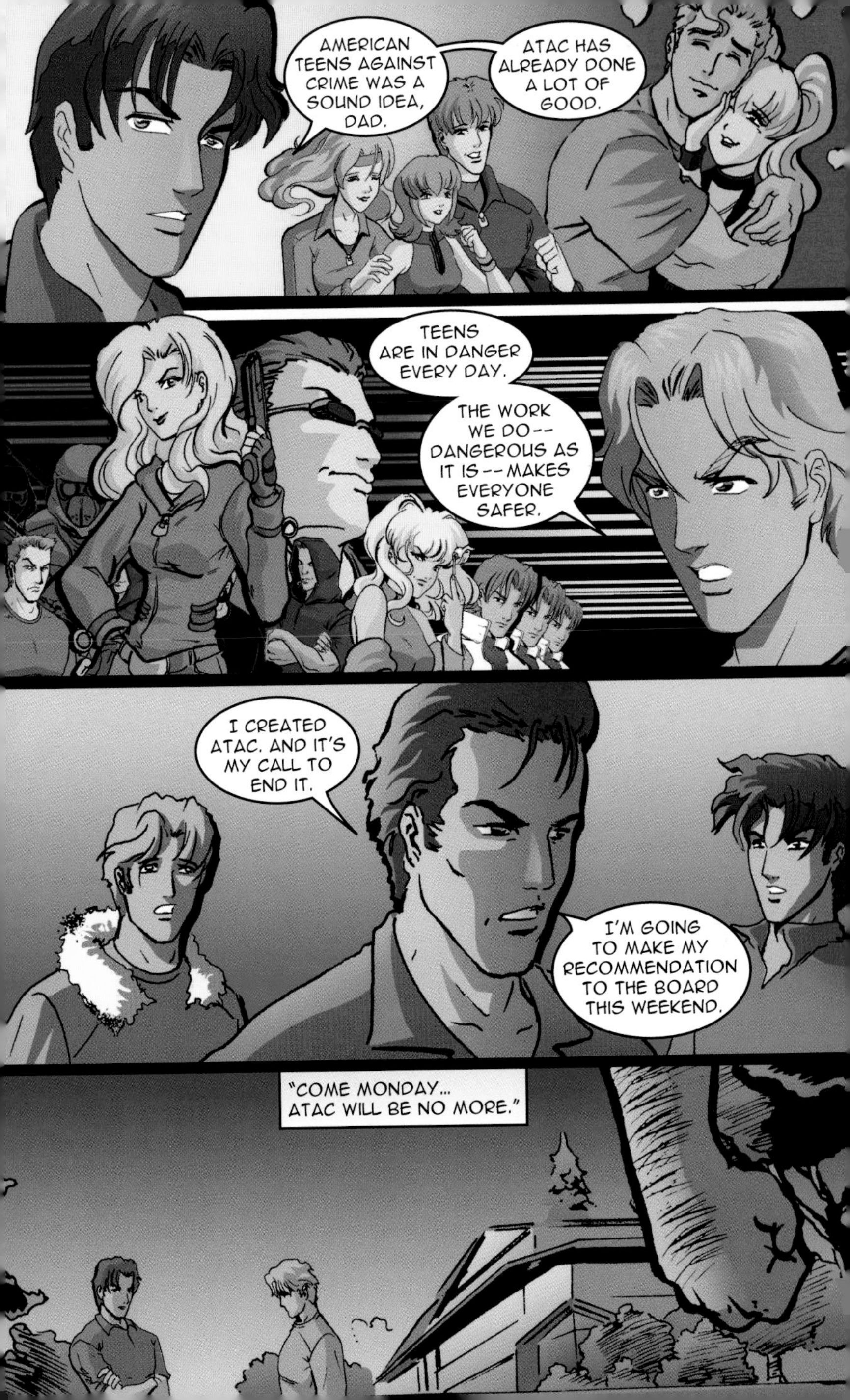
AMERICAN TEENS AGAINST CRIME WAS A SOUND IDEA, DAD.
ATAC HAS ALREADY DONE A LOT OF GOOD.
TEENS ARE IN DANGER EVERY DAY.
THE WORK WE DO-- DANGEROUS AS IT IS--MAKES EVERYONE SAFER.
I CREATED ATAC. AND IT'S MY CALL TO END IT.
I'M GOING TO MAKE MY RECOMMENDATION TO THE BOARD THIS WEEKEND.
"COME MONDAY... ATAC WILL BE NO MORE."

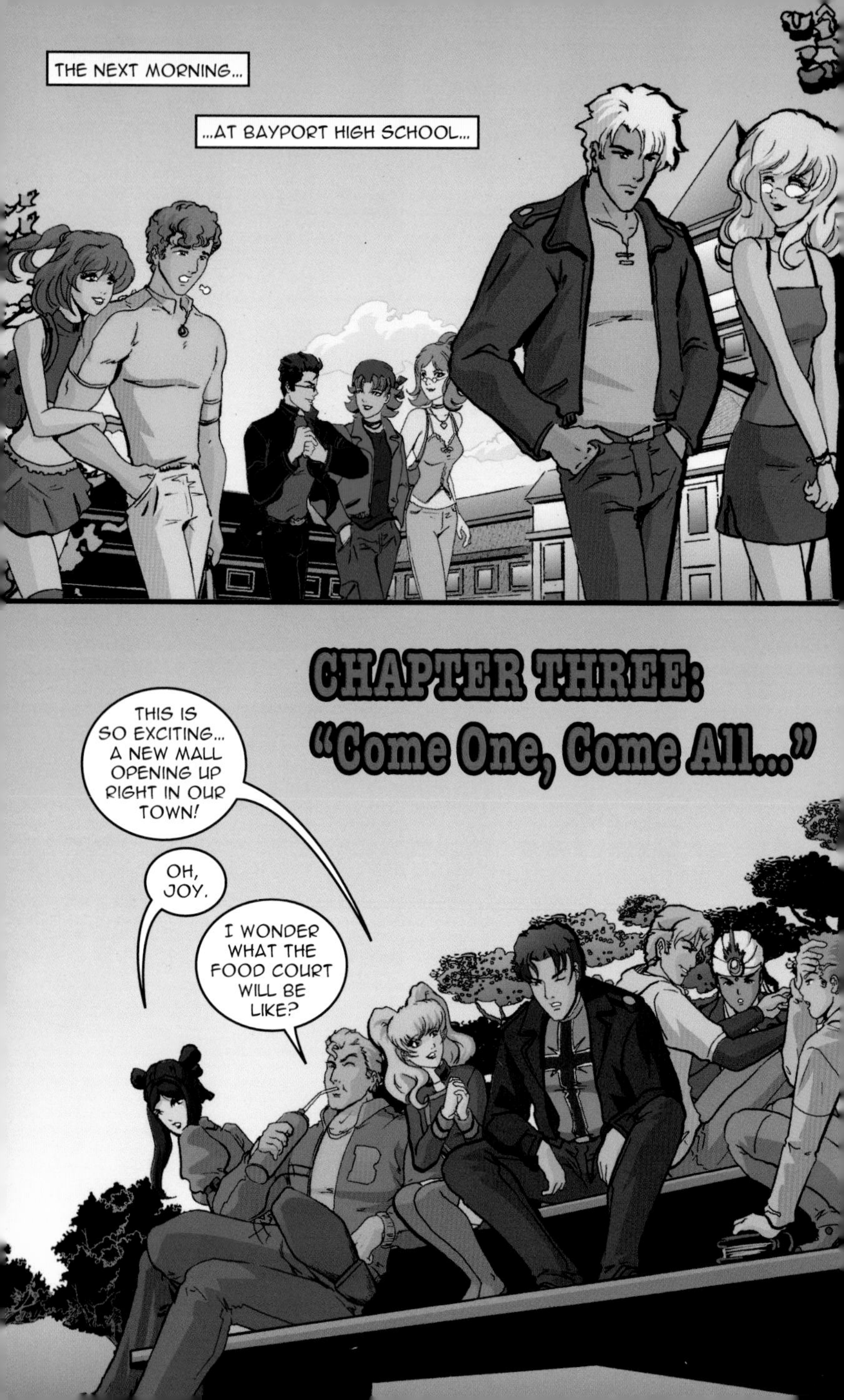
THE NEXT MORNING...
...AT BAYPORT HIGH SCHOOL...
CHAPTER THREE:
"Come One, Come All..."
THIS IS SO EXCITING... A NEW MALL OPENING UP RIGHT IN OUR TOWN!
OH, JOY.
I WONDER WHAT THE FOOD COURT WILL BE LIKE?

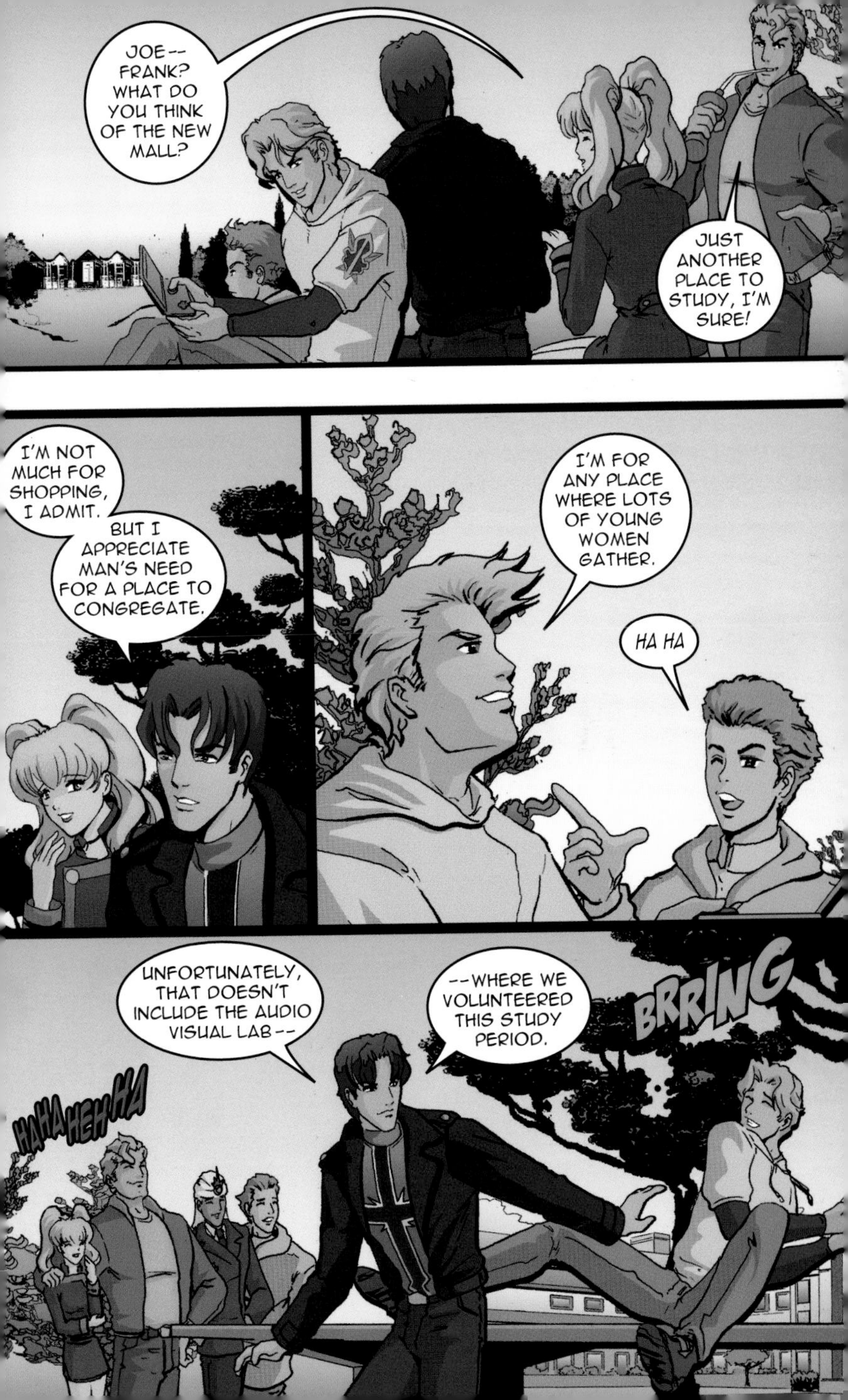
JOE-- FRANK? WHAT DO YOU THINK OF THE NEW MALL?
JUST ANOTHER PLACE TO STUDY, I'M SURE!
I'M NOT MUCH FOR SHOPPING, I ADMIT.
BUT I APPRECIATE MAN'S NEED FOR A PLACE TO CONGREGATE.
I'M FOR ANY PLACE WHERE LOTS OF YOUNG WOMEN GATHER.
HA HA
UNFORTUNATELY, THAT DOESN'T INCLUDE THE AUDIO VISUAL LAB--
--WHERE WE VOLUNTEERED THIS STUDY PERIOD.
BRRING
HAHAHEHHA

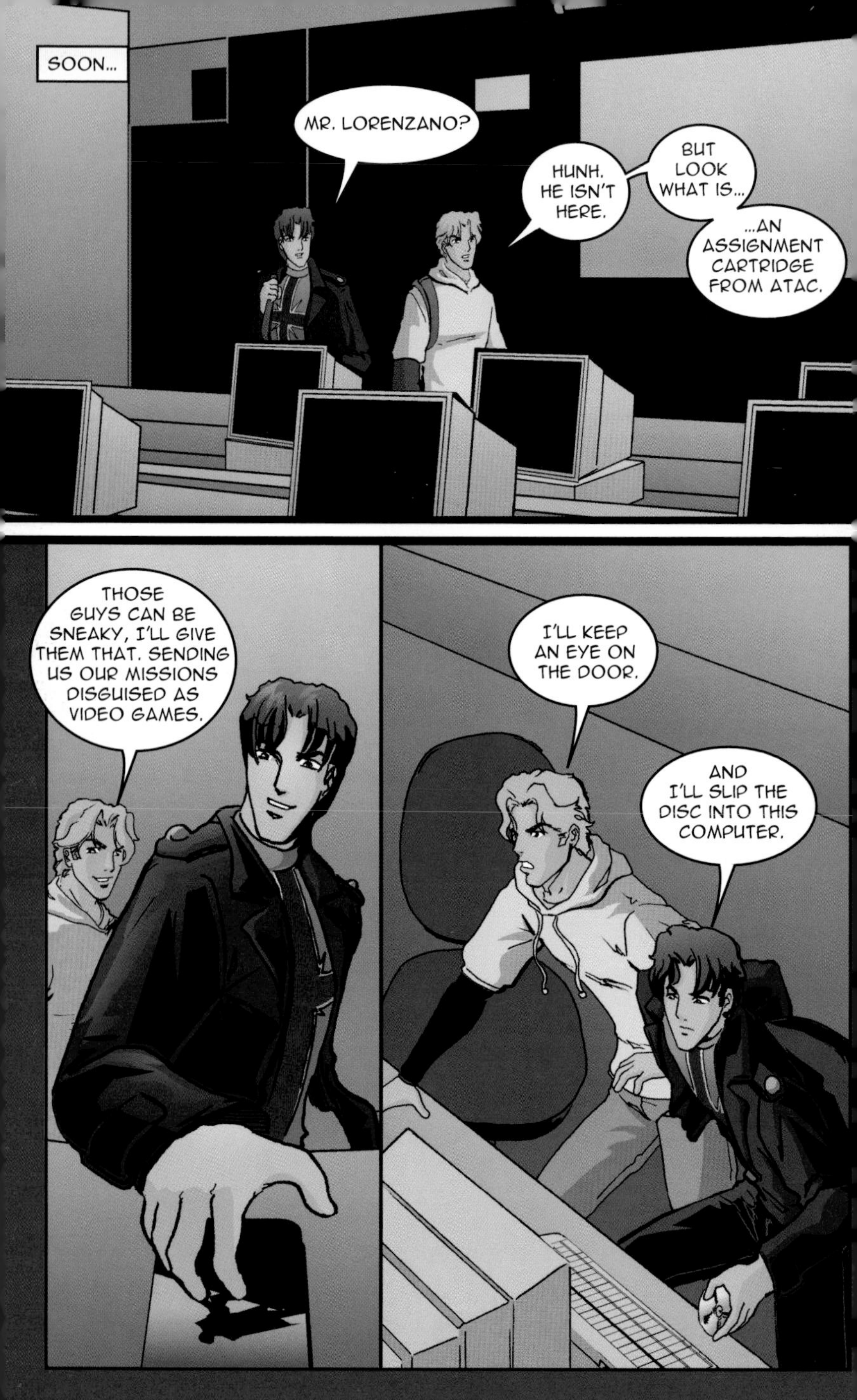
SOON...
MR. LORENZANO?
HUNH. HE ISN'T HERE.
BUT LOOK WHAT IS...
...AN ASSIGNMENT CARTRIDGE FROM ATAC.
THOSE GUYS CAN BE SNEAKY, I'LL GIVE THEM THAT. SENDING US OUR MISSIONS DISGUISED AS VIDEO GAMES.
I'LL KEEP AN EYE ON THE DOOR.
AND I'LL SLIP THE DISC INTO THIS COMPUTER.

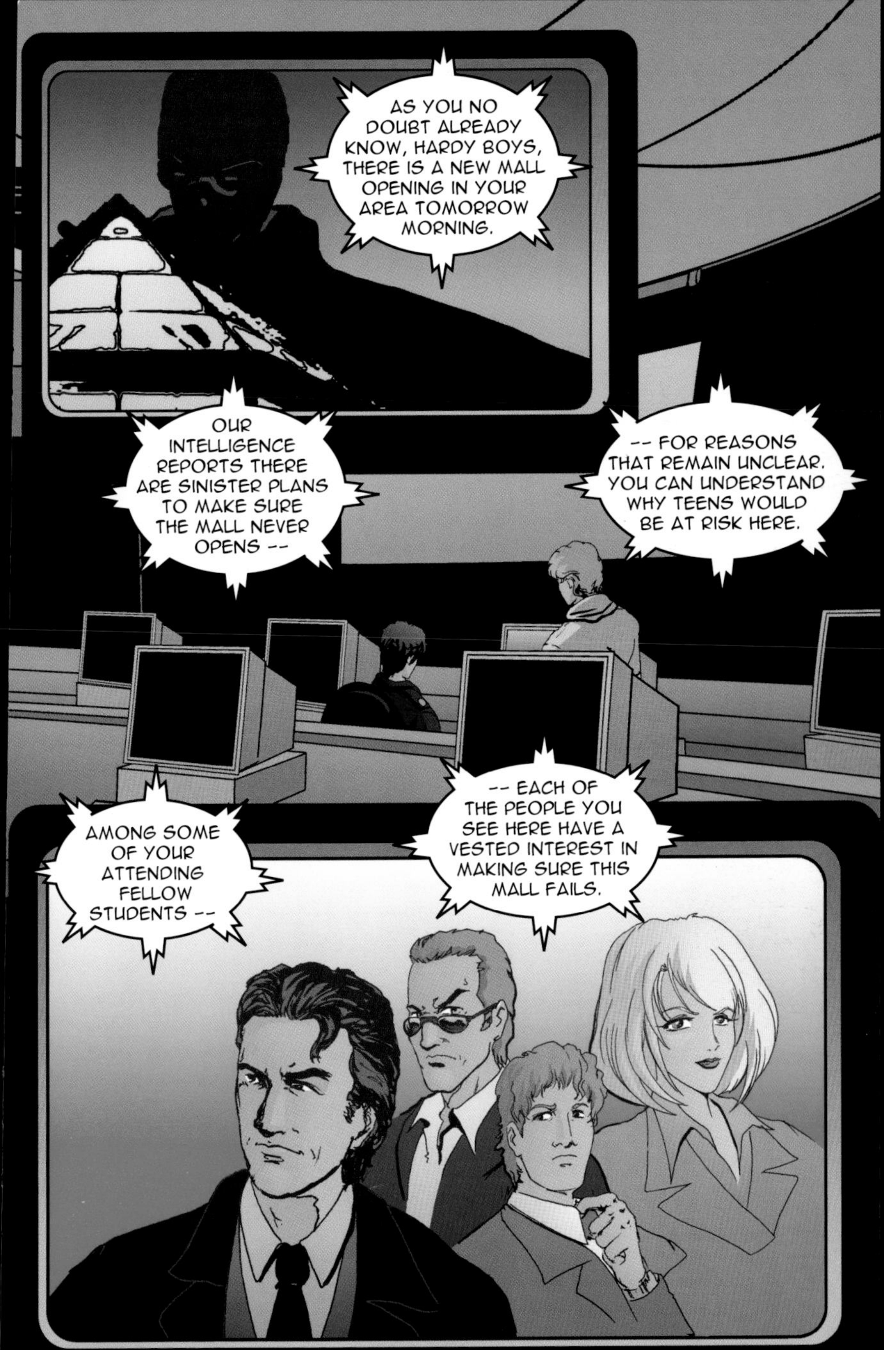
AS YOU NO DOUBT ALREADY KNOW, HARDY BOYS, THERE IS A NEW MALL OPENING IN YOUR AREA TOMORROW MORNING.
OUR INTELLIGENCE REPORTS THERE ARE SINISTER PLANS TO MAKE SURE THE MALL NEVER OPENS --
-- FOR REASONS THAT REMAIN UNCLEAR. YOU CAN UNDERSTAND WHY TEENS WOULD BE AT RISK HERE.
AMONG SOME OF YOUR ATTENDING FELLOW STUDENTS --
-- EACH OF THE PEOPLE YOU SEE HERE HAVE A VESTED INTEREST IN MAKING SURE THIS MALL FAILS.

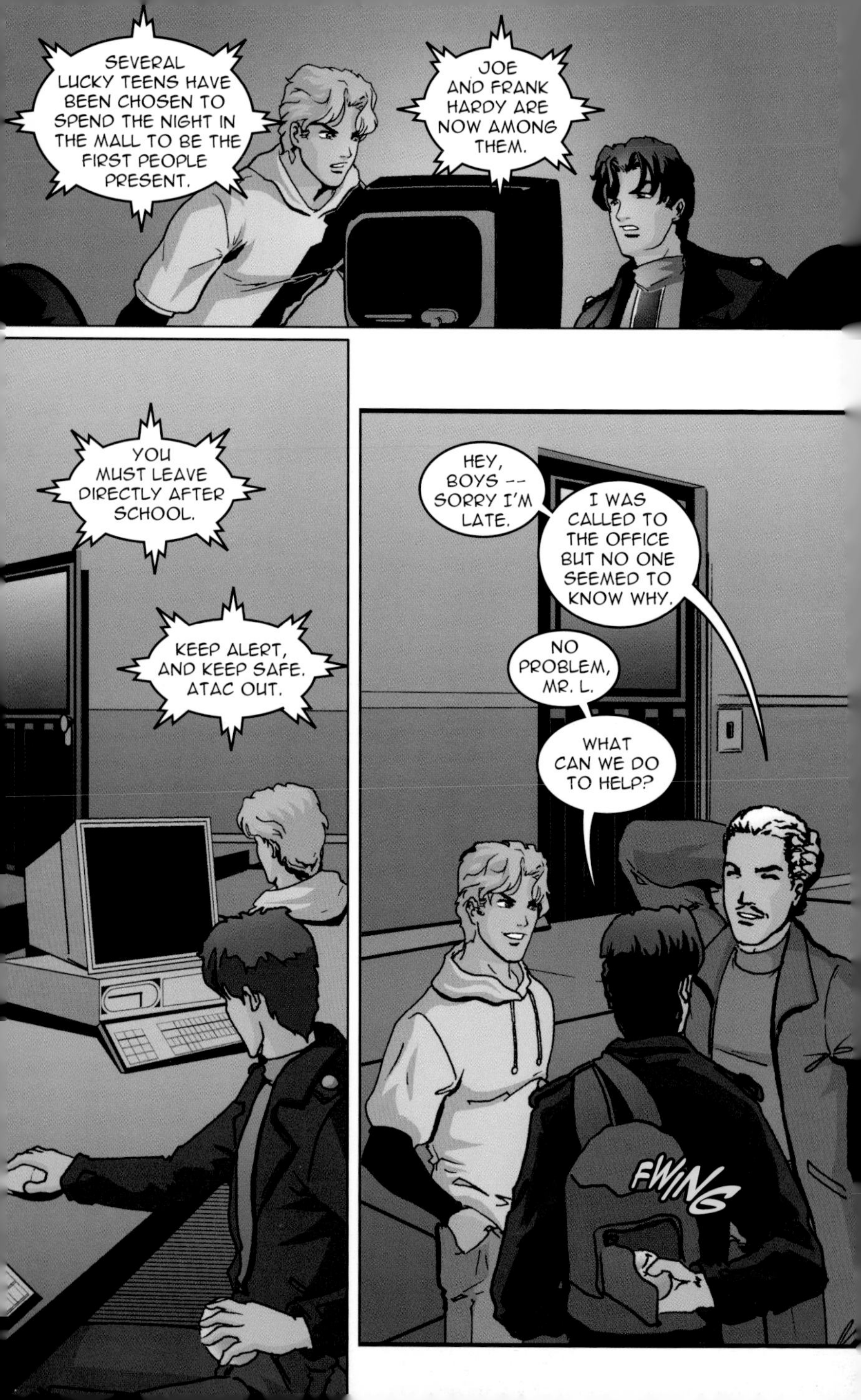
SEVERAL LUCKY TEENS HAVE BEEN CHOSEN TO SPEND THE NIGHT IN THE MALL TO BE THE FIRST PEOPLE PRESENT.
JOE AND FRANK HARDY ARE NOW AMONG THEM.
YOU MUST LEAVE DIRECTLY AFTER SCHOOL.
KEEP ALERT, AND KEEP SAFE. ATAC OUT.
HEY, BOYS -- SORRY I'M LATE.
I WAS CALLED TO THE OFFICE BUT NO ONE SEEMED TO KNOW WHY.
NO PROBLEM, MR. L.
WHAT CAN WE DO TO HELP?
FWING

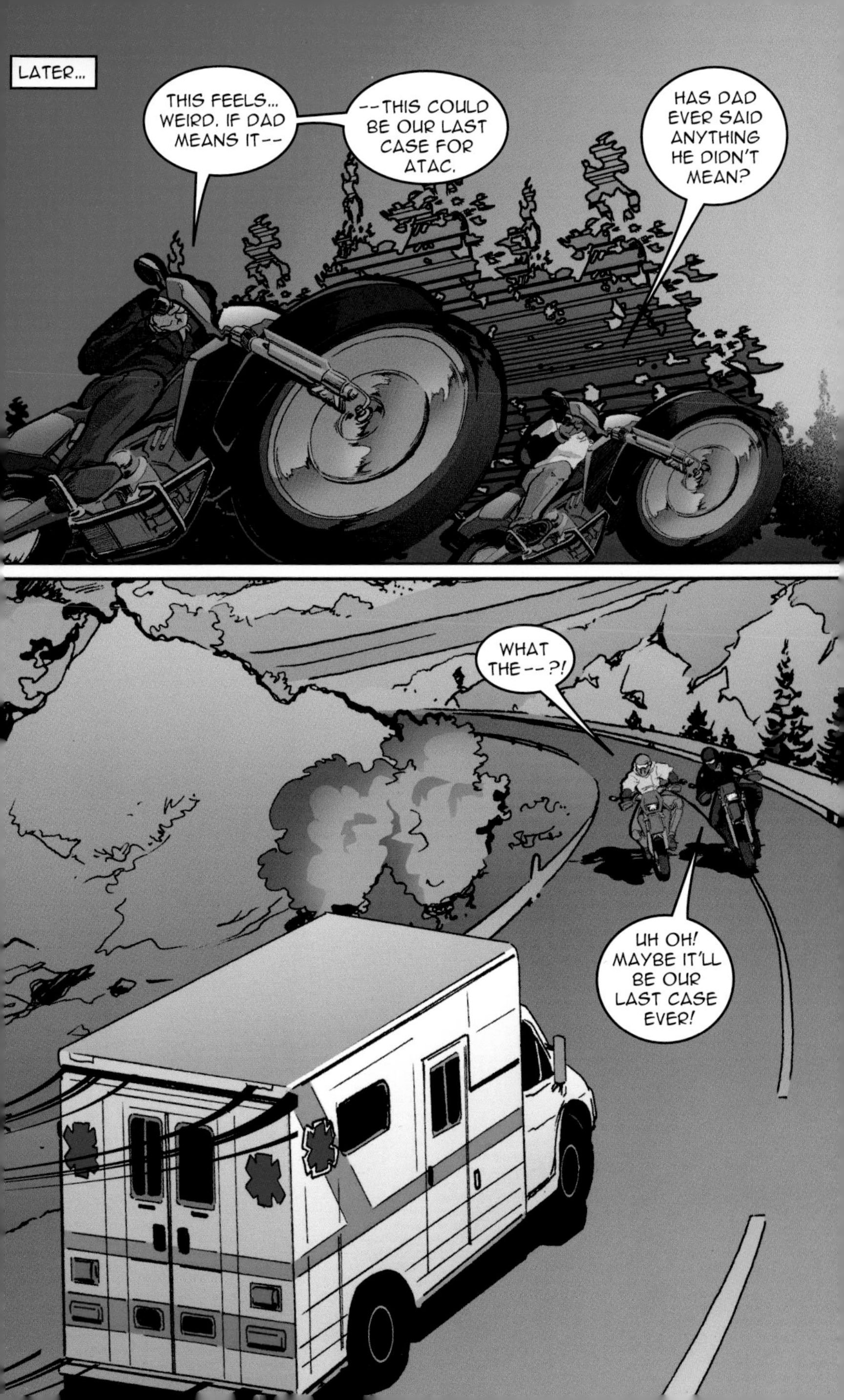
LATER...
THIS FEELS... WEIRD. IF DAD MEANS IT--
--THIS COULD BE OUR LAST CASE FOR ATAC.
HAS DAD EVER SAID ANYTHING HE DIDN'T MEAN?
WHAT THE--?!
UH OH! MAYBE IT'LL BE OUR LAST CASE EVER!

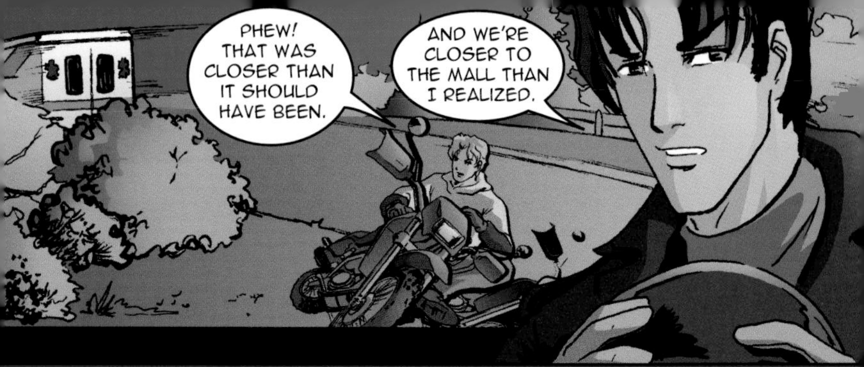
PHEW! THAT WAS CLOSER THAN IT SHOULD HAVE BEEN.
AND WE'RE CLOSER TO THE MALL THAN I REALIZED.

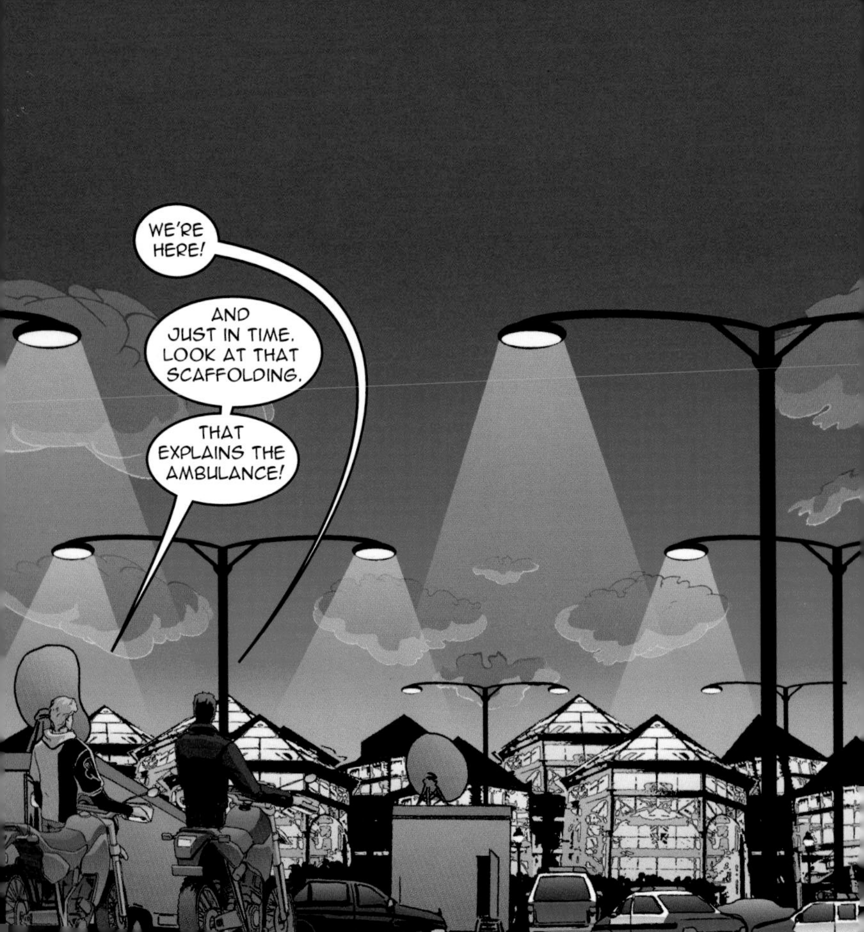
WE'RE HERE!
AND JUST IN TIME. LOOK AT THAT SCAFFOLDING.
THAT EXPLAINS THE AMBULANCE!

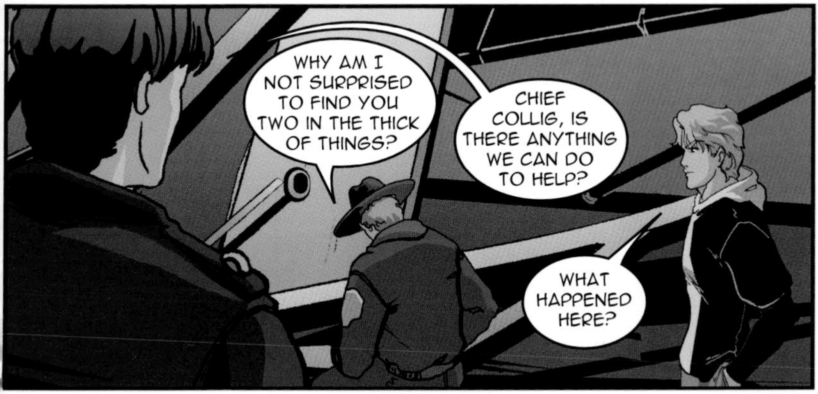
WHY AM I NOT SURPRISED TO FIND YOU TWO IN THE THICK OF THINGS?
CHIEF COLLIG, IS THERE ANYTHING WE CAN DO TO HELP?
WHAT HAPPENED HERE?

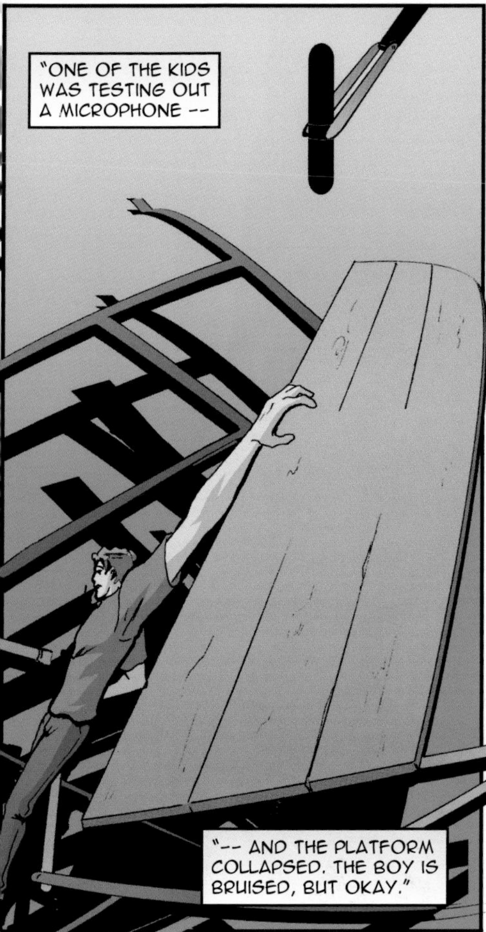
"ONE OF THE KIDS WAS TESTING OUT A MICROPHONE --
"-- AND THE PLATFORM COLLAPSED. THE BOY IS BRUISED, BUT OKAY."

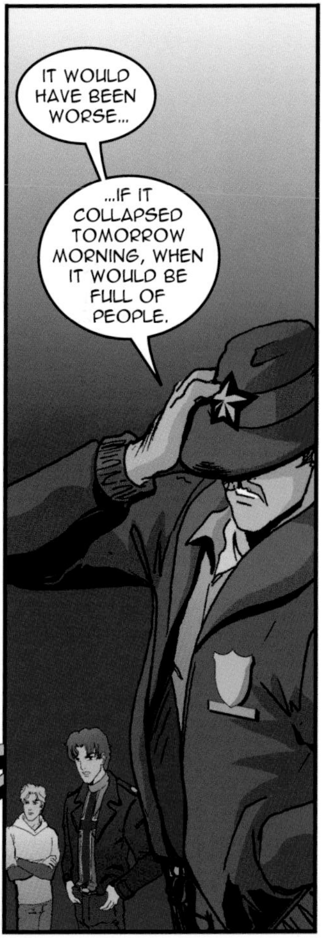
IT WOULD HAVE BEEN WORSE...
...IF IT COLLAPSED TOMORROW MORNING, WHEN IT WOULD BE FULL OF PEOPLE.

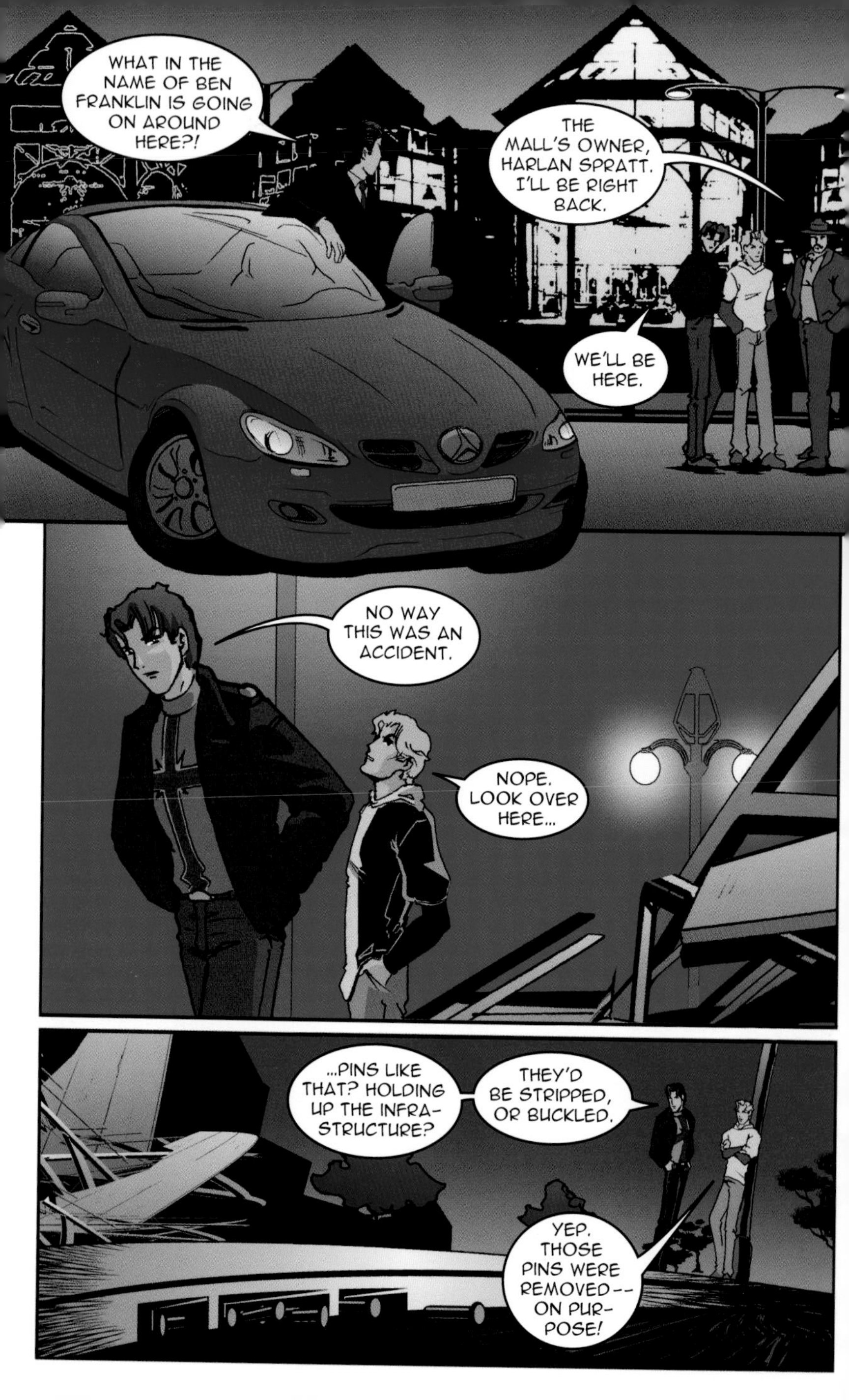
WHAT IN THE NAME OF BEN FRANKLIN IS GOING ON AROUND HERE?!
THE MALL'S OWNER, HARLAN SPRATT. I'LL BE RIGHT BACK.
WE'LL BE HERE.
NO WAY THIS WAS AN ACCIDENT.
NOPE. LOOK OVER HERE...
...PINS LIKE THAT? HOLDING UP THE INFRA-STRUCTURE?
THEY'D BE STRIPPED, OR BUCKLED.
YEP. THOSE PINS WERE REMOVED-- ON PUR-POSE!

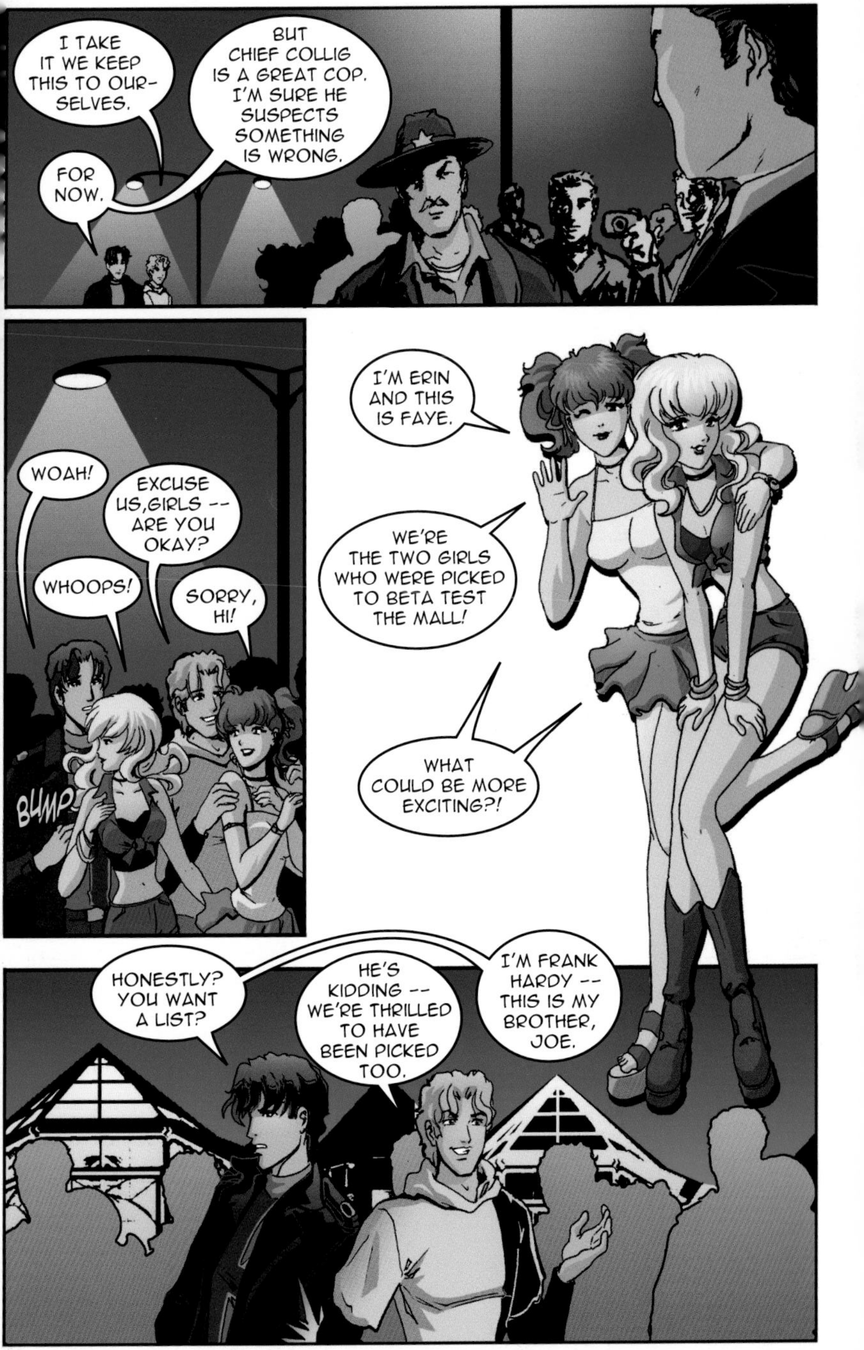
I TAKE IT WE KEEP THIS TO OURSELVES.
FOR NOW.
BUT CHIEF COLLIG IS A GREAT COP. I'M SURE HE SUSPECTS SOMETHING IS WRONG.
WOAH!
EXCUSE US,GIRLS -- ARE YOU OKAY?
WHOOPS!
SORRY, HI!
BUMP
I'M ERIN AND THIS IS FAYE.
WE'RE THE TWO GIRLS WHO WERE PICKED TO BETA TEST THE MALL!
WHAT COULD BE MORE EXCITING?!
HONESTLY? YOU WANT A LIST?
HE'S KIDDING -- WE'RE THRILLED TO HAVE BEEN PICKED TOO.
I'M FRANK HARDY -- THIS IS MY BROTHER, JOE.

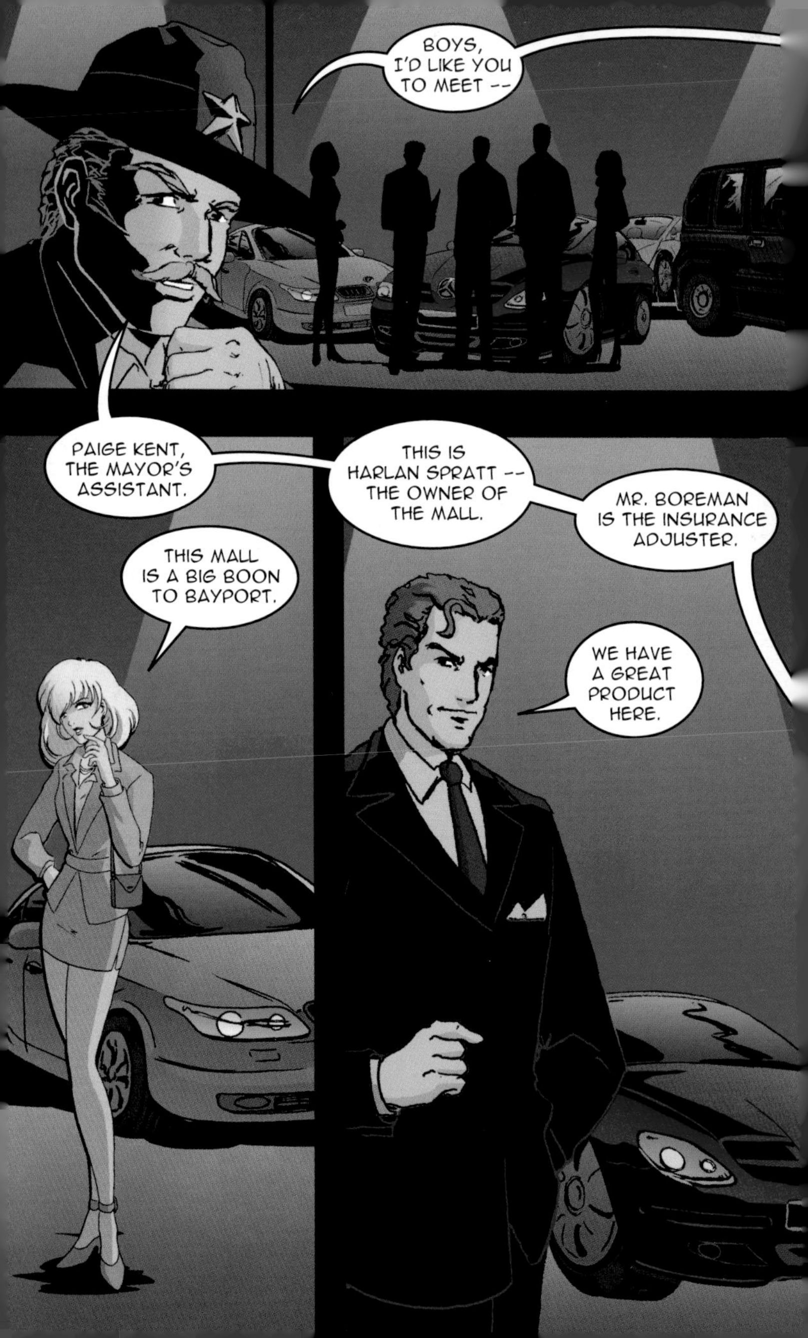
BOYS, I'D LIKE YOU TO MEET --
PAIGE KENT, THE MAYOR'S ASSISTANT.
THIS MALL IS A BIG BOON TO BAYPORT.
THIS IS HARLAN SPRATT -- THE OWNER OF THE MALL.
MR. BOREMAN IS THE INSURANCE ADJUSTER.
WE HAVE A GREAT PRODUCT HERE.

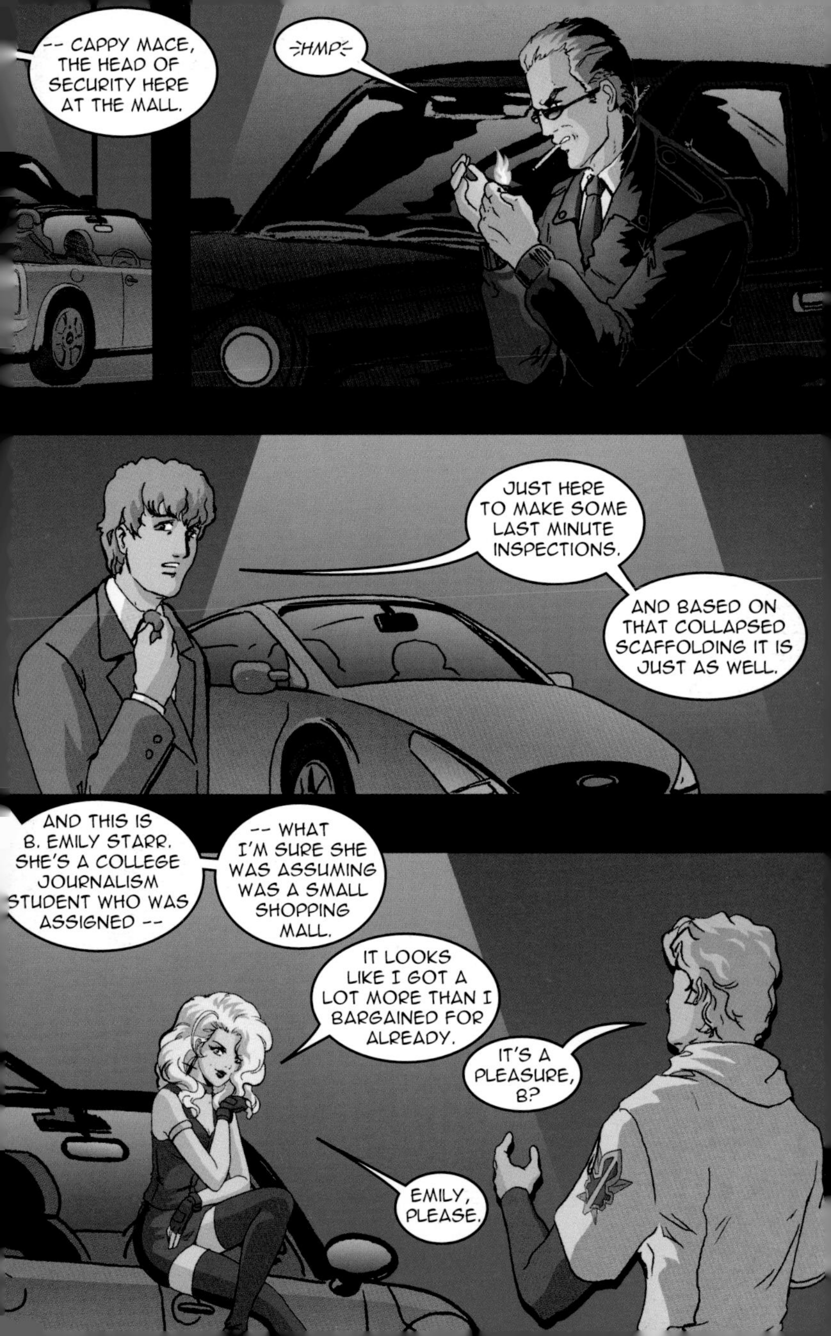
-- CAPPY MACE, THE HEAD OF SECURITY HERE AT THE MALL.
HMP
JUST HERE TO MAKE SOME LAST MINUTE INSPECTIONS.
AND BASED ON THAT COLLAPSED SCAFFOLDING IT IS JUST AS WELL.
AND THIS IS B. EMILY STARR. SHE'S A COLLEGE JOURNALISM STUDENT WHO WAS ASSIGNED --
-- WHAT I'M SURE SHE WAS ASSUMING WAS A SMALL SHOPPING MALL.
IT LOOKS LIKE I GOT A LOT MORE THAN I BARGAINED FOR ALREADY.
IT'S A PLEASURE, B?
EMILY, PLEASE.

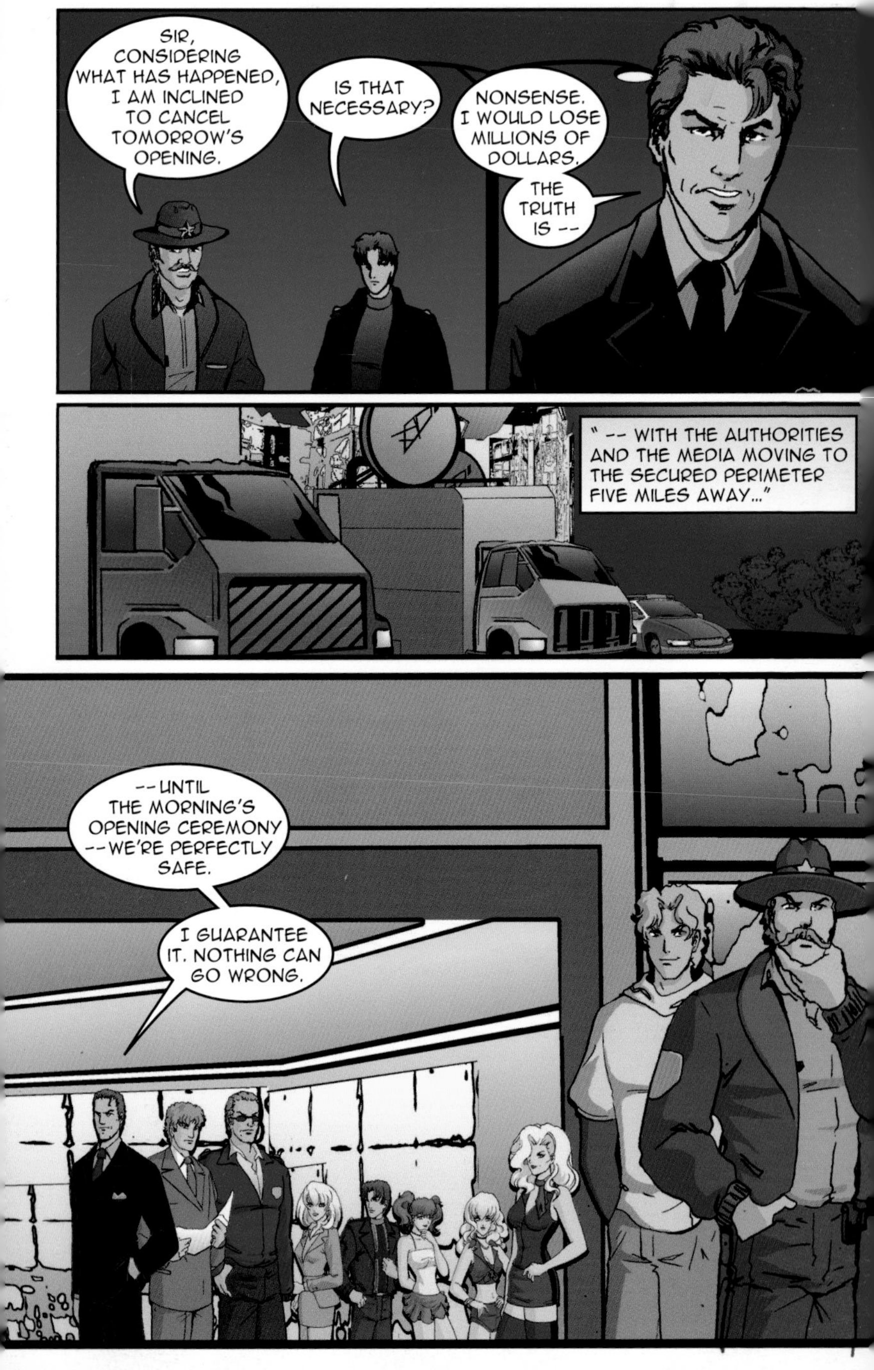
SIR, CONSIDERING WHAT HAS HAPPENED, I AM INCLINED TO CANCEL TOMORROW'S OPENING.
IS THAT NECESSARY?
NONSENSE. I WOULD LOSE MILLIONS OF DOLLARS.
THE TRUTH IS --
" -- WITH THE AUTHORITIES AND THE MEDIA MOVING TO THE SECURED PERIMETER FIVE MILES AWAY..."
--UNTIL THE MORNING'S OPENING CEREMONY --WE'RE PERFECTLY SAFE.
I GUARANTEE IT. NOTHING CAN GO WRONG.

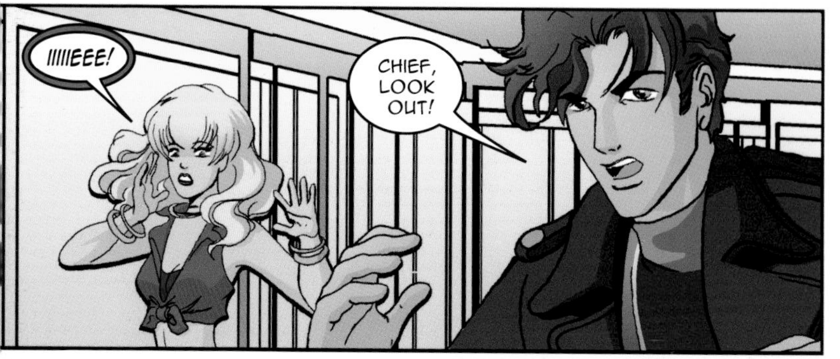
IIIIIEEE!
CHIEF, LOOK OUT!

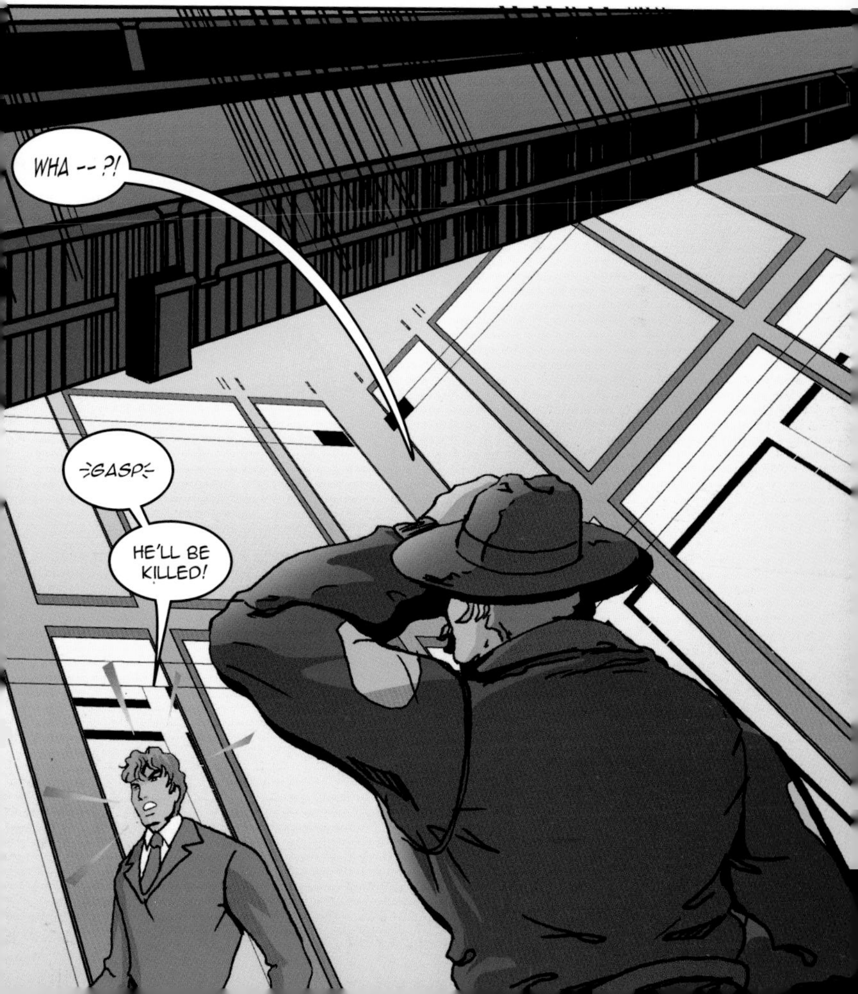
WHA -- ?!
GASP
HE'LL BE KILLED!

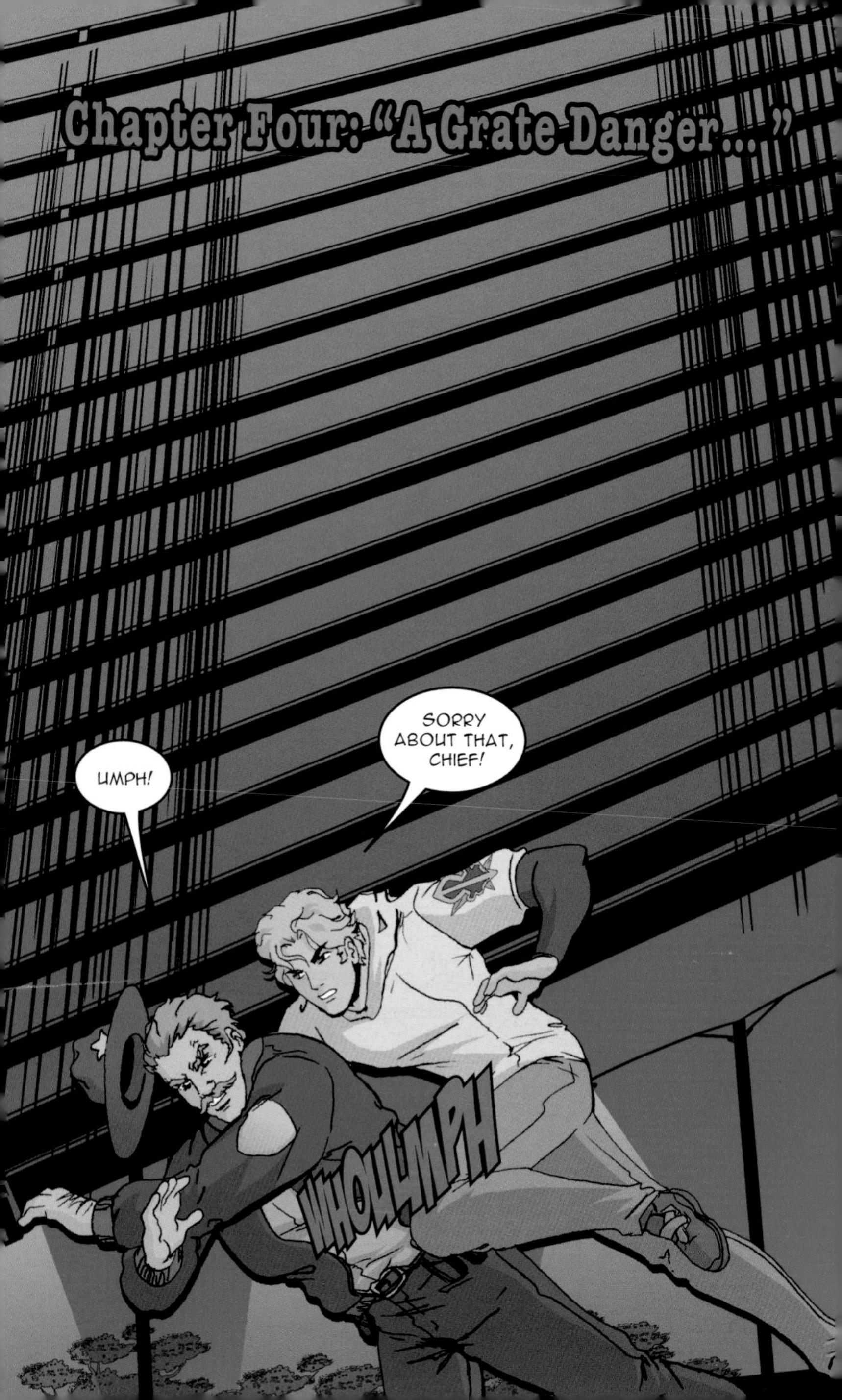
Chapter Four: "A Grate Danger..."
UMPH!
SORRY ABOUT THAT, CHIEF!
WHOULMPH

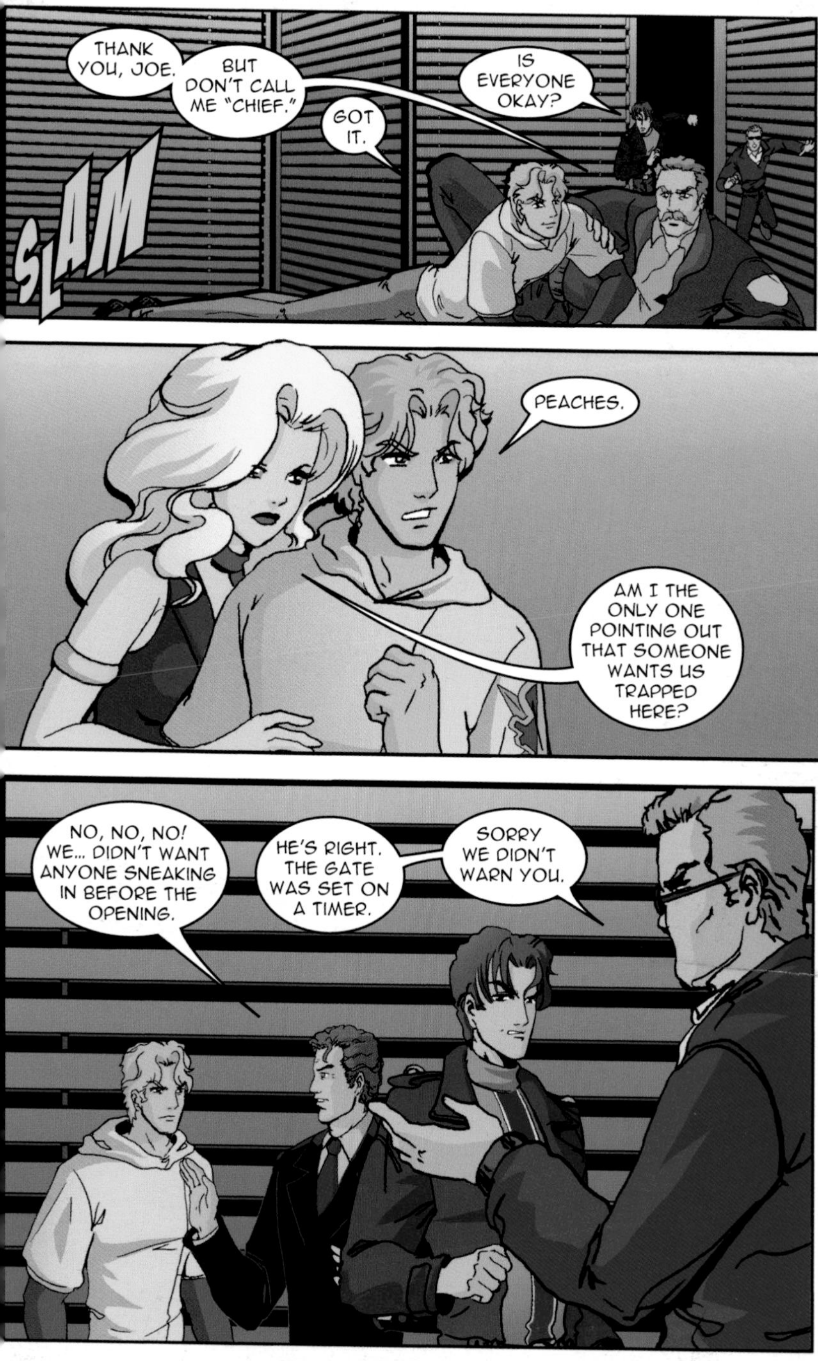
THANK YOU, JOE.
BUT DON'T CALL ME "CHIEF."
GOT IT.
IS EVERYONE OKAY?
SLAM
PEACHES.
AM I THE ONLY ONE POINTING OUT THAT SOMEONE WANTS US TRAPPED HERE?
NO, NO, NO! WE... DIDN'T WANT ANYONE SNEAKING IN BEFORE THE OPENING.
HE'S RIGHT. THE GATE WAS SET ON A TIMER.
SORRY WE DIDN'T WARN YOU.

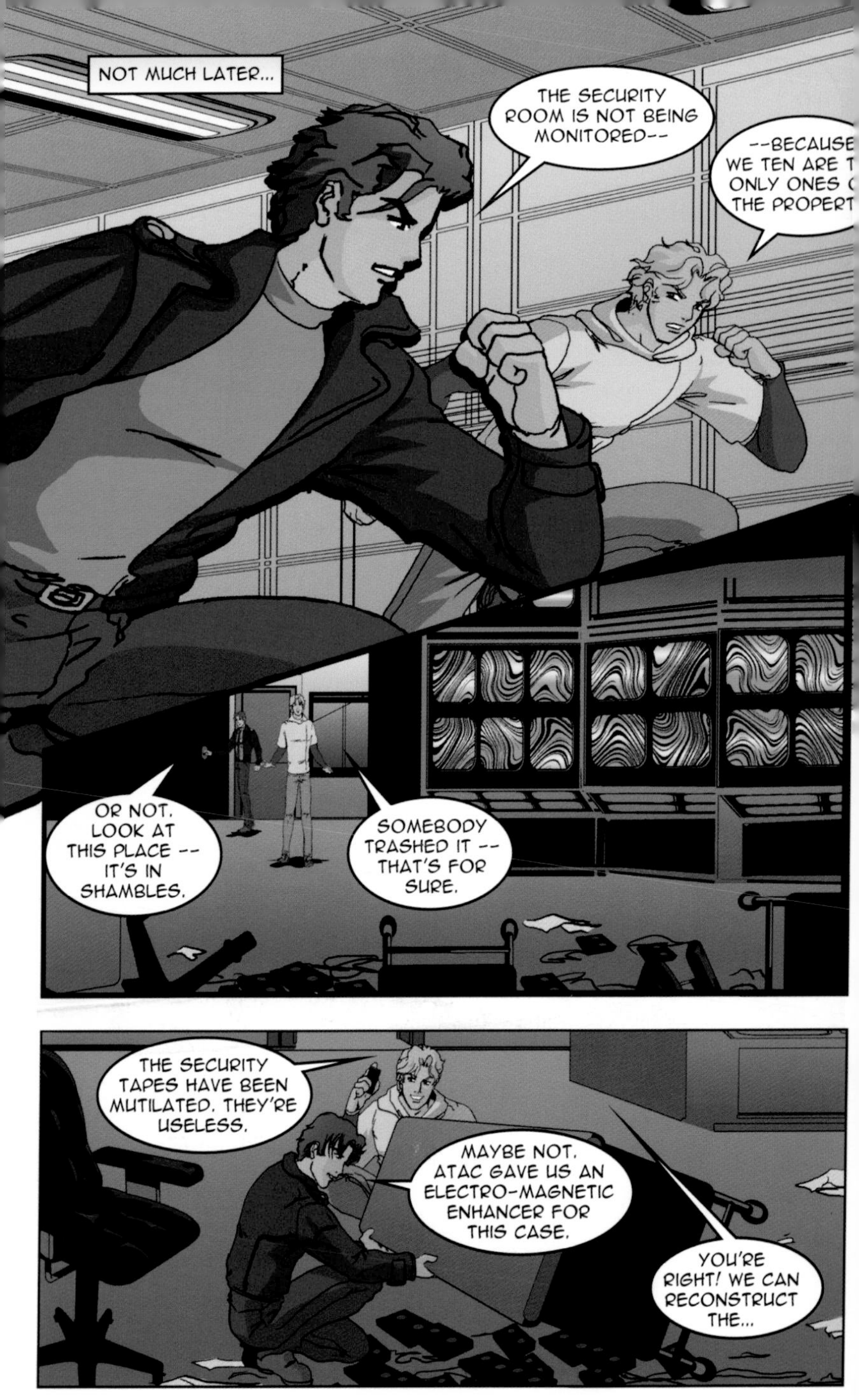

NOT MUCH LATER...
THE SECURITY ROOM IS NOT BEING MONITORED--
--BECAUSE WE TEN ARE T ONLY ONES C THE PROPERT
OR NOT. LOOK AT THIS PLACE -- IT'S IN SHAMBLES.
SOMEBODY TRASHED IT -- THAT'S FOR SURE.
THE SECURITY TAPES HAVE BEEN MUTILATED. THEY'RE USELESS.
MAYBE NOT. ATAC GAVE US AN ELECTRO-MAGNETIC ENHANCER FOR THIS CASE.
YOU'RE RIGHT! WE CAN RECONSTRUCT THE...

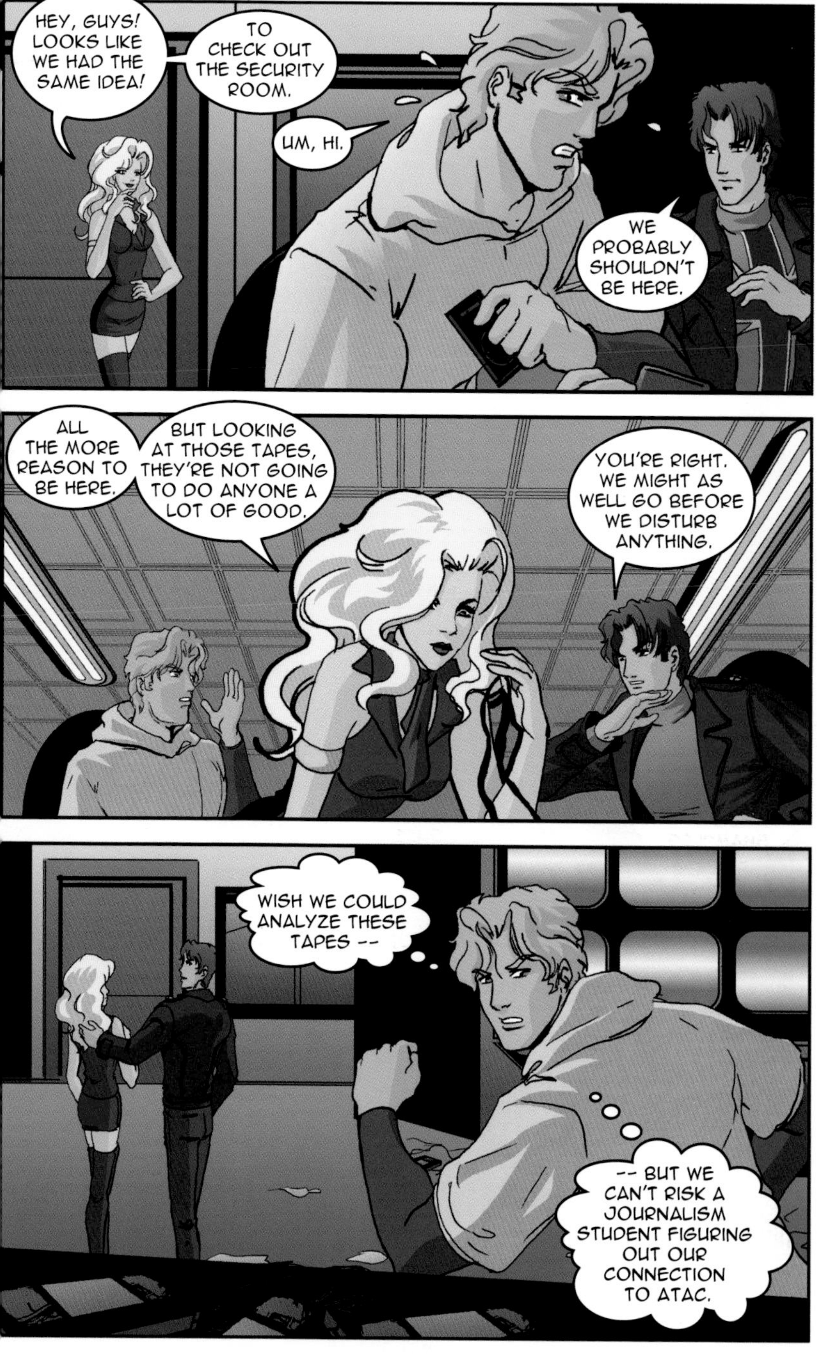
HEY, GUYS! LOOKS LIKE WE HAD THE SAME IDEA!
TO CHECK OUT THE SECURITY ROOM.
UM, HI.
WE PROBABLY SHOULDN'T BE HERE.
ALL THE MORE REASON TO BE HERE.
BUT LOOKING AT THOSE TAPES, THEY'RE NOT GOING TO DO ANYONE A LOT OF GOOD.
YOU'RE RIGHT. WE MIGHT AS WELL GO BEFORE WE DISTURB ANYTHING.
WISH WE COULD ANALYZE THESE TAPES --
-- BUT WE CAN'T RISK A JOURNALISM STUDENT FIGURING OUT OUR CONNECTION TO ATAC.

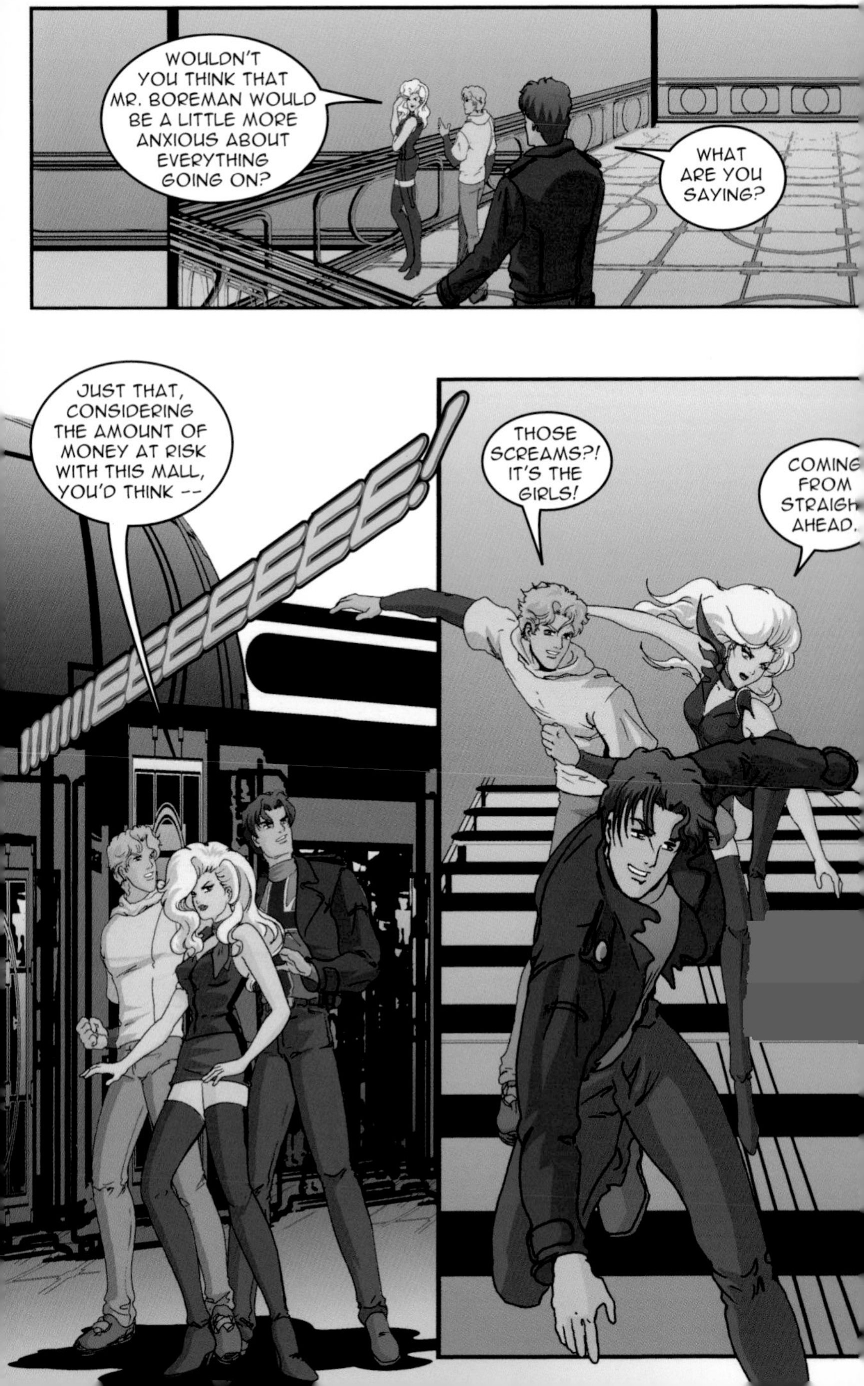
WOULDN'T YOU THINK THAT MR. BOREMAN WOULD BE A LITTLE MORE ANXIOUS ABOUT EVERYTHING GOING ON?
WHAT ARE YOU SAYING?
JUST THAT, CONSIDERING THE AMOUNT OF MONEY AT RISK WITH THIS MALL, YOU'D THINK --
IIIIIIEEEEEEEEEEEE!!
THOSE SCREAMS?! IT'S THE GIRLS!
COMING FROM STRAIGH AHEAD.

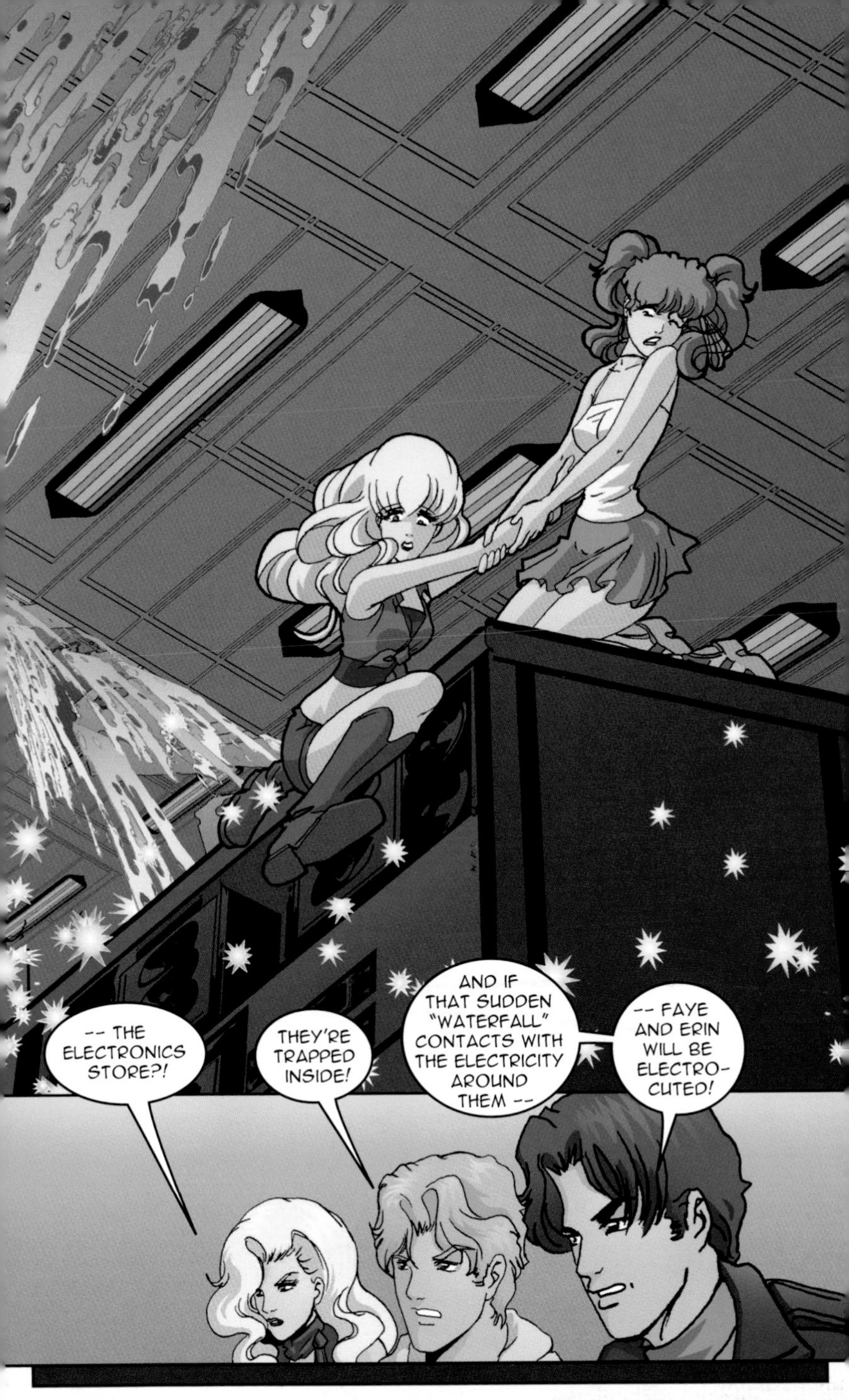
-- THE ELECTRONICS STORE?!
THEY'RE TRAPPED INSIDE!
AND IF THAT SUDDEN "WATERFALL" CONTACTS WITH THE ELECTRICITY AROUND THEM --
-- FAYE AND ERIN WILL BE ELECTRO-CUTED!

CHAPTER FIVE: "Rain of Terror!"

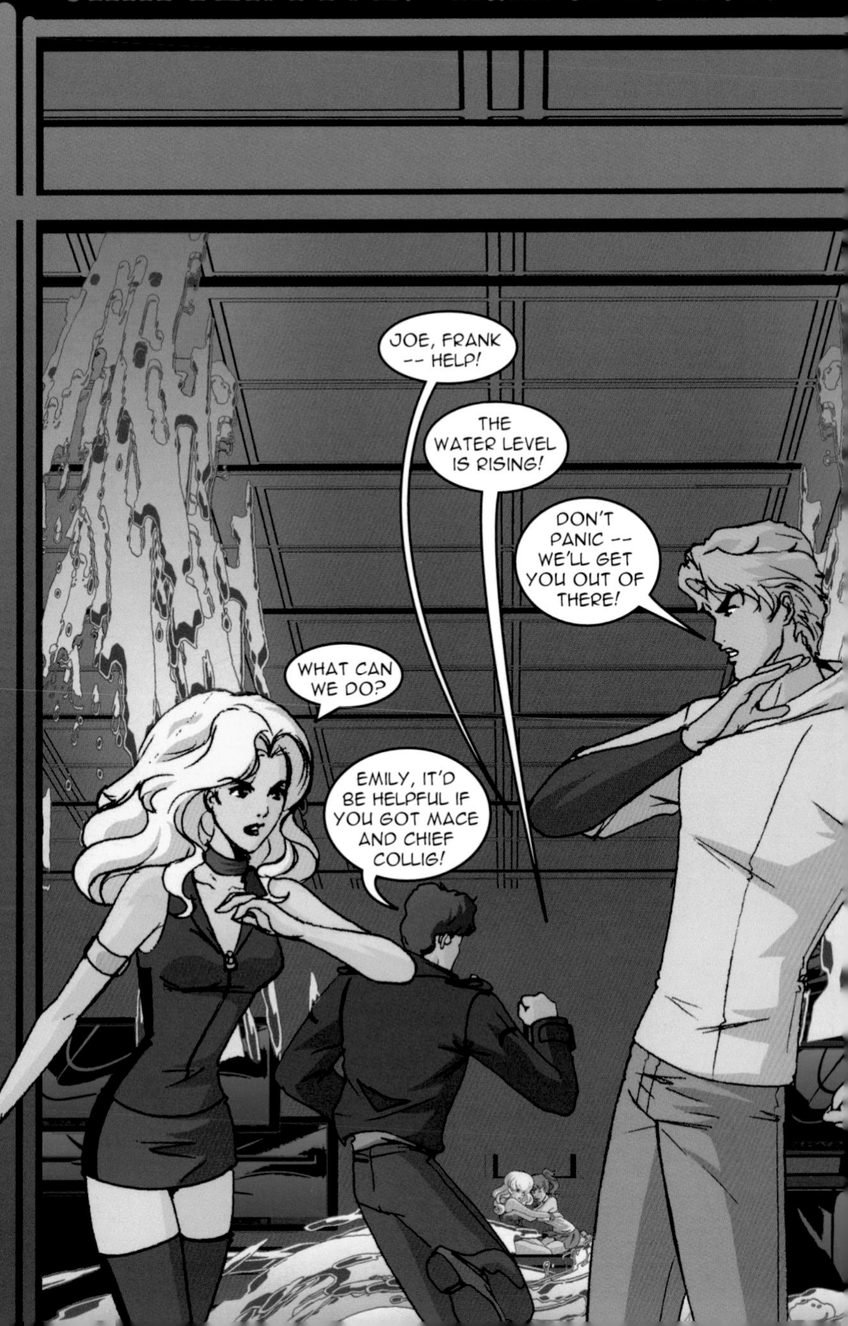

JOE, FRANK -- HELP!
THE WATER LEVEL IS RISING!
DON'T PANIC -- WE'LL GET YOU OUT OF THERE!
WHAT CAN WE DO?
EMILY, IT'D BE HELPFUL IF YOU GOT MACE AND CHIEF COLLIG!

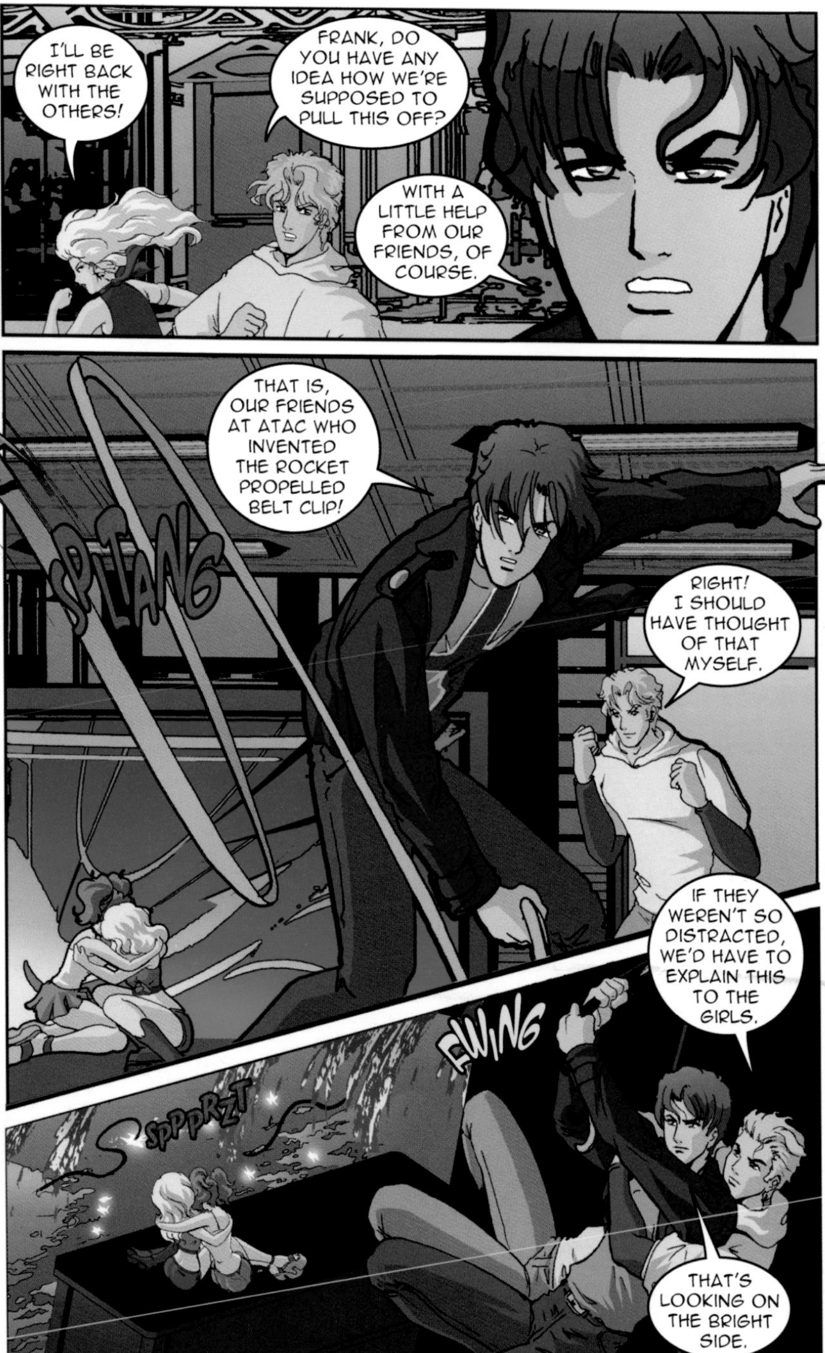

I'LL BE RIGHT BACK WITH THE OTHERS!
FRANK, DO YOU HAVE ANY IDEA HOW WE'RE SUPPOSED TO PULL THIS OFF?
WITH A LITTLE HELP FROM OUR FRIENDS, OF COURSE.
THAT IS, OUR FRIENDS AT ATAC WHO INVENTED THE ROCKET PROPELLED BELT CLIP!
SPLANG
RIGHT! I SHOULD HAVE THOUGHT OF THAT MYSELF.
IF THEY WEREN'T SO DISTRACTED, WE'D HAVE TO EXPLAIN THIS TO THE GIRLS.
FWING
SpPpRzT
THAT'S LOOKING ON THE BRIGHT SIDE.

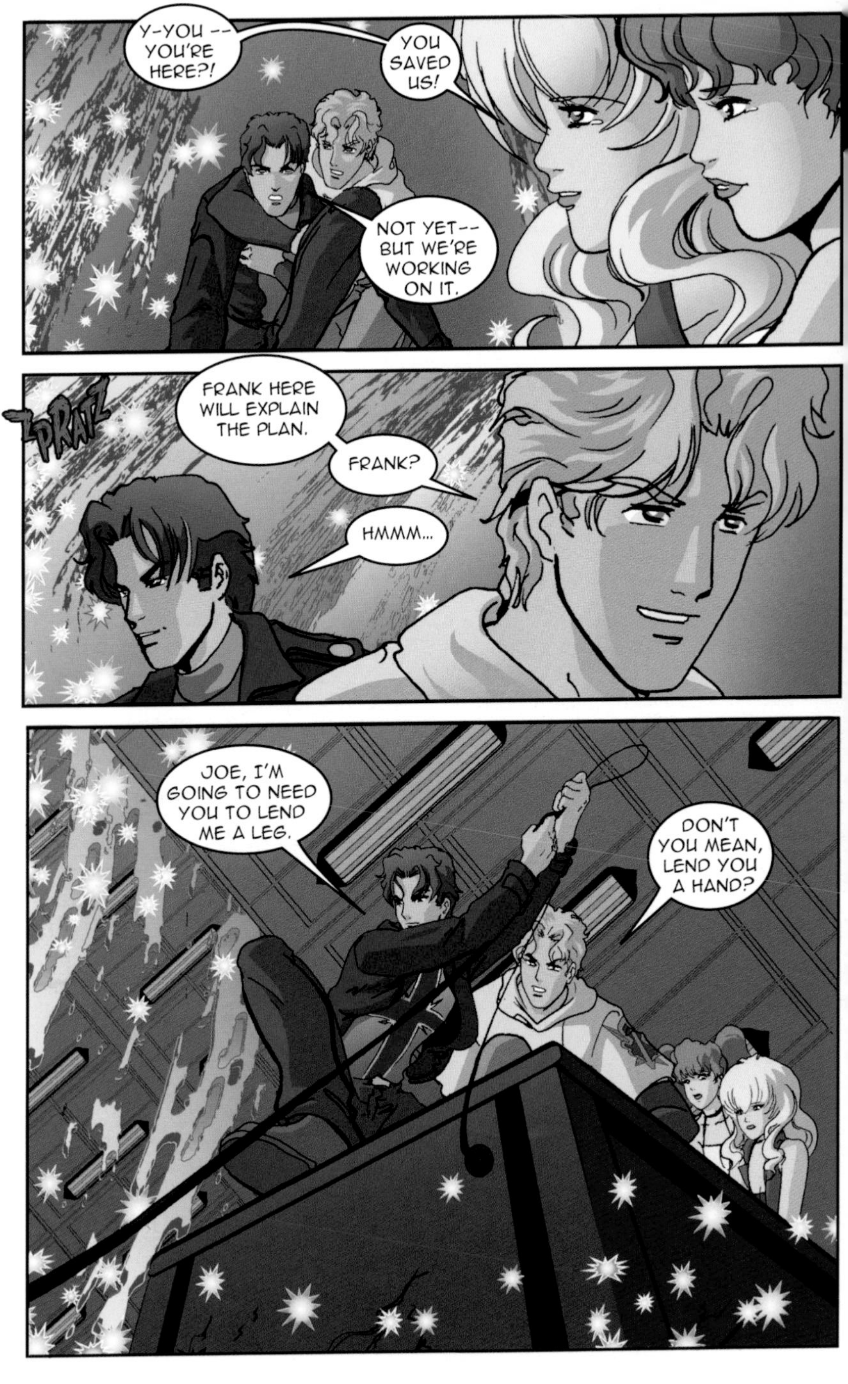
Y-YOU -- YOU'RE HERE?!
YOU SAVED US!
NOT YET-- BUT WE'RE WORKING ON IT.
ZPRATZ
FRANK HERE WILL EXPLAIN THE PLAN.
FRANK?
HMMM...
JOE, I'M GOING TO NEED YOU TO LEND ME A LEG.
DON'T YOU MEAN, LEND YOU A HAND?

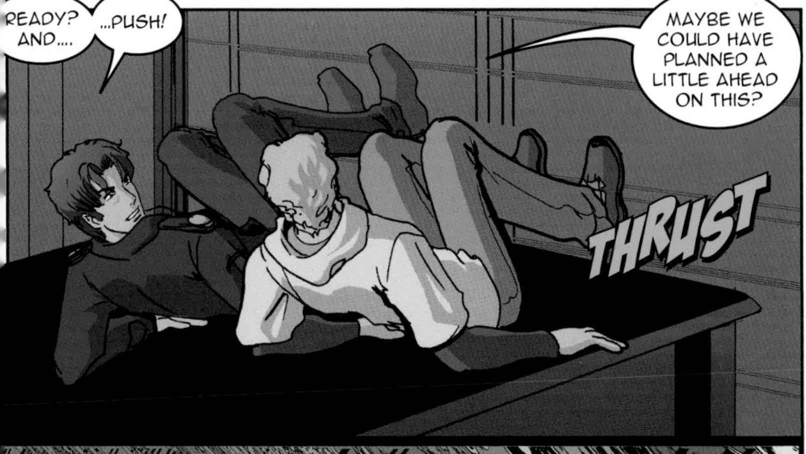
READY? AND....
...PUSH!
MAYBE WE COULD HAVE PLANNED A LITTLE AHEAD ON THIS?
THRUST

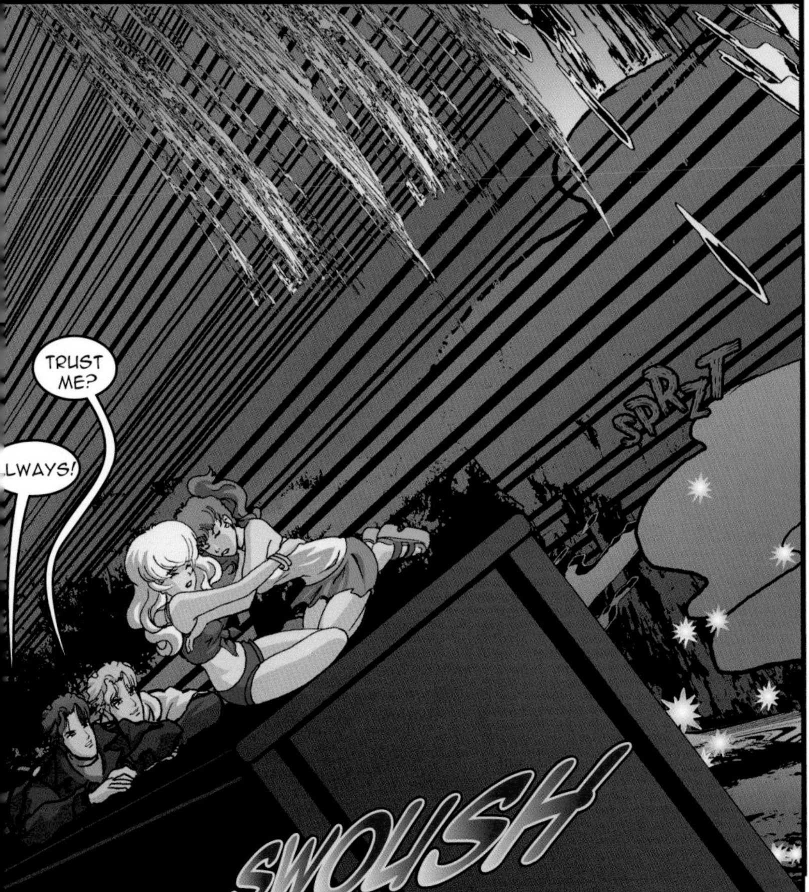
SPRZT
TRUST ME?
LWAYS!
SWOUSH

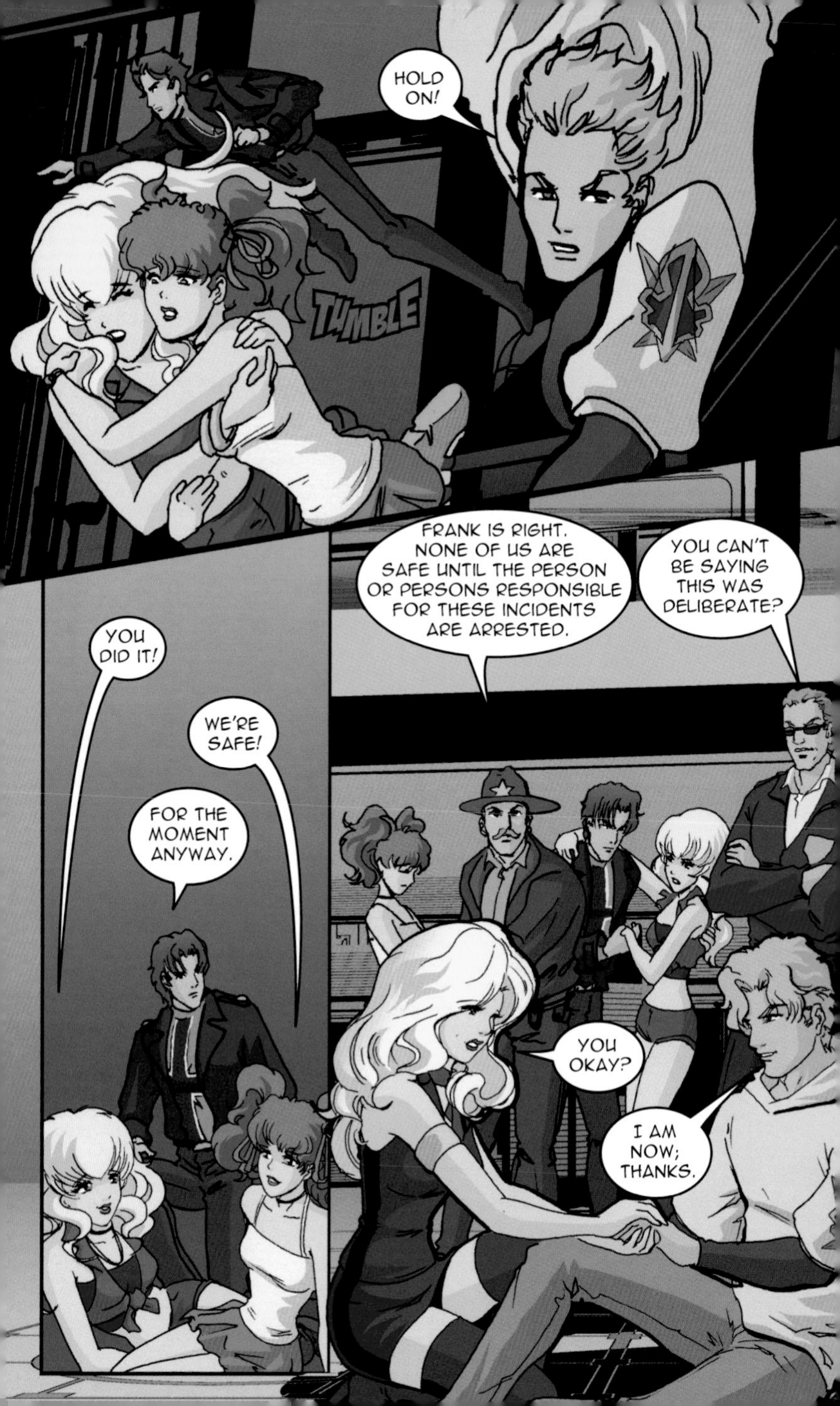
HOLD ON!
TUMBLE
FRANK IS RIGHT. NONE OF US ARE SAFE UNTIL THE PERSON OR PERSONS RESPONSIBLE FOR THESE INCIDENTS ARE ARRESTED.
YOU CAN'T BE SAYING THIS WAS DELIBERATE?
YOU DID IT!
WE'RE SAFE!
FOR THE MOMENT ANYWAY.
YOU OKAY?
I AM NOW; THANKS.

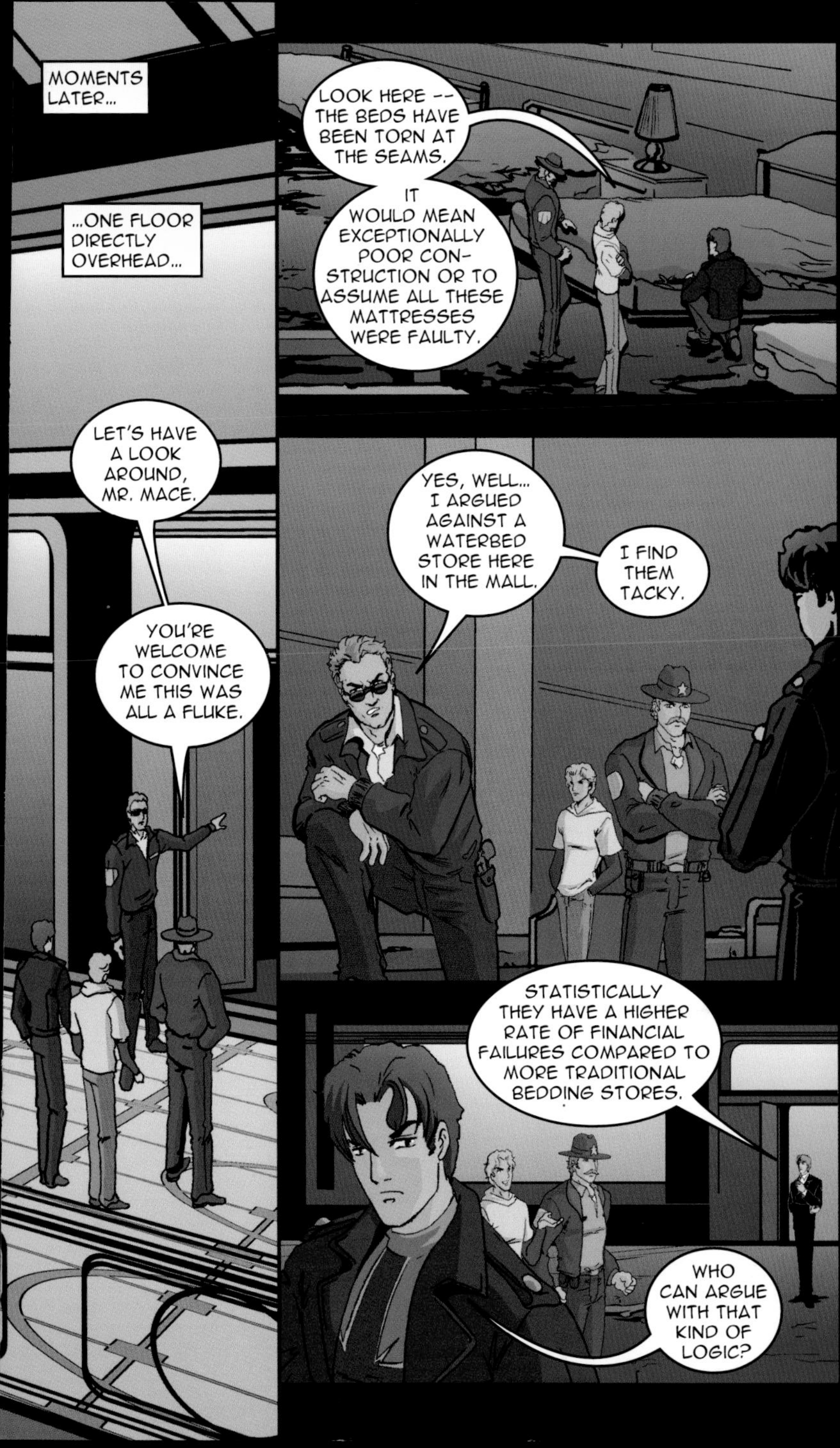

MOMENTS LATER...
LOOK HERE -- THE BEDS HAVE BEEN TORN AT THE SEAMS.
IT WOULD MEAN EXCEPTIONALLY POOR CON-STRUCTION OR TO ASSUME ALL THESE MATTRESSES WERE FAULTY.
...ONE FLOOR DIRECTLY OVERHEAD...
LET'S HAVE A LOOK AROUND, MR. MACE.
YOU'RE WELCOME TO CONVINCE ME THIS WAS ALL A FLUKE.
YES, WELL... I ARGUED AGAINST A WATERBED STORE HERE IN THE MALL.
I FIND THEM TACKY.
STATISTICALLY THEY HAVE A HIGHER RATE OF FINANCIAL FAILURES COMPARED TO MORE TRADITIONAL BEDDING STORES.
WHO CAN ARGUE WITH THAT KIND OF LOGIC?

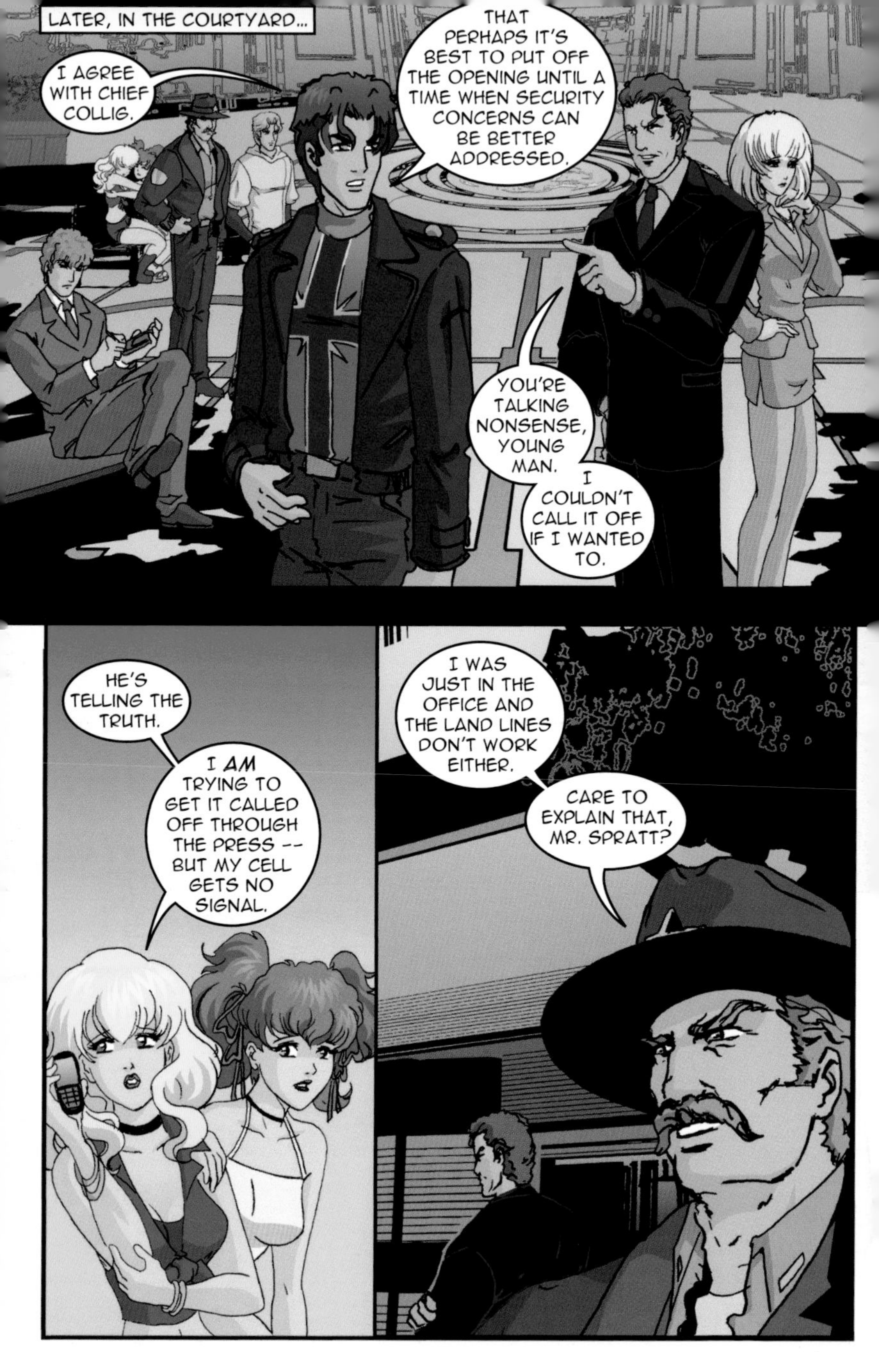
LATER, IN THE COURTYARD...
I AGREE WITH CHIEF COLLIG.
THAT PERHAPS IT'S BEST TO PUT OFF THE OPENING UNTIL A TIME WHEN SECURITY CONCERNS CAN BE BETTER ADDRESSED.
YOU'RE TALKING NONSENSE, YOUNG MAN.
I COULDN'T CALL IT OFF IF I WANTED TO.
HE'S TELLING THE TRUTH.
I *AM* TRYING TO GET IT CALLED OFF THROUGH THE PRESS -- BUT MY CELL GETS NO SIGNAL.
I WAS JUST IN THE OFFICE AND THE LAND LINES DON'T WORK EITHER.
CARE TO EXPLAIN THAT, MR. SPRATT?

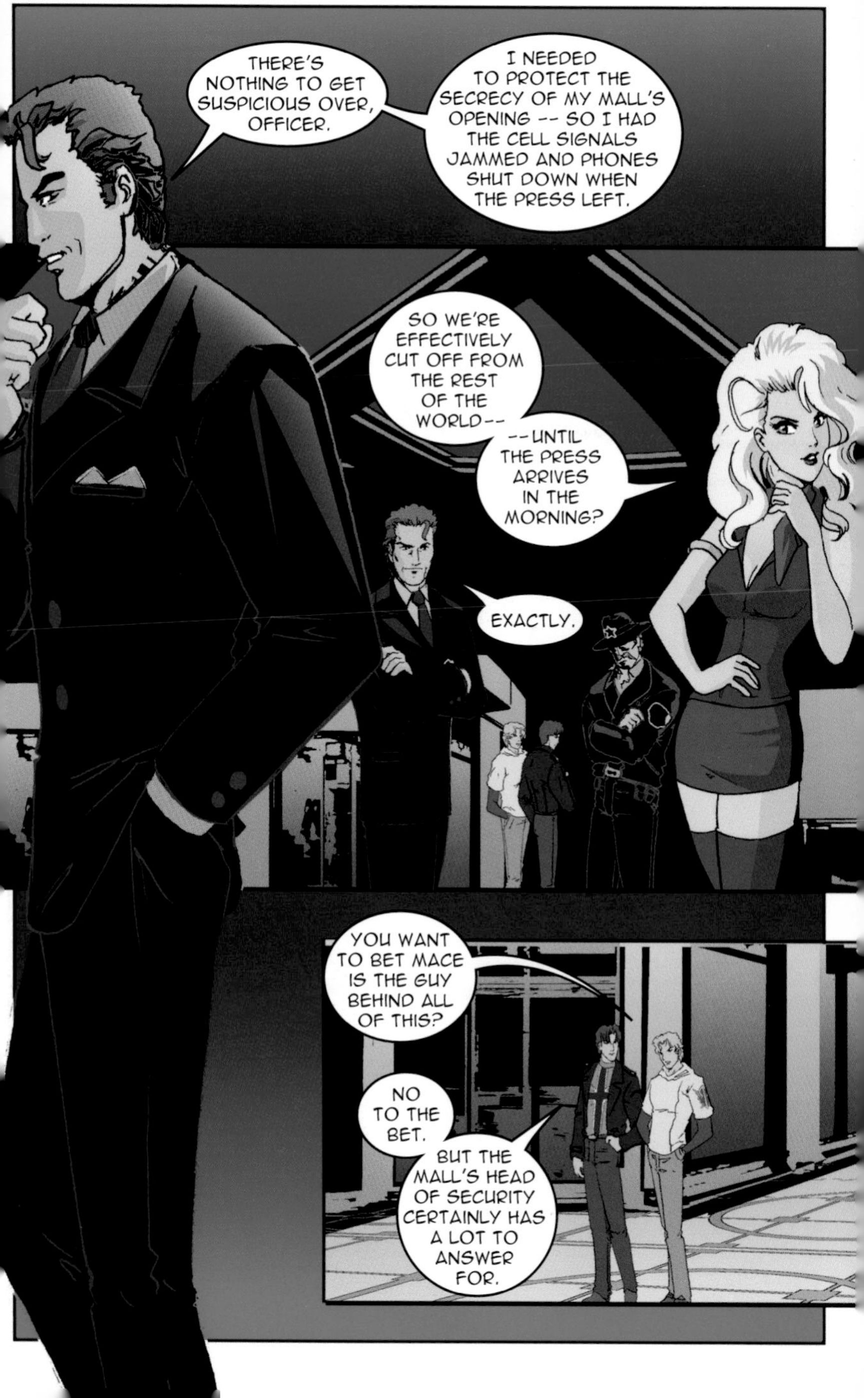
THERE'S NOTHING TO GET SUSPICIOUS OVER, OFFICER.
I NEEDED TO PROTECT THE SECRECY OF MY MALL'S OPENING -- SO I HAD THE CELL SIGNALS JAMMED AND PHONES SHUT DOWN WHEN THE PRESS LEFT.
SO WE'RE EFFECTIVELY CUT OFF FROM THE REST OF THE WORLD--
--UNTIL THE PRESS ARRIVES IN THE MORNING?
EXACTLY.
YOU WANT TO BET MACE IS THE GUY BEHIND ALL OF THIS?
NO TO THE BET.
BUT THE MALL'S HEAD OF SECURITY CERTAINLY HAS A LOT TO ANSWER FOR.

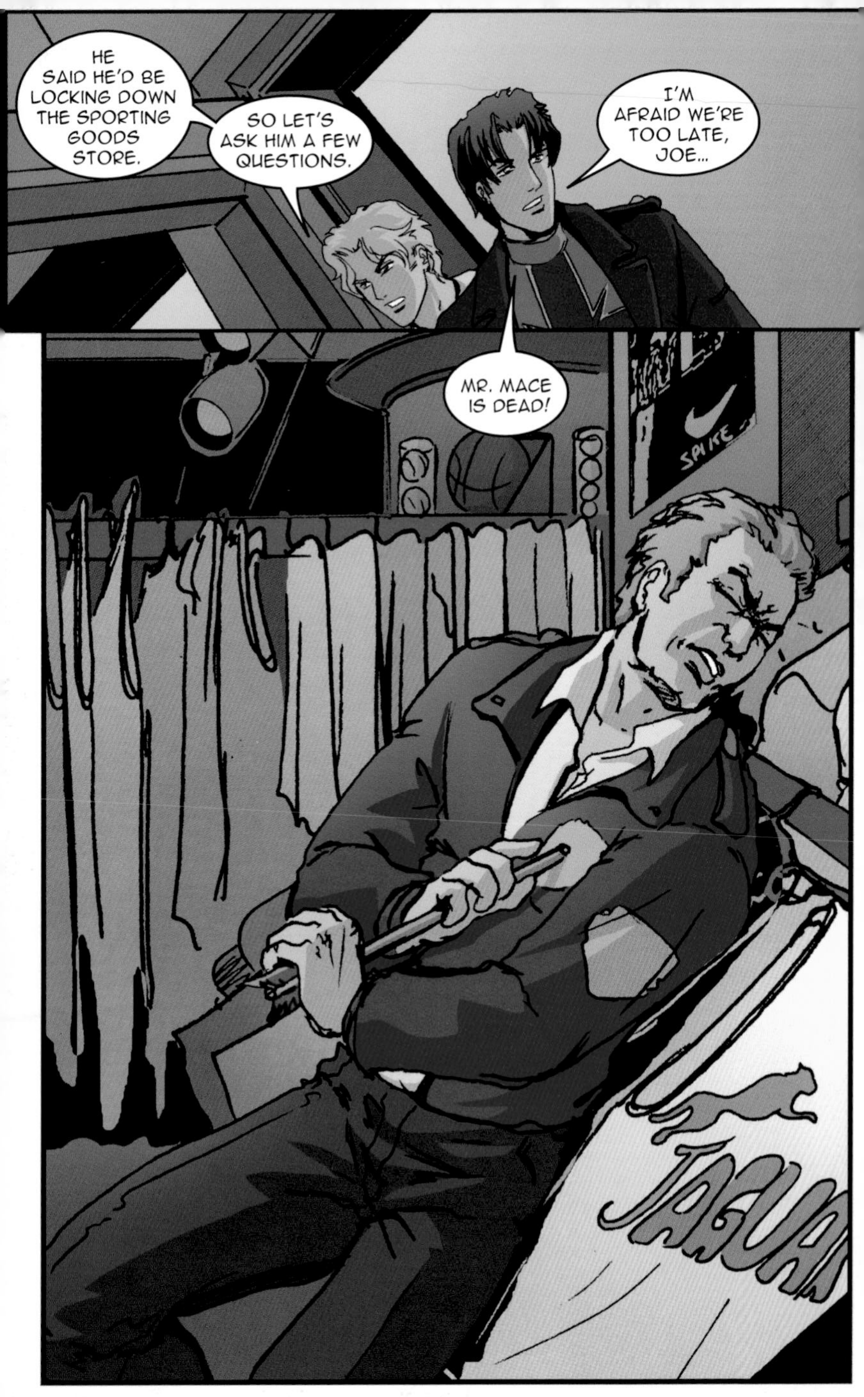
HE SAID HE'D BE LOCKING DOWN THE SPORTING GOODS STORE.
SO LET'S ASK HIM A FEW QUESTIONS.
I'M AFRAID WE'RE TOO LATE, JOE...
MR. MACE IS DEAD!
SPIKE
JAGUA

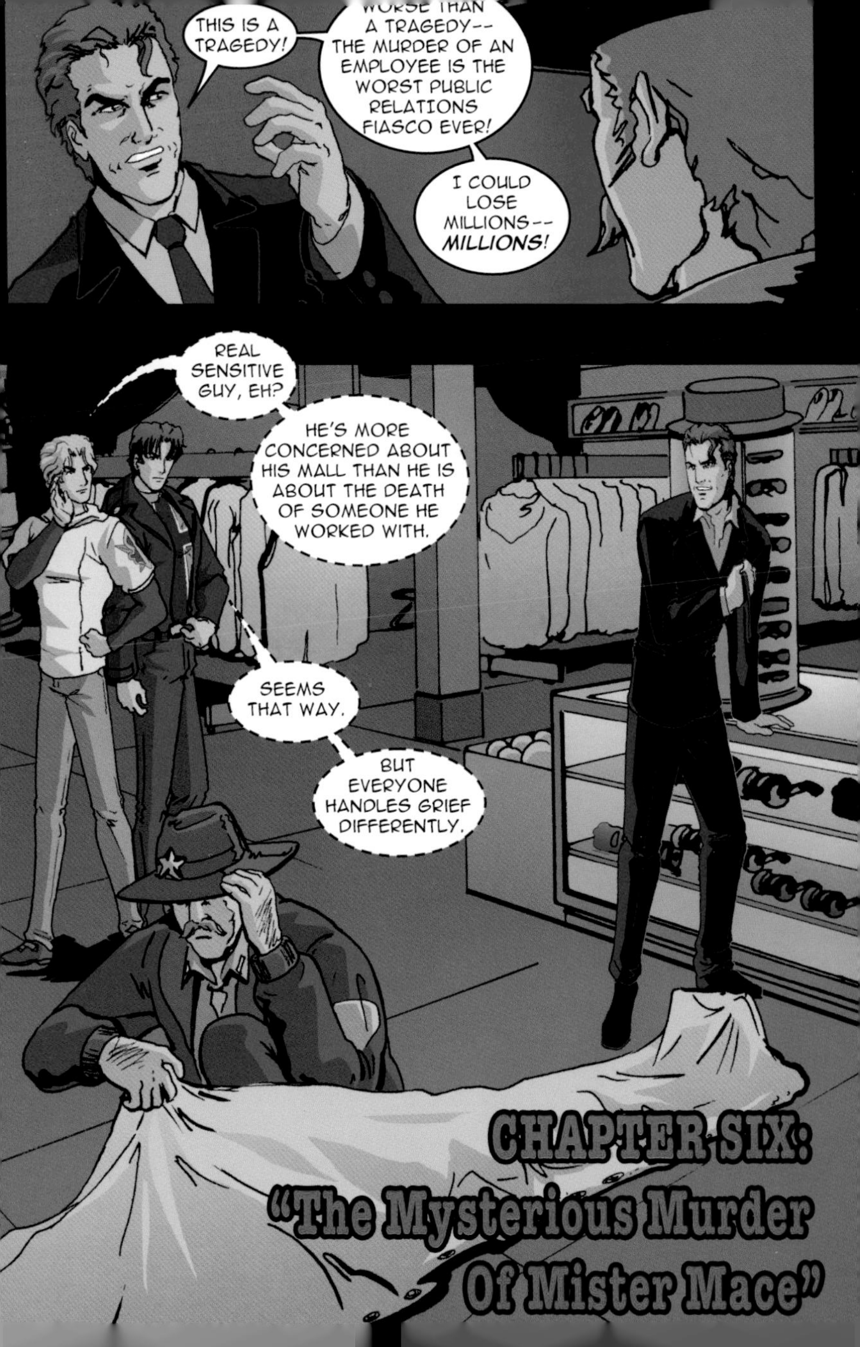
THIS IS A TRAGEDY!
WORSE THAN A TRAGEDY-- THE MURDER OF AN EMPLOYEE IS THE WORST PUBLIC RELATIONS FIASCO EVER!
I COULD LOSE MILLIONS-- MILLIONS!
REAL SENSITIVE GUY, EH?
HE'S MORE CONCERNED ABOUT HIS MALL THAN HE IS ABOUT THE DEATH OF SOMEONE HE WORKED WITH.
SEEMS THAT WAY.
BUT EVERYONE HANDLES GRIEF DIFFERENTLY.
CHAPTER SIX:
"The Mysterious Murder Of Mister Mace"

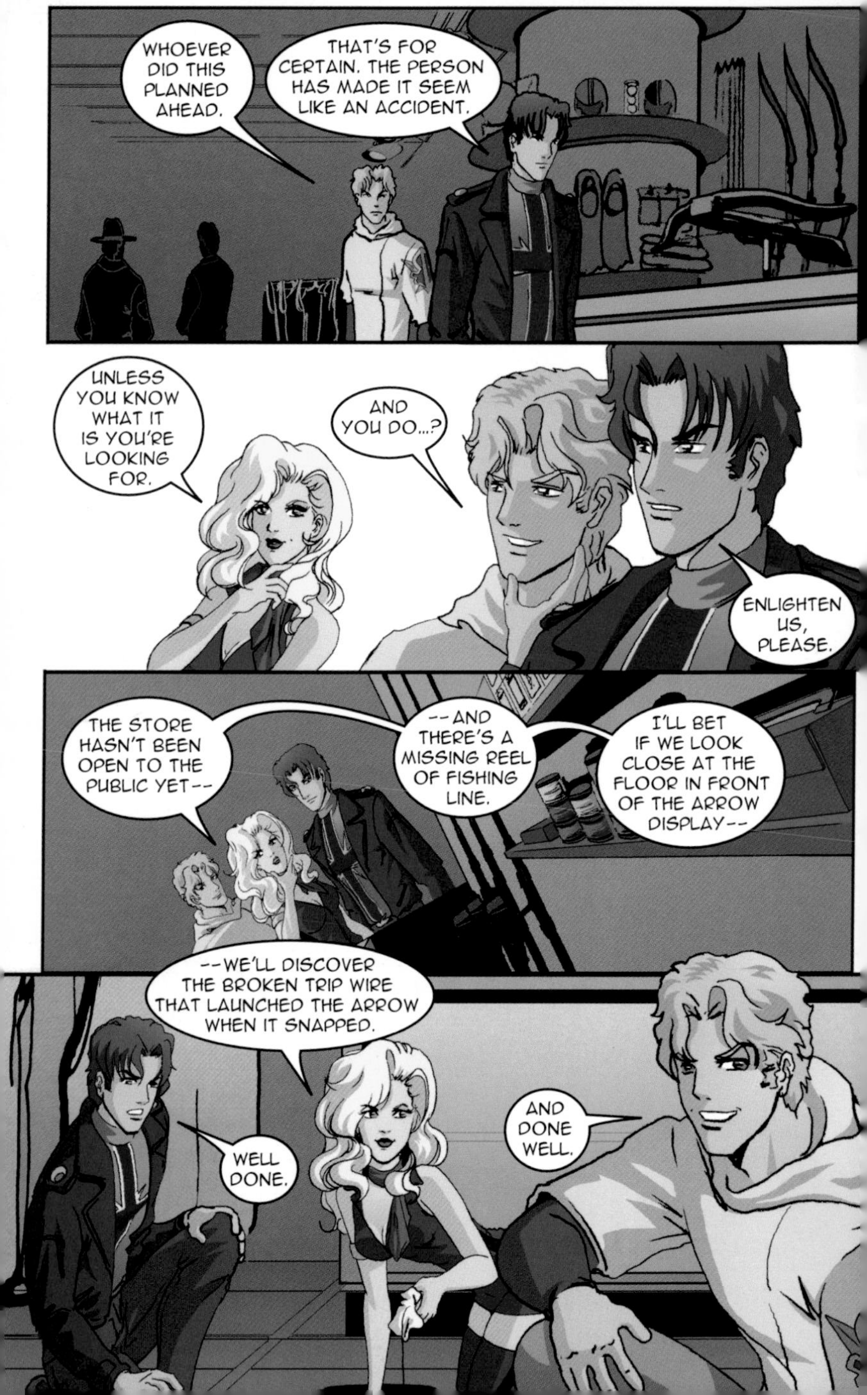
WHOEVER DID THIS PLANNED AHEAD.
THAT'S FOR CERTAIN. THE PERSON HAS MADE IT SEEM LIKE AN ACCIDENT.
UNLESS YOU KNOW WHAT IT IS YOU'RE LOOKING FOR.
AND YOU DO...?
ENLIGHTEN US, PLEASE.
THE STORE HASN'T BEEN OPEN TO THE PUBLIC YET--
--AND THERE'S A MISSING REEL OF FISHING LINE.
I'LL BET IF WE LOOK CLOSE AT THE FLOOR IN FRONT OF THE ARROW DISPLAY--
--WE'LL DISCOVER THE BROKEN TRIP WIRE THAT LAUNCHED THE ARROW WHEN IT SNAPPED.
WELL DONE.
AND DONE WELL.

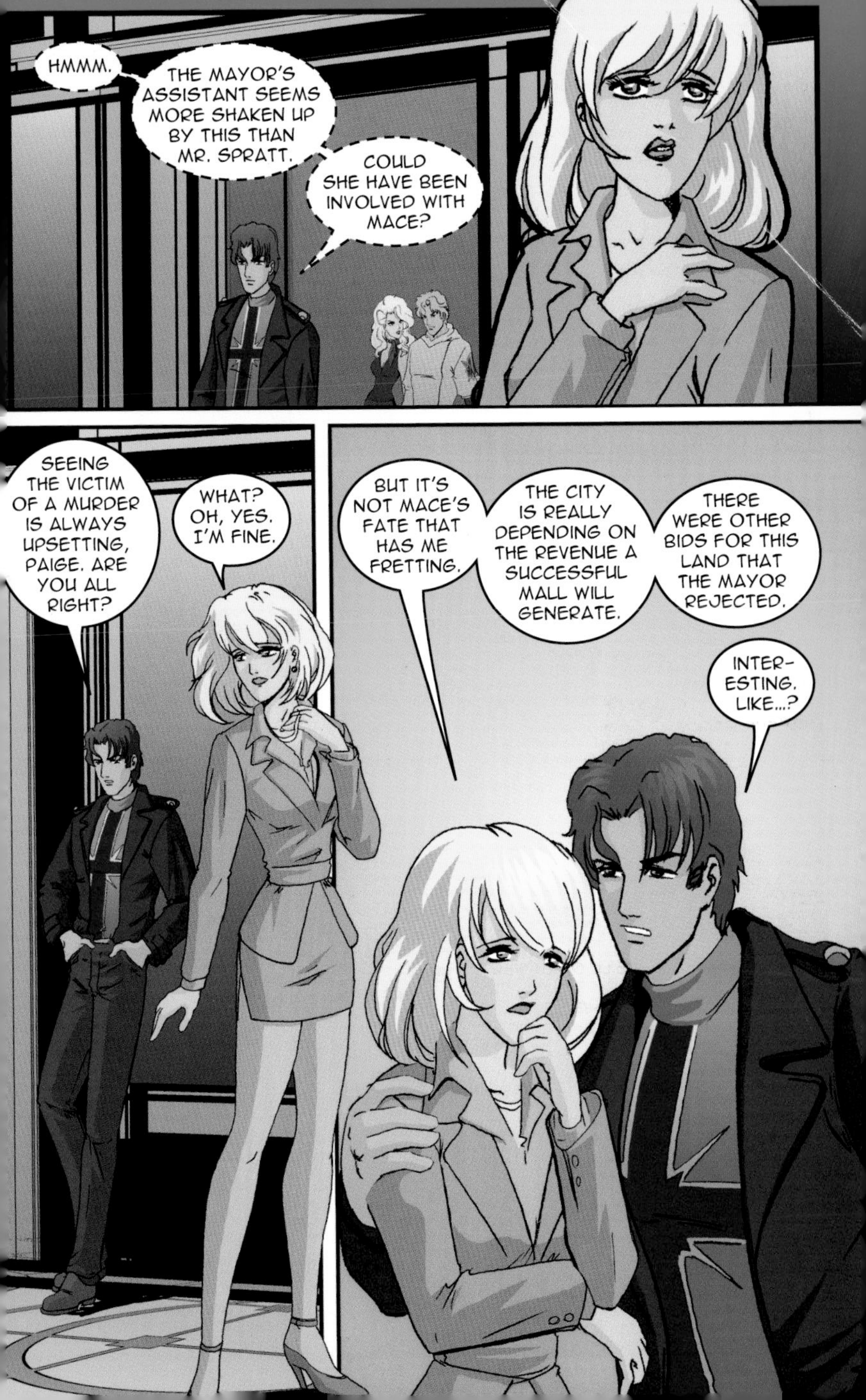
HMMM.
THE MAYOR'S ASSISTANT SEEMS MORE SHAKEN UP BY THIS THAN MR. SPRATT.
COULD SHE HAVE BEEN INVOLVED WITH MACE?
SEEING THE VICTIM OF A MURDER IS ALWAYS UPSETTING, PAIGE. ARE YOU ALL RIGHT?
WHAT? OH, YES. I'M FINE.
BUT IT'S NOT MACE'S FATE THAT HAS ME FRETTING.
THE CITY IS REALLY DEPENDING ON THE REVENUE A SUCCESSFUL MALL WILL GENERATE.
THERE WERE OTHER BIDS FOR THIS LAND THAT THE MAYOR REJECTED.
INTER-ESTING. LIKE...?

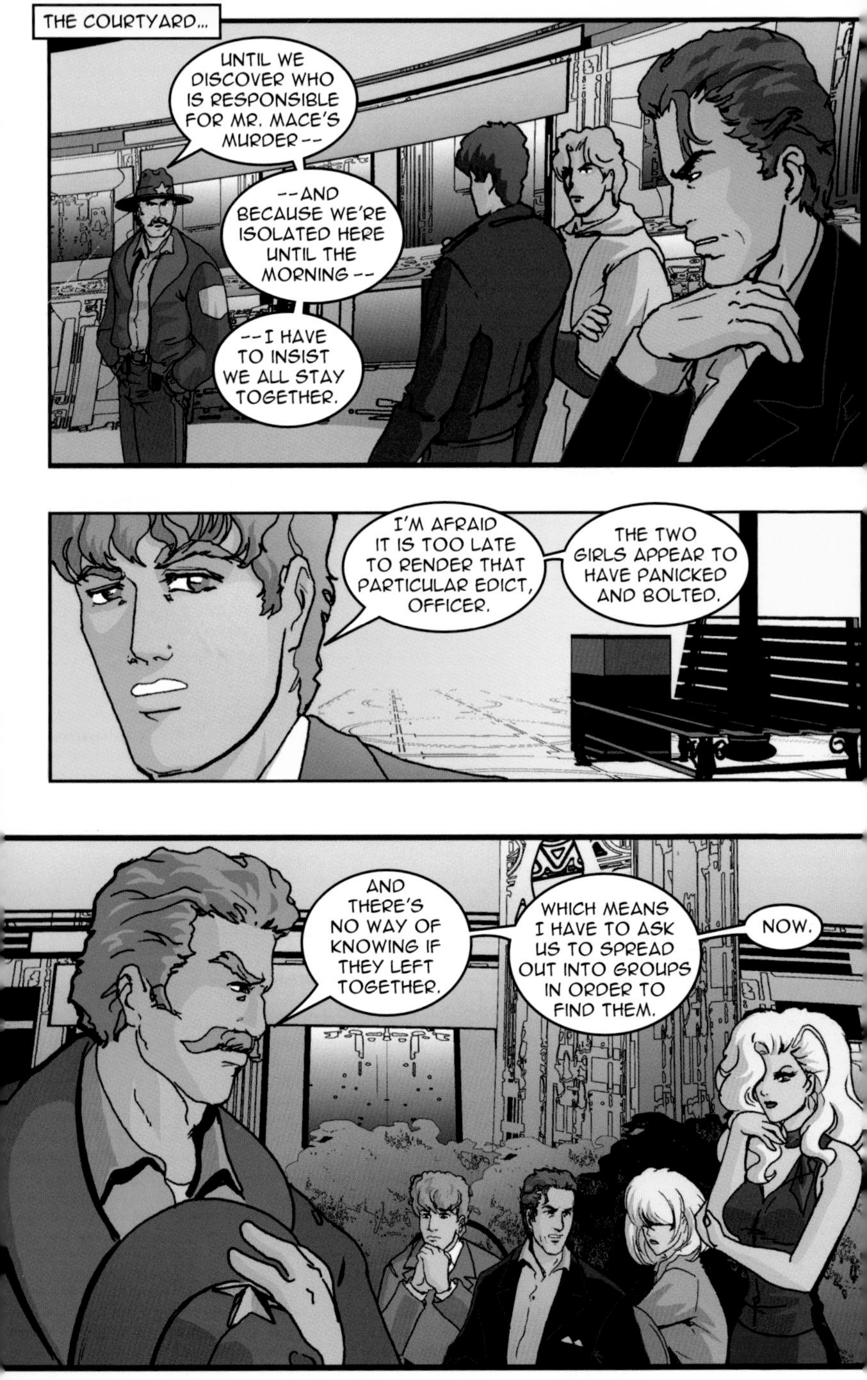
THE COURTYARD...
UNTIL WE DISCOVER WHO IS RESPONSIBLE FOR MR. MACE'S MURDER--
--AND BECAUSE WE'RE ISOLATED HERE UNTIL THE MORNING--
--I HAVE TO INSIST WE ALL STAY TOGETHER.
I'M AFRAID IT IS TOO LATE TO RENDER THAT PARTICULAR EDICT, OFFICER.
THE TWO GIRLS APPEAR TO HAVE PANICKED AND BOLTED.
AND THERE'S NO WAY OF KNOWING IF THEY LEFT TOGETHER.
WHICH MEANS I HAVE TO ASK US TO SPREAD OUT INTO GROUPS IN ORDER TO FIND THEM.
NOW.

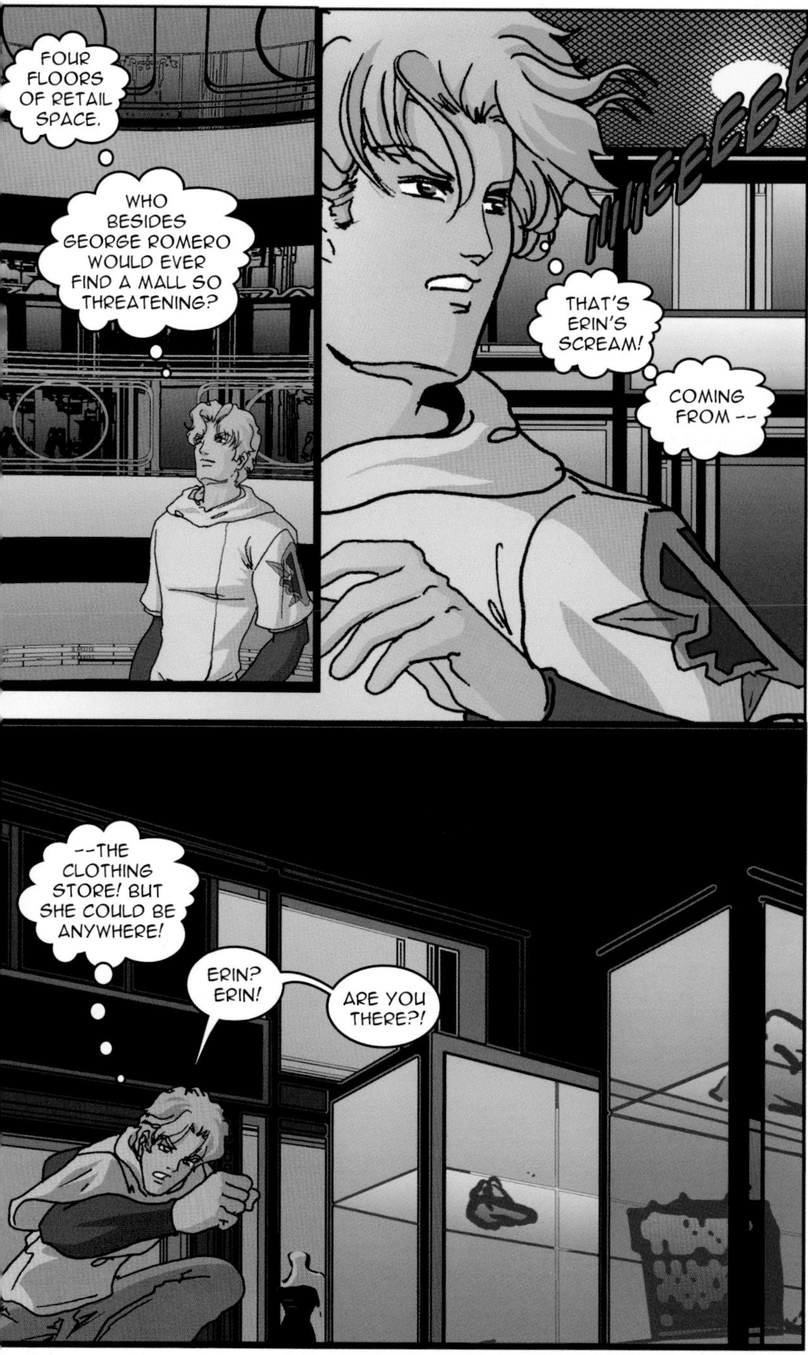
FOUR FLOORS OF RETAIL SPACE.
WHO BESIDES GEORGE ROMERO WOULD EVER FIND A MALL SO THREATENING?
MMEEEEEEE
THAT'S ERIN'S SCREAM!
COMING FROM --
--THE CLOTHING STORE! BUT SHE COULD BE ANYWHERE!
ERIN? ERIN!
ARE YOU THERE?!

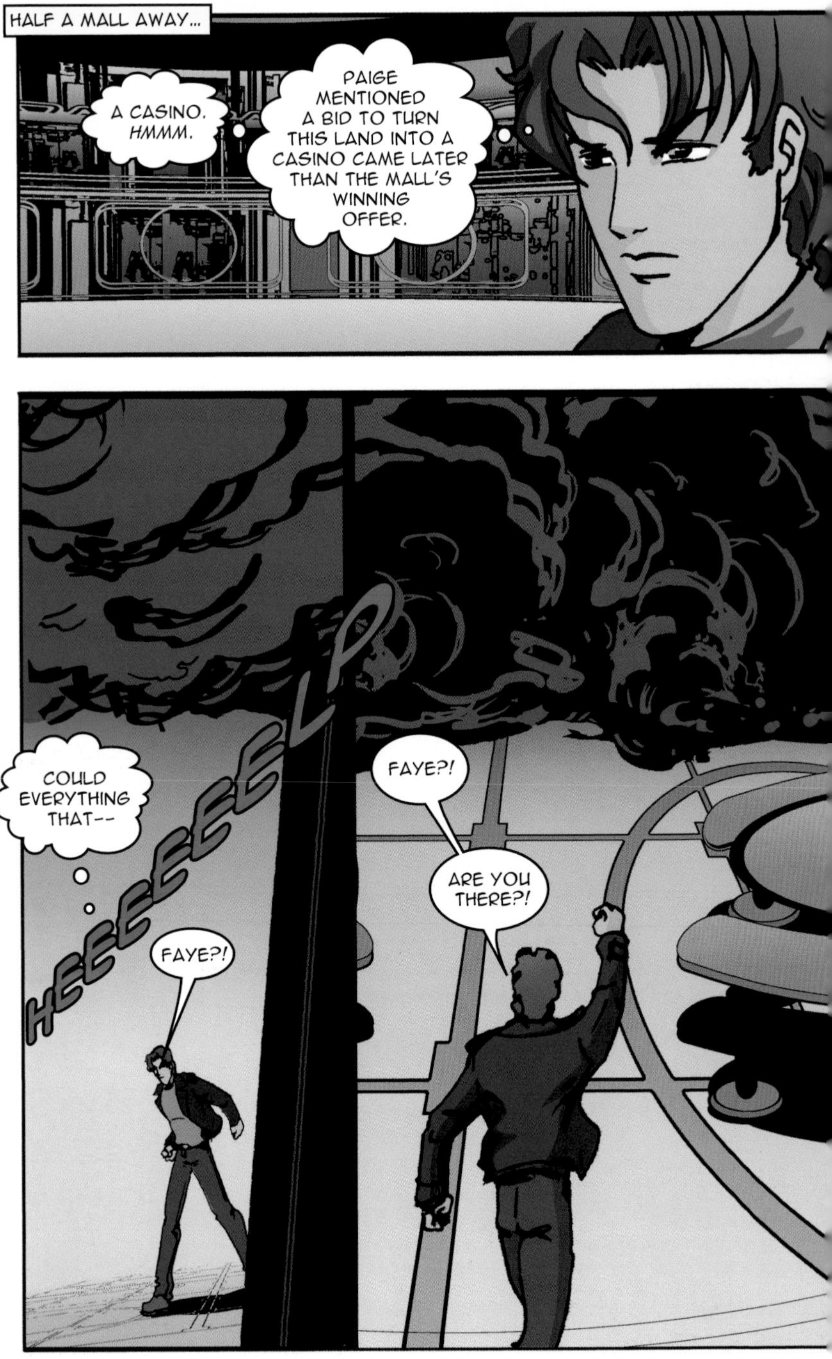

HALF A MALL AWAY...
A CASINO. HMMM.
PAIGE MENTIONED A BID TO TURN THIS LAND INTO A CASINO CAME LATER THAN THE MALL'S WINNING OFFER.
COULD EVERYTHING THAT--
HEEEEEEELP
FAYE?!
FAYE?!
ARE YOU THERE?!

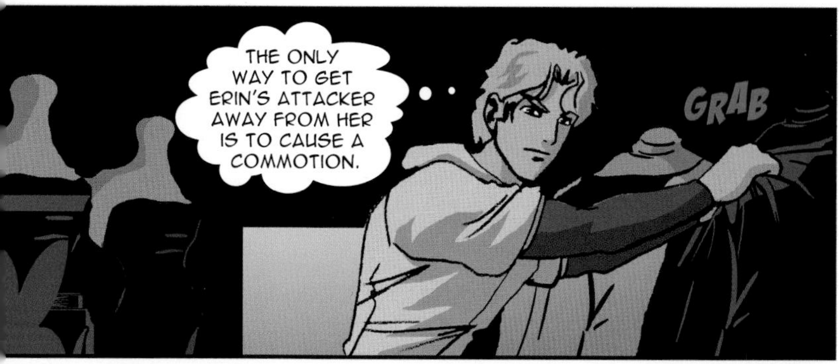

THE ONLY WAY TO GET ERIN'S ATTACKER AWAY FROM HER IS TO CAUSE A COMMOTION.
GRAB

CHAPTER SEVEN:
"A Danger Most Alarming..."

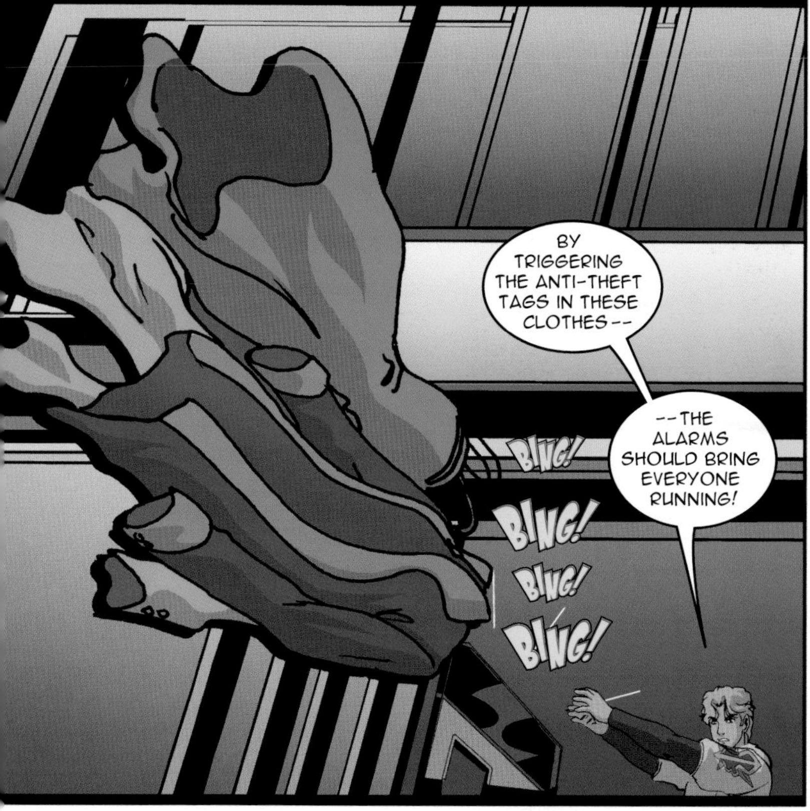

BY TRIGGERING THE ANTI-THEFT TAGS IN THESE CLOTHES --
--THE ALARMS SHOULD BRING EVERYONE RUNNING!
BING!
BING!
BING!
BING!

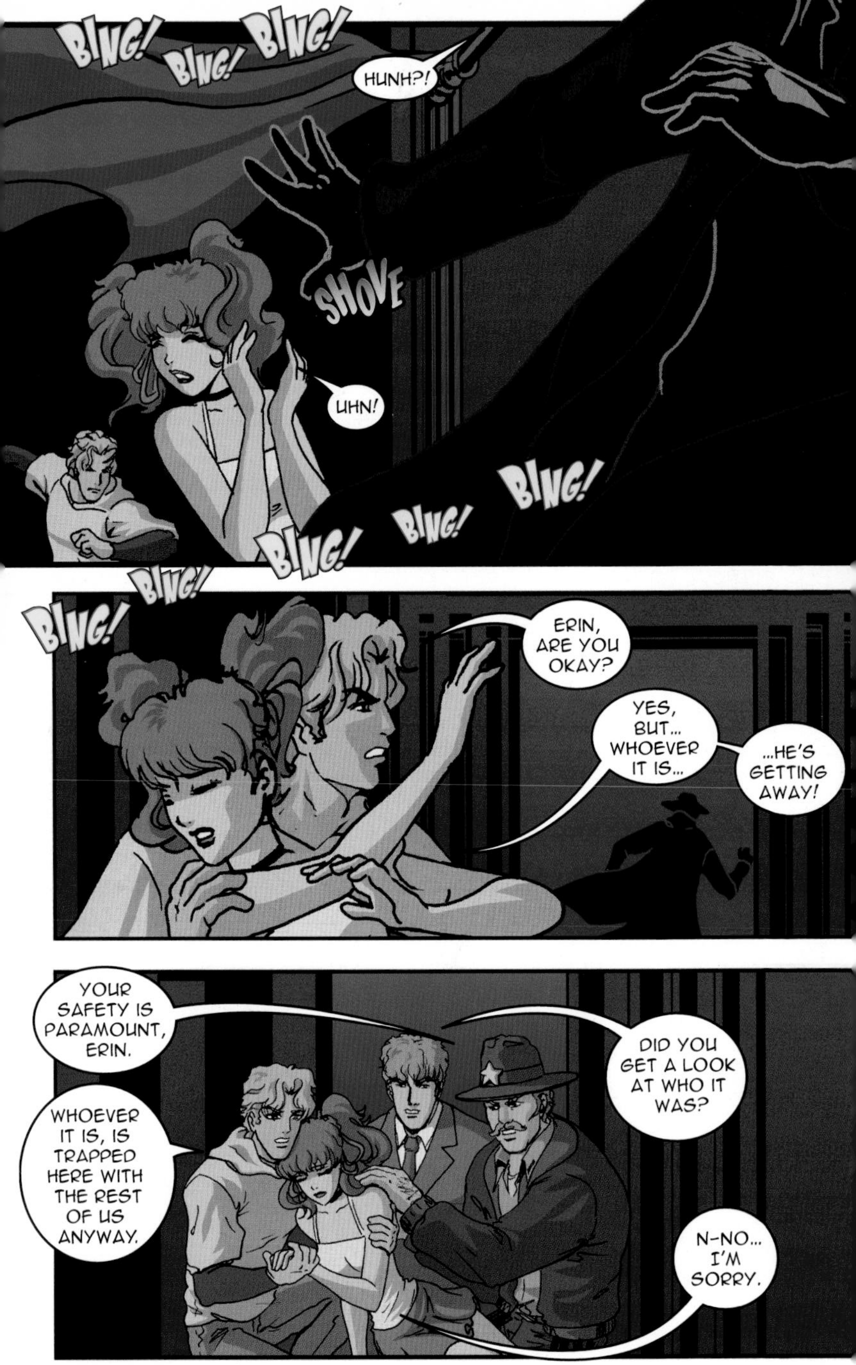
BING! BING! BING!
HUNH?!
SHOVE
UHN!
BING! BING! BING!
BING! BING!
ERIN, ARE YOU OKAY?
YES, BUT... WHOEVER IT IS...
...HE'S GETTING AWAY!
YOUR SAFETY IS PARAMOUNT, ERIN.
DID YOU GET A LOOK AT WHO IT WAS?
WHOEVER IT IS, IS TRAPPED HERE WITH THE REST OF US ANYWAY.
N-NO... I'M SORRY.

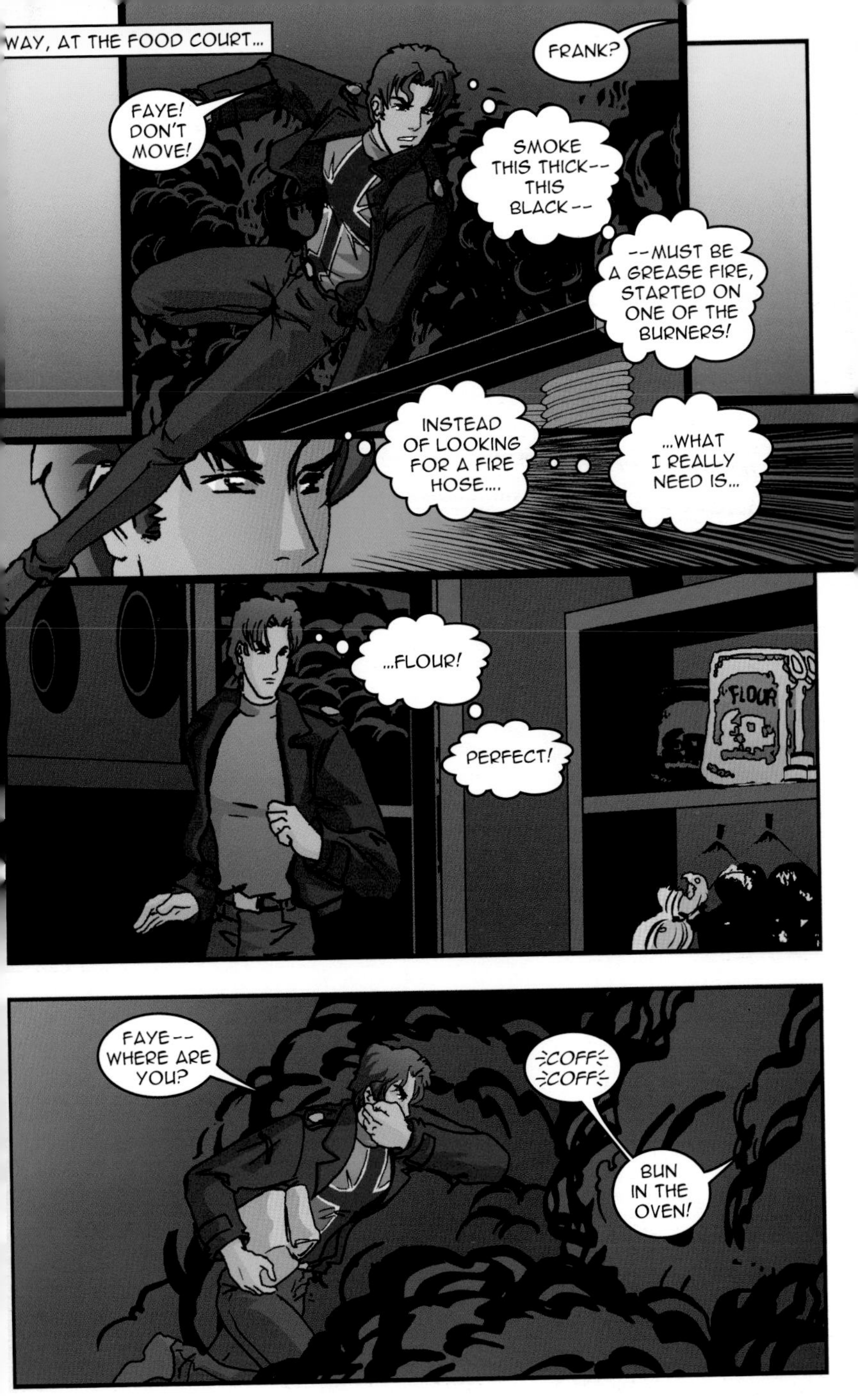

WAY, AT THE FOOD COURT...
FRANK?
FAYE! DON'T MOVE!
SMOKE THIS THICK-- THIS BLACK--
--MUST BE A GREASE FIRE, STARTED ON ONE OF THE BURNERS!
INSTEAD OF LOOKING FOR A FIRE HOSE....
...WHAT I REALLY NEED IS...
...FLOUR!
PERFECT!
FLOUR
FAYE-- WHERE ARE YOU?
COFF COFF
BUN IN THE OVEN!

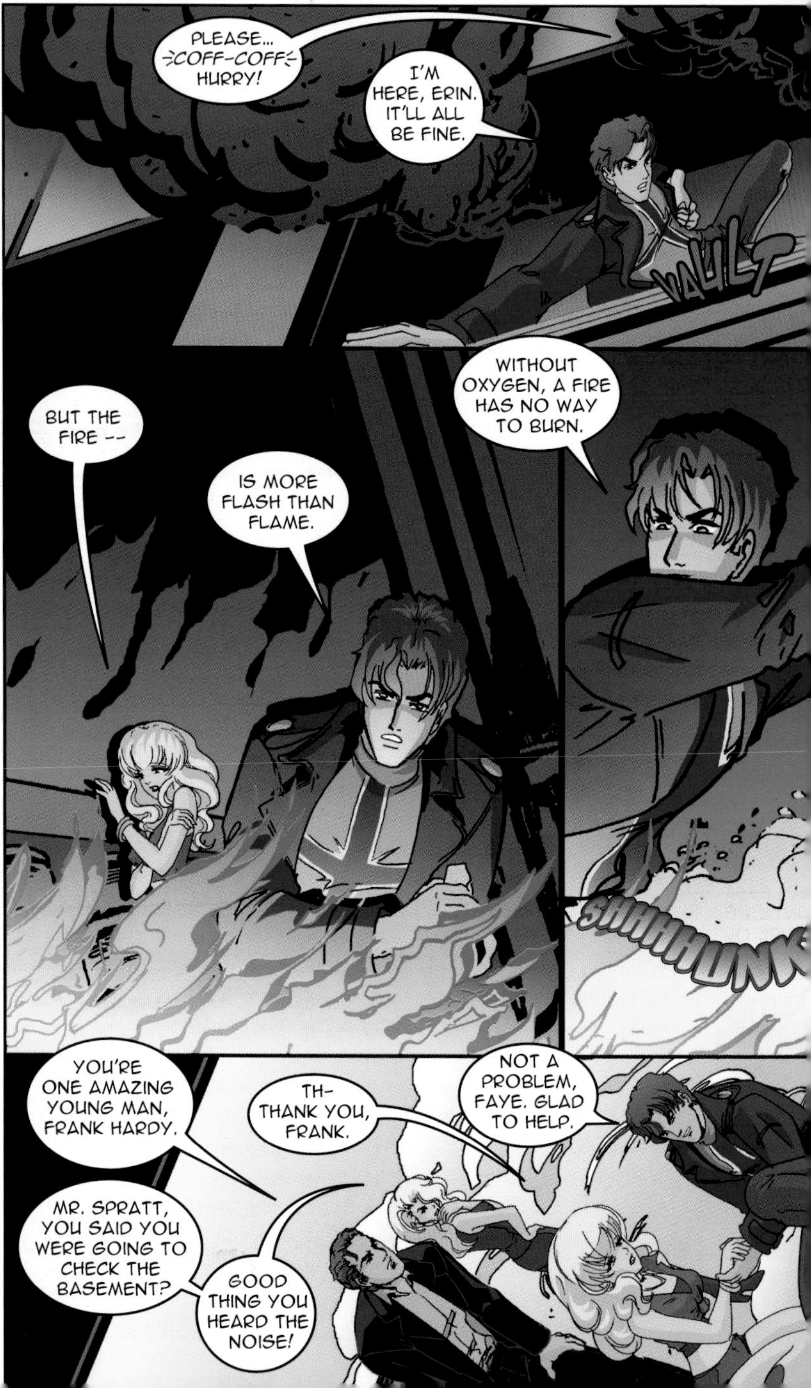
PLEASE... ≈COFF-COFF≈ HURRY!
I'M HERE, ERIN. IT'LL ALL BE FINE.
VAULT
BUT THE FIRE --
IS MORE FLASH THAN FLAME.
WITHOUT OXYGEN, A FIRE HAS NO WAY TO BURN.
SHHHHUNK
YOU'RE ONE AMAZING YOUNG MAN, FRANK HARDY.
TH- THANK YOU, FRANK.
NOT A PROBLEM, FAYE. GLAD TO HELP.
MR. SPRATT, YOU SAID YOU WERE GOING TO CHECK THE BASEMENT?
GOOD THING YOU HEARD THE NOISE!

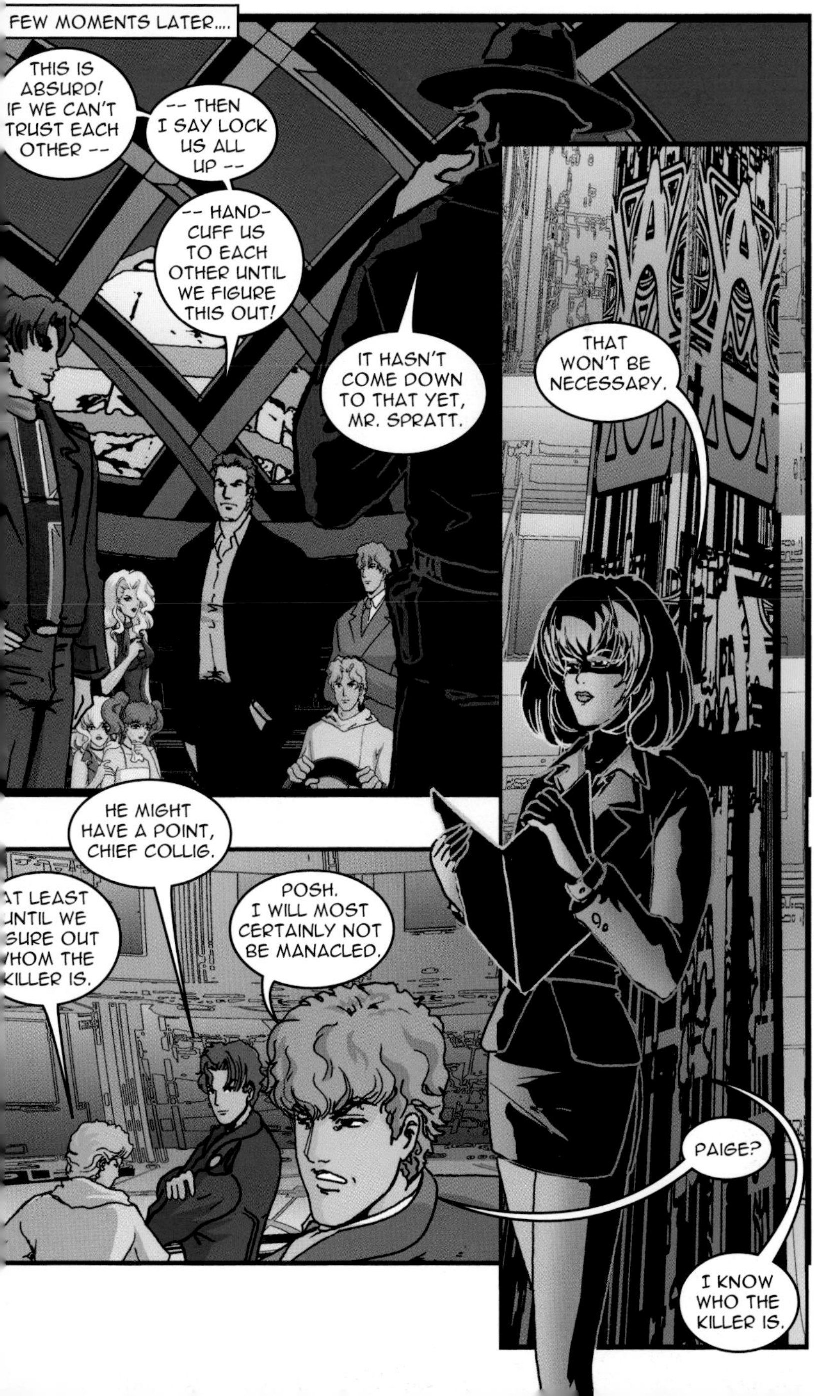
FEW MOMENTS LATER....
THIS IS ABSURD! IF WE CAN'T TRUST EACH OTHER --
-- THEN I SAY LOCK US ALL UP --
-- HAND-CUFF US TO EACH OTHER UNTIL WE FIGURE THIS OUT!
IT HASN'T COME DOWN TO THAT YET, MR. SPRATT.
THAT WON'T BE NECESSARY.
HE MIGHT HAVE A POINT, CHIEF COLLIG.
AT LEAST UNTIL WE FIGURE OUT WHOM THE KILLER IS.
POSH. I WILL MOST CERTAINLY NOT BE MANACLED.
PAIGE?
I KNOW WHO THE KILLER IS.

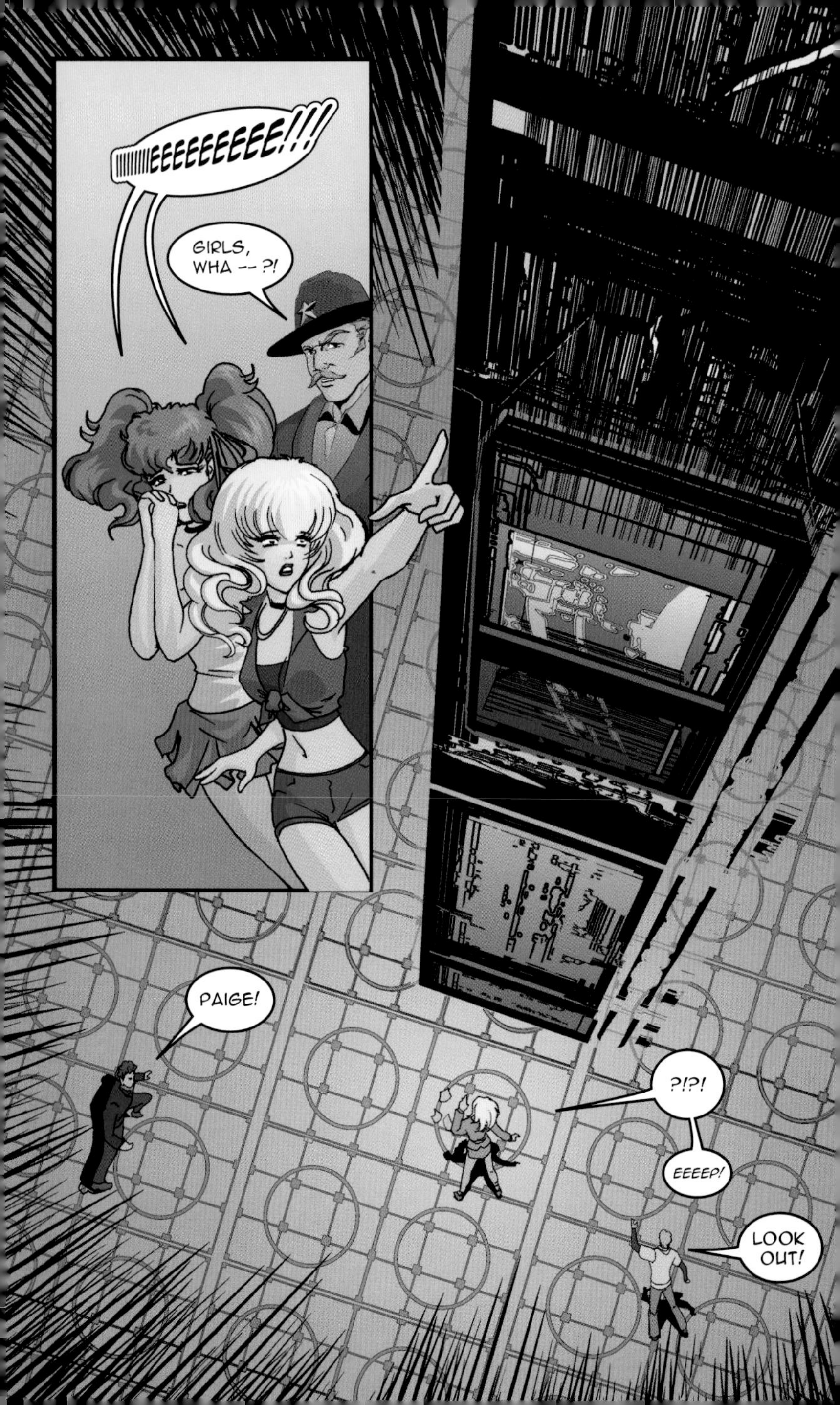

IIIIIIIIIEEEEEEEEEE!!!
GIRLS, WHA -- ?!
PAIGE!
?!?!
EEEEP!
LOOK OUT!

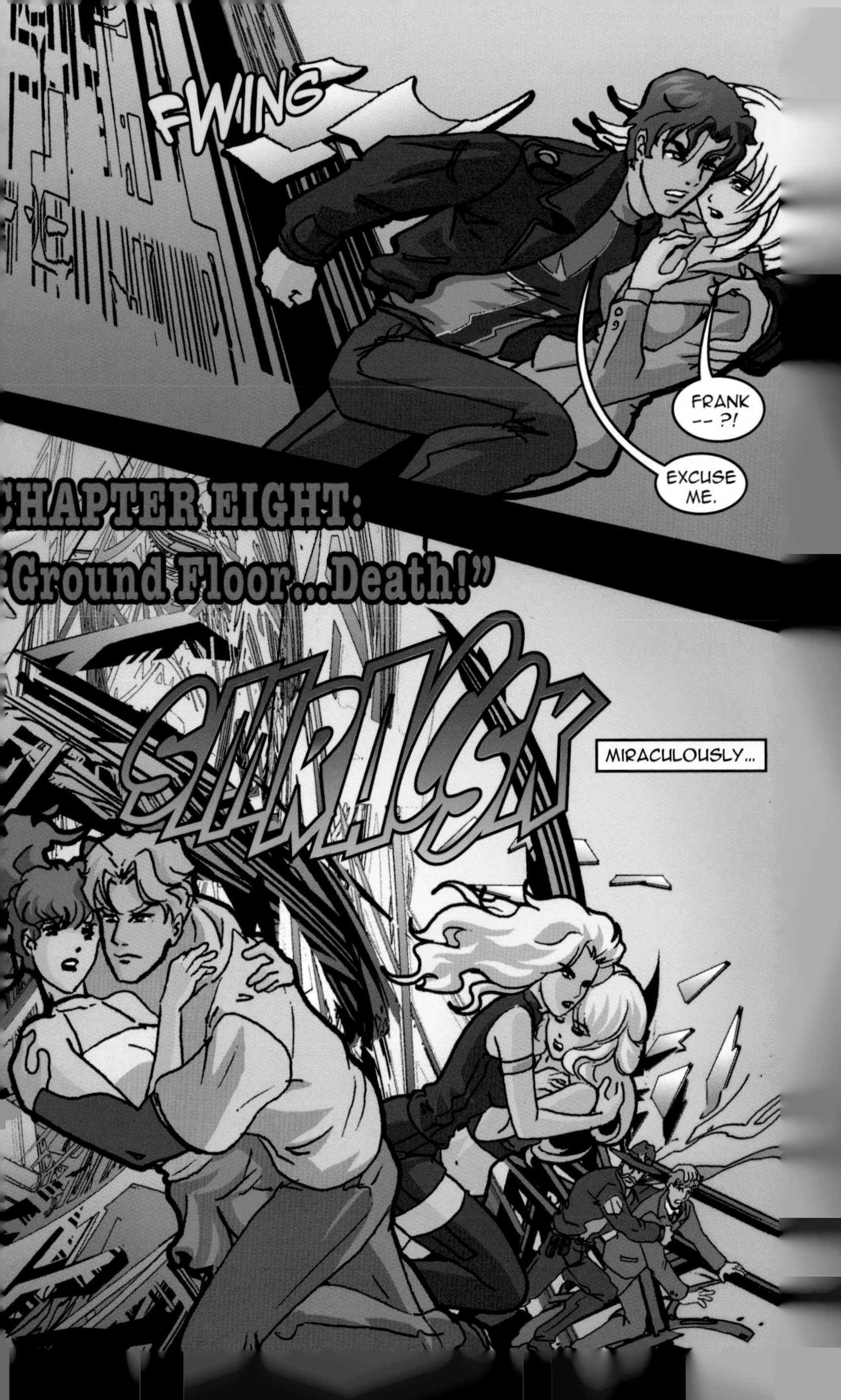
FWING
FRANK -- ?!
EXCUSE ME.
CHAPTER EIGHT:
"Ground Floor...Death!"
MIRACULOUSLY...

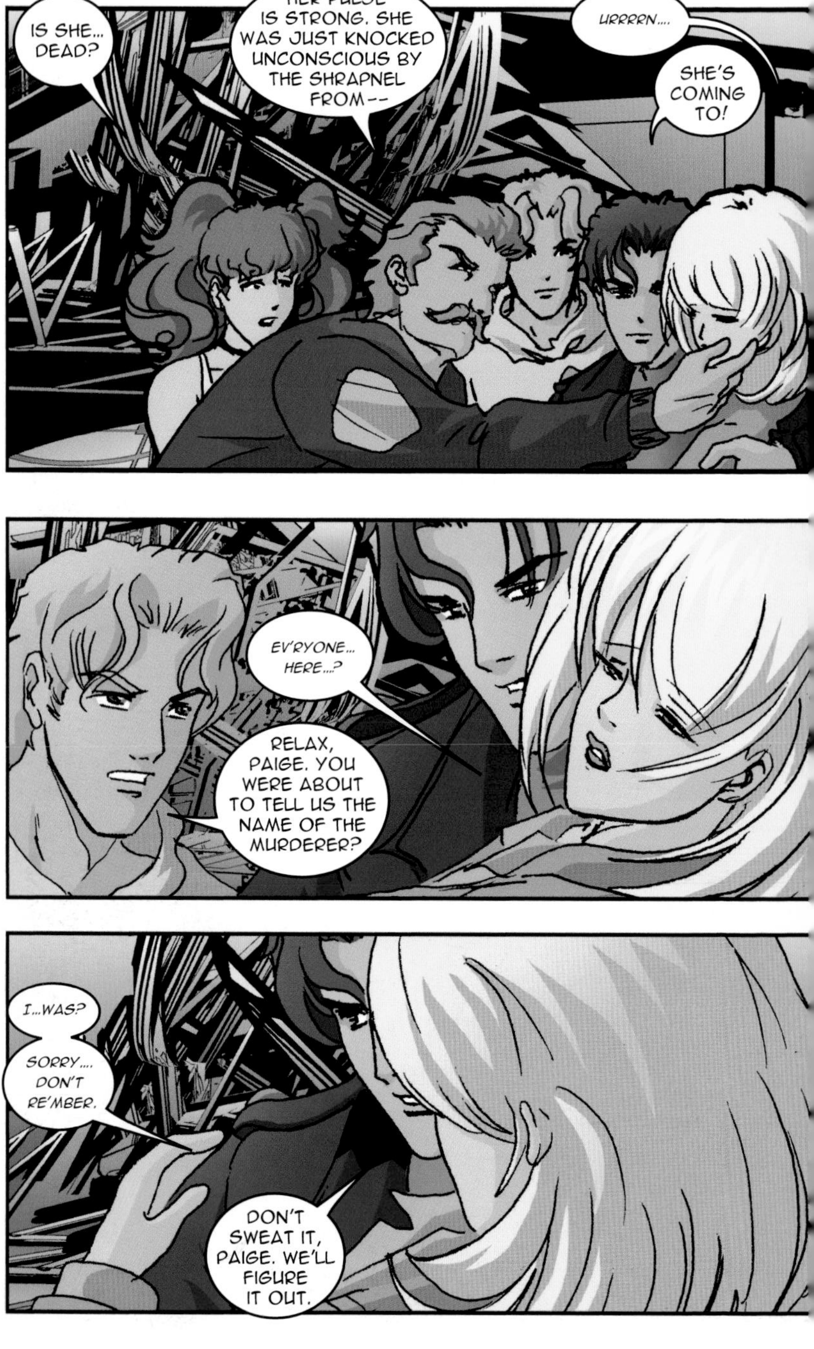
IS SHE... DEAD?
HER PULSE IS STRONG. SHE WAS JUST KNOCKED UNCONSCIOUS BY THE SHRAPNEL FROM--
URRRRN....
SHE'S COMING TO!
EV'RYONE... HERE...?
RELAX, PAIGE. YOU WERE ABOUT TO TELL US THE NAME OF THE MURDERER?
I...WAS?
SORRY.... DON'T RE'MBER.
DON'T SWEAT IT, PAIGE. WE'LL FIGURE IT OUT.

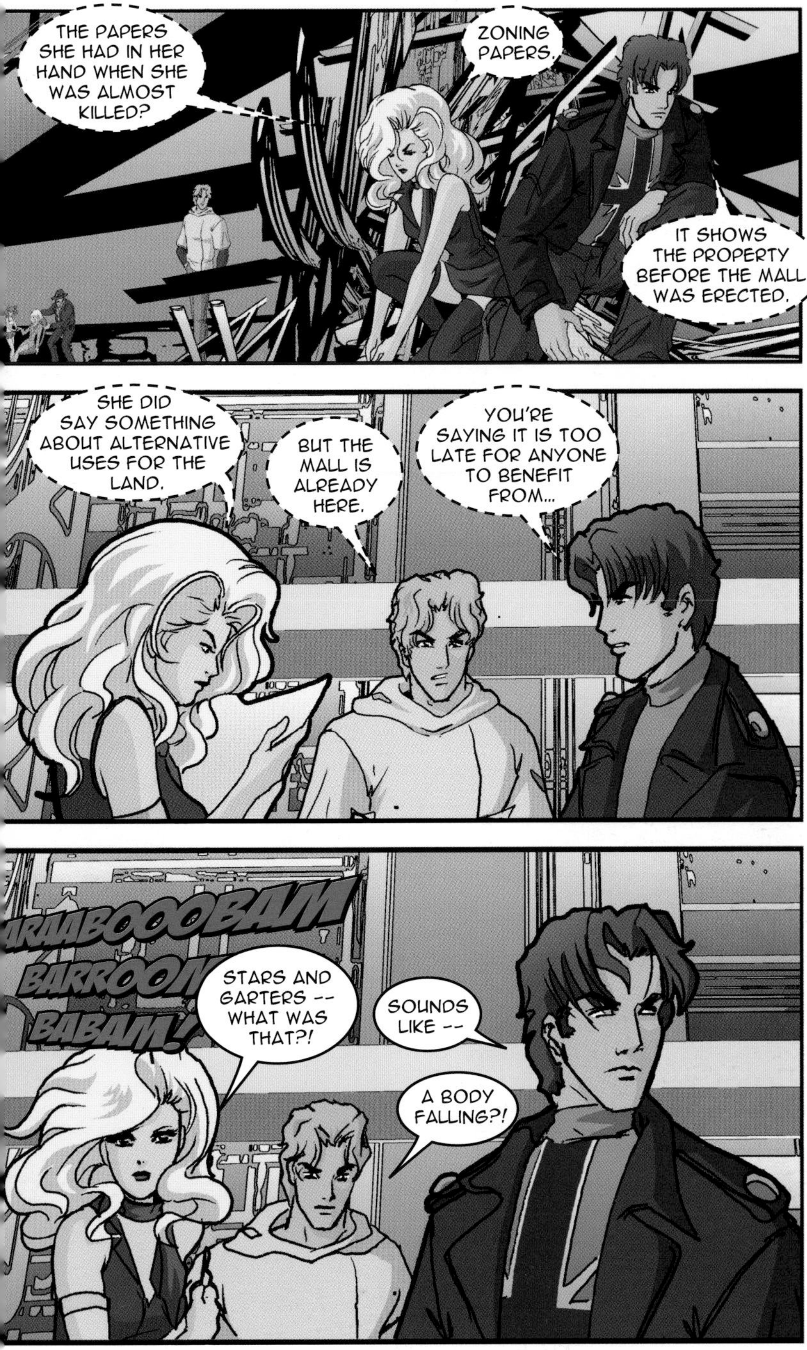
THE PAPERS SHE HAD IN HER HAND WHEN SHE WAS ALMOST KILLED?
ZONING PAPERS.
IT SHOWS THE PROPERTY BEFORE THE MALL WAS ERECTED.
SHE DID SAY SOMETHING ABOUT ALTERNATIVE USES FOR THE LAND.
BUT THE MALL IS ALREADY HERE.
YOU'RE SAYING IT IS TOO LATE FOR ANYONE TO BENEFIT FROM...
ARAAABOOOOBAM
BARROOM
BABAM!
STARS AND GARTERS -- WHAT WAS THAT?!
SOUNDS LIKE --
A BODY FALLING?!

IT'S MR. BOREMAN!

I GUESS IT IS POSSIBLE THIS WAS AN ACCIDENT.

WE'LL WORRY ABOUT THE "HOW" IN A MOMENT -- AFTER WE MAKE SURE HE'S OKAY.

HE'S UNCONSCIOUS, BUT I DON'T FEEL ANY BROKEN BONES. IF HE WAKES UP, HE SHOULD BE FINE.

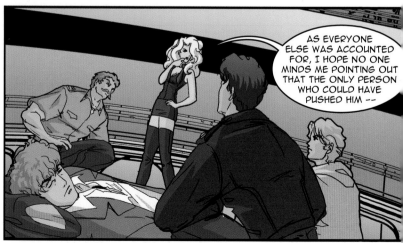

AS EVERYONE ELSE WAS ACCOUNTED FOR, I HOPE NO ONE MINDS ME POINTING OUT THAT THE ONLY PERSON WHO COULD HAVE PUSHED HIM --

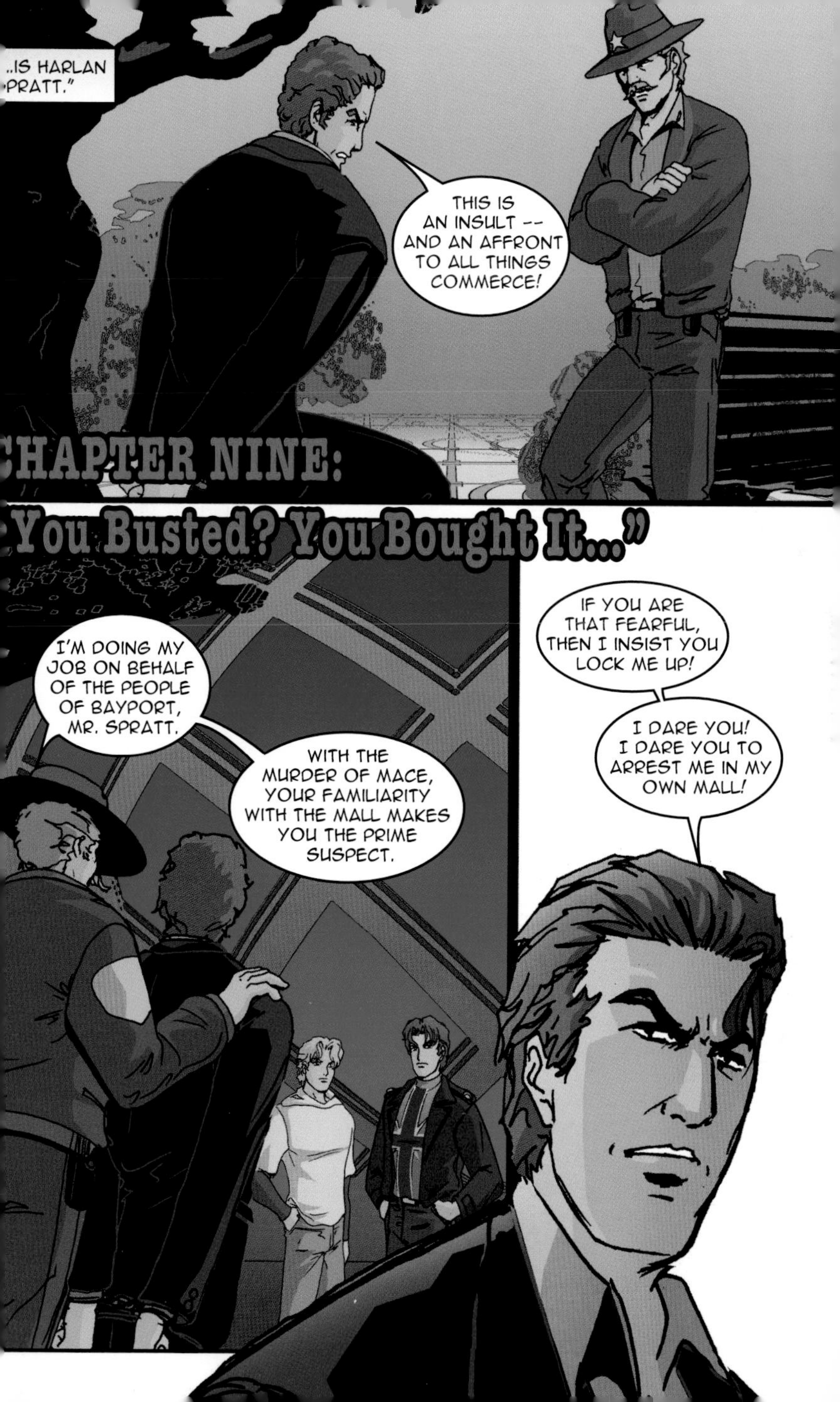
..IS HARLAN
PRATT."
THIS IS AN INSULT -- AND AN AFFRONT TO ALL THINGS COMMERCE!
CHAPTER NINE:
"You Busted? You Bought It..."
I'M DOING MY JOB ON BEHALF OF THE PEOPLE OF BAYPORT, MR. SPRATT.
WITH THE MURDER OF MACE, YOUR FAMILIARITY WITH THE MALL MAKES YOU THE PRIME SUSPECT.
IF YOU ARE THAT FEARFUL, THEN I INSIST YOU LOCK ME UP!
I DARE YOU! I DARE YOU TO ARREST ME IN MY OWN MALL!

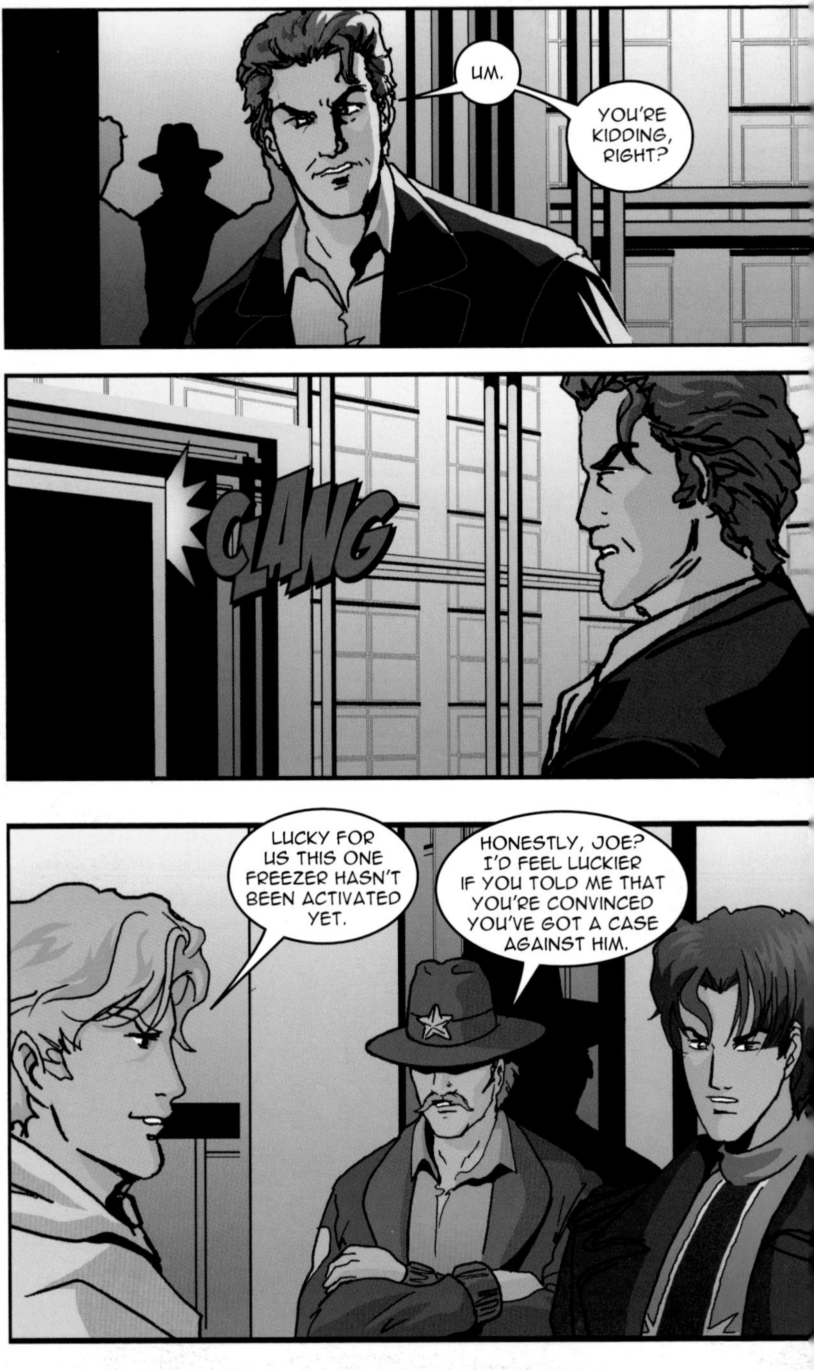
UM.
YOU'RE KIDDING, RIGHT?
CLANG
LUCKY FOR US THIS ONE FREEZER HASN'T BEEN ACTIVATED YET.
HONESTLY, JOE? I'D FEEL LUCKIER IF YOU TOLD ME THAT YOU'RE CONVINCED YOU'VE GOT A CASE AGAINST HIM.

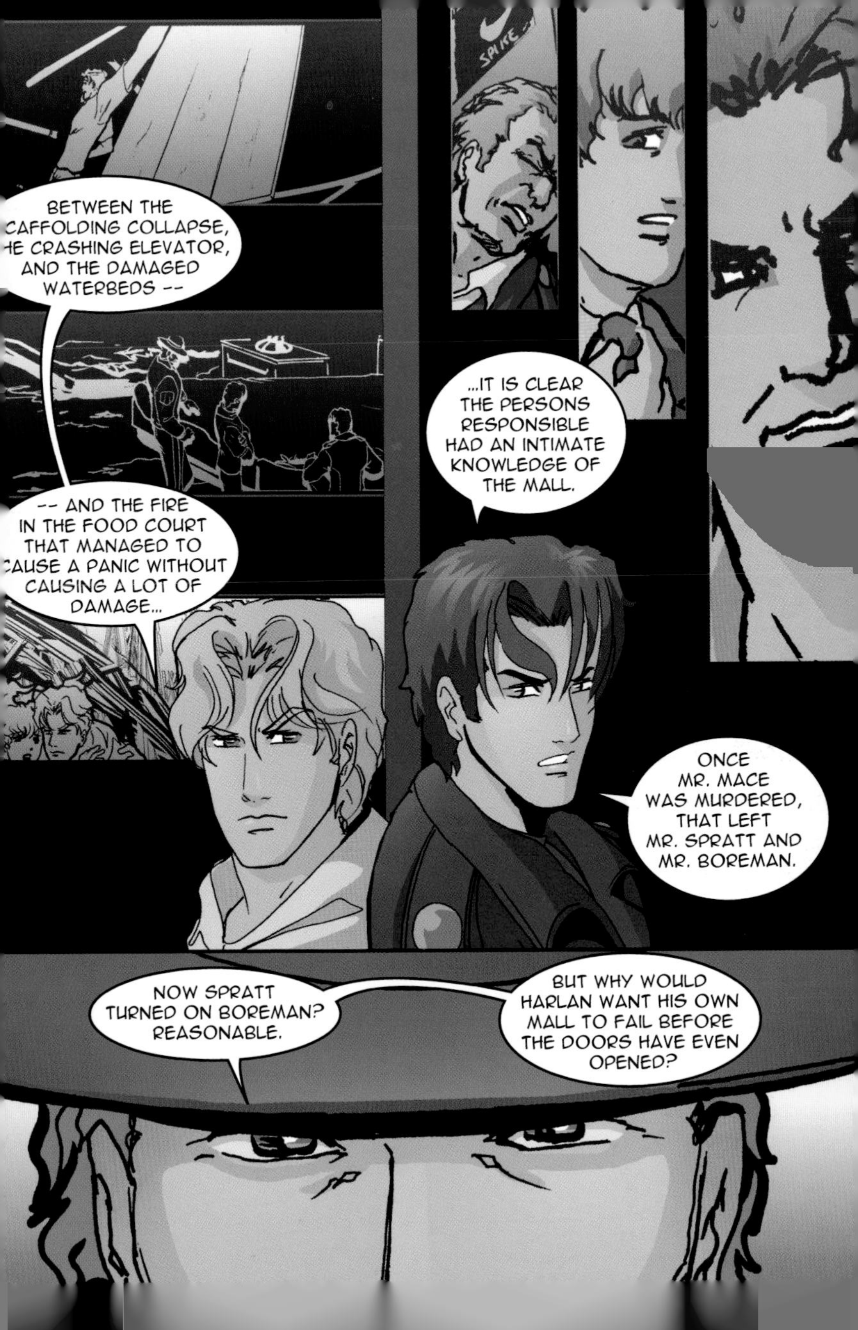
BETWEEN THE CAFFOLDING COLLAPSE, HE CRASHING ELEVATOR, AND THE DAMAGED WATERBEDS --
...IT IS CLEAR THE PERSONS RESPONSIBLE HAD AN INTIMATE KNOWLEDGE OF THE MALL.
-- AND THE FIRE IN THE FOOD COURT THAT MANAGED TO AUSE A PANIC WITHOUT CAUSING A LOT OF DAMAGE...
ONCE MR. MACE WAS MURDERED, THAT LEFT MR. SPRATT AND MR. BOREMAN.
NOW SPRATT TURNED ON BOREMAN? REASONABLE.
BUT WHY WOULD HARLAN WANT HIS OWN MALL TO FAIL BEFORE THE DOORS HAVE EVEN OPENED?

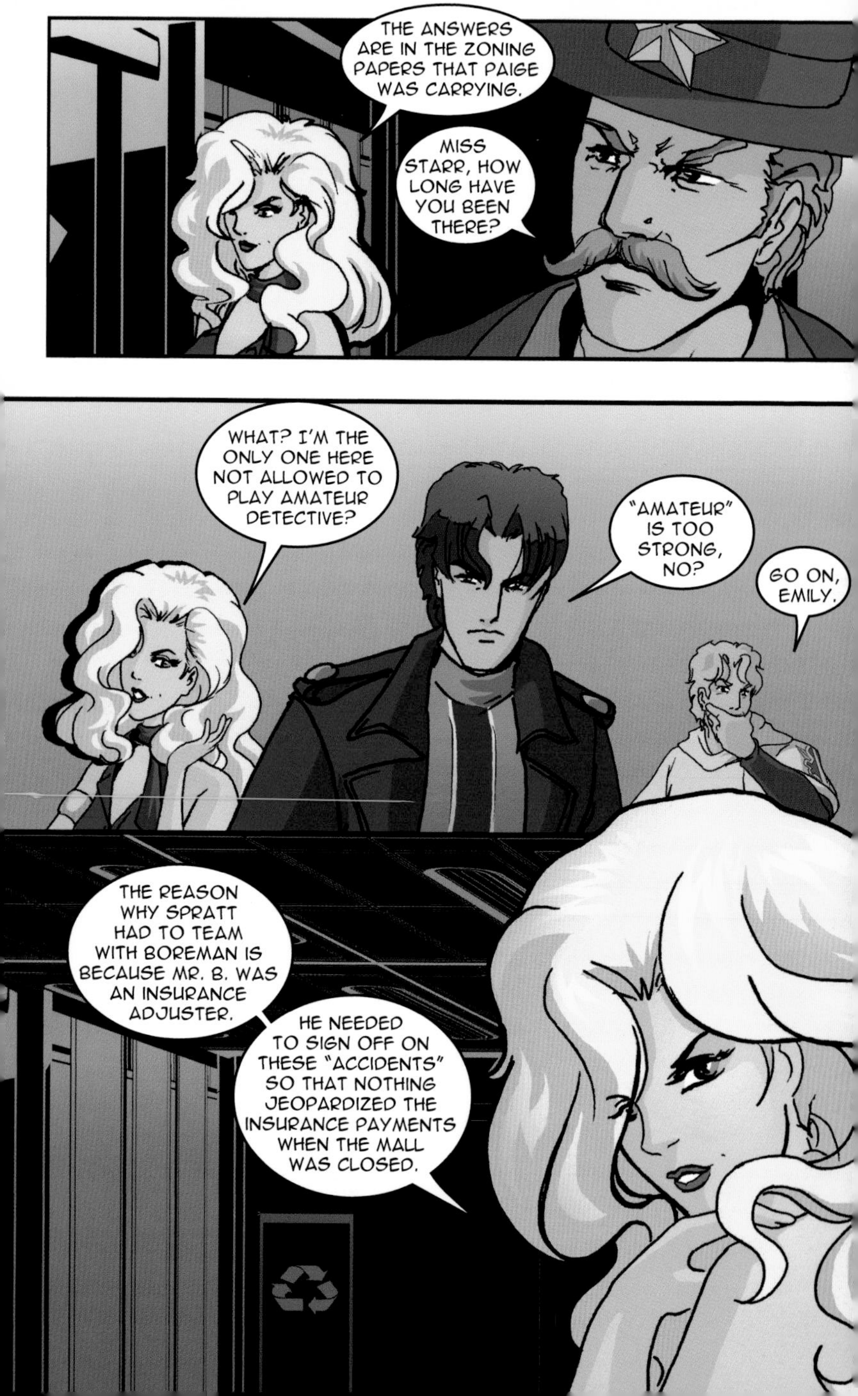
THE ANSWERS ARE IN THE ZONING PAPERS THAT PAIGE WAS CARRYING.
MISS STARR, HOW LONG HAVE YOU BEEN THERE?
WHAT? I'M THE ONLY ONE HERE NOT ALLOWED TO PLAY AMATEUR DETECTIVE?
"AMATEUR" IS TOO STRONG, NO?
GO ON, EMILY.
THE REASON WHY SPRATT HAD TO TEAM WITH BOREMAN IS BECAUSE MR. B. WAS AN INSURANCE ADJUSTER.
HE NEEDED TO SIGN OFF ON THESE "ACCIDENTS" SO THAT NOTHING JEOPARDIZED THE INSURANCE PAYMENTS WHEN THE MALL WAS CLOSED.

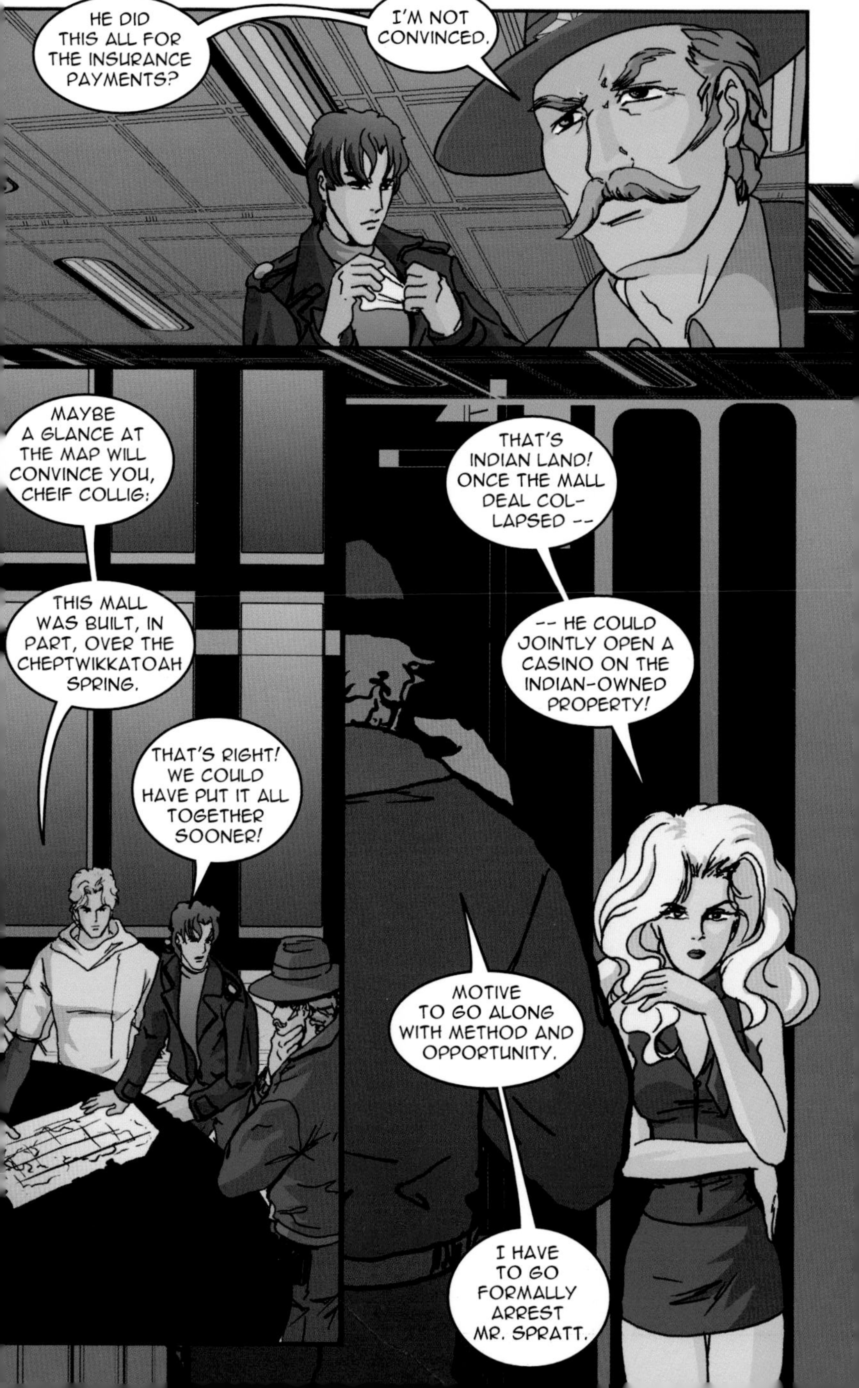
HE DID THIS ALL FOR THE INSURANCE PAYMENTS?
I'M NOT CONVINCED.
MAYBE A GLANCE AT THE MAP WILL CONVINCE YOU, CHEIF COLLIG:
THIS MALL WAS BUILT, IN PART, OVER THE CHEPTWIKKATOAH SPRING.
THAT'S RIGHT! WE COULD HAVE PUT IT ALL TOGETHER SOONER!
THAT'S INDIAN LAND! ONCE THE MALL DEAL COL-LAPSED --
-- HE COULD JOINTLY OPEN A CASINO ON THE INDIAN-OWNED PROPERTY!
MOTIVE TO GO ALONG WITH METHOD AND OPPORTUNITY.
I HAVE TO GO FORMALLY ARREST MR. SPRATT.

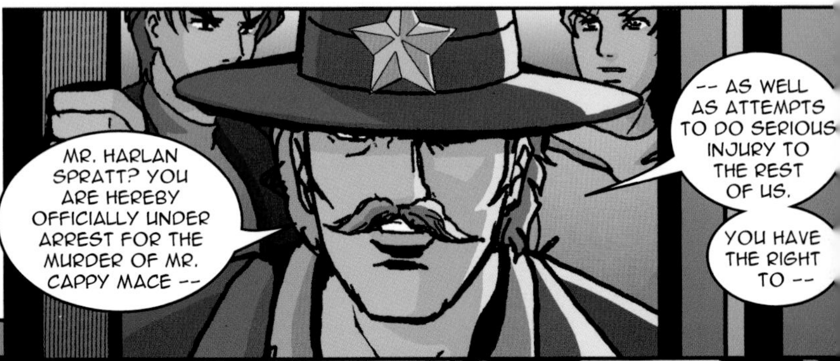
MR. HARLAN SPRATT? YOU ARE HEREBY OFFICIALLY UNDER ARREST FOR THE MURDER OF MR. CAPPY MACE --
-- AS WELL AS ATTEMPTS TO DO SERIOUS INJURY TO THE REST OF US.
YOU HAVE THE RIGHT TO --

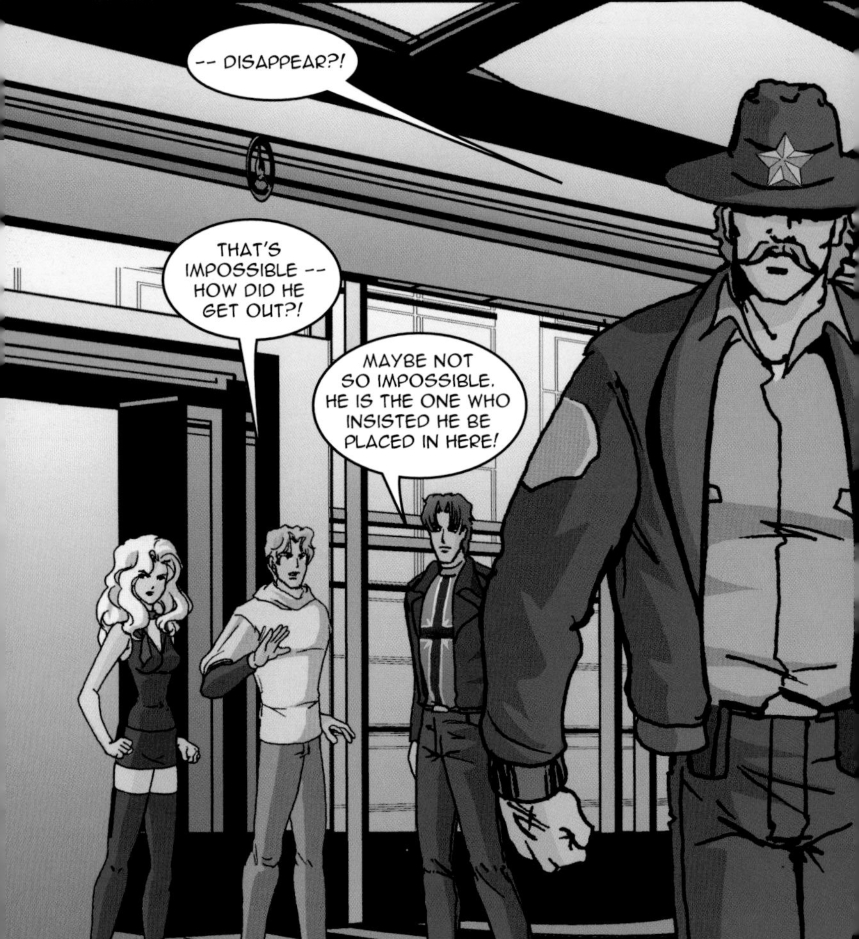
-- DISAPPEAR?!
THAT'S IMPOSSIBLE -- HOW DID HE GET OUT?!
MAYBE NOT SO IMPOSSIBLE. HE IS THE ONE WHO INSISTED HE BE PLACED IN HERE!

CHAPTER TEN:
"Attention, Shoppers..."

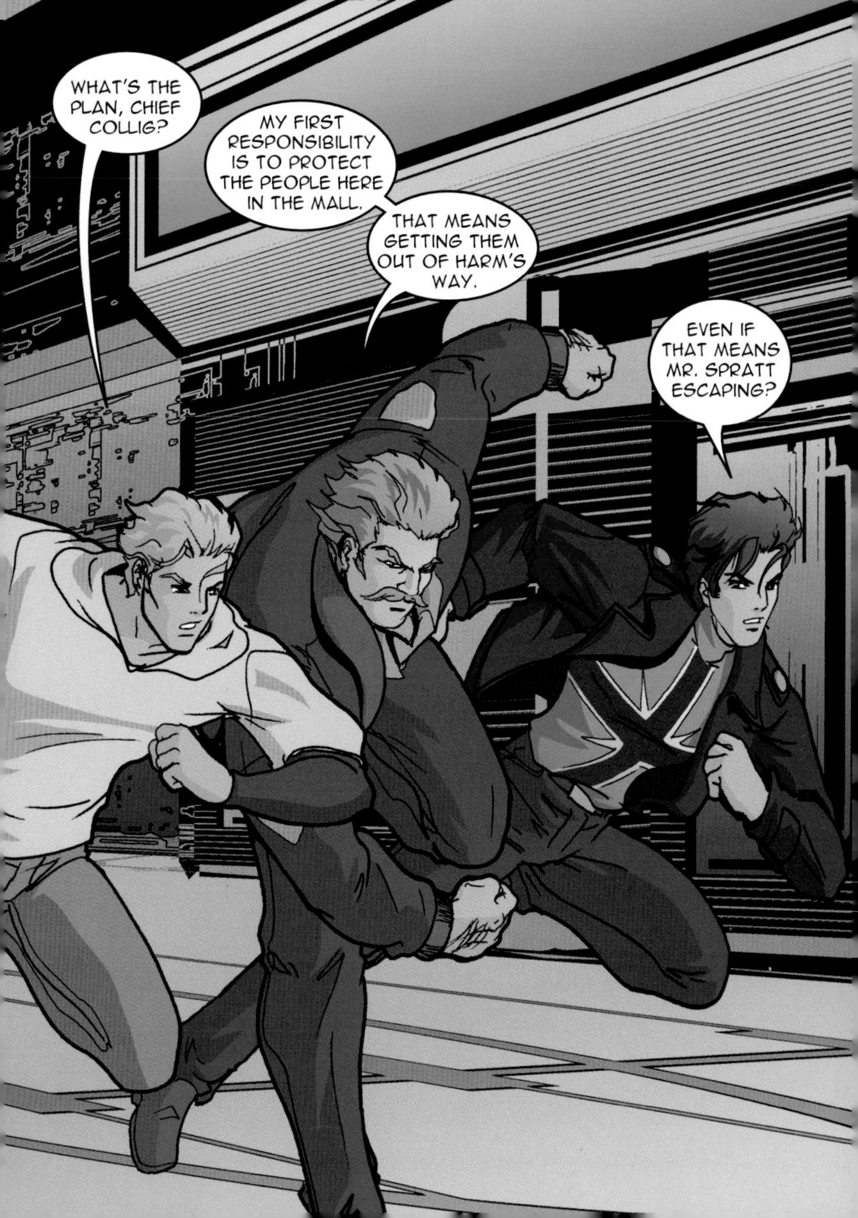
WHAT'S THE PLAN, CHIEF COLLIG?
MY FIRST RESPONSIBILITY IS TO PROTECT THE PEOPLE HERE IN THE MALL.
THAT MEANS GETTING THEM OUT OF HARM'S WAY.
EVEN IF THAT MEANS MR. SPRATT ESCAPING?

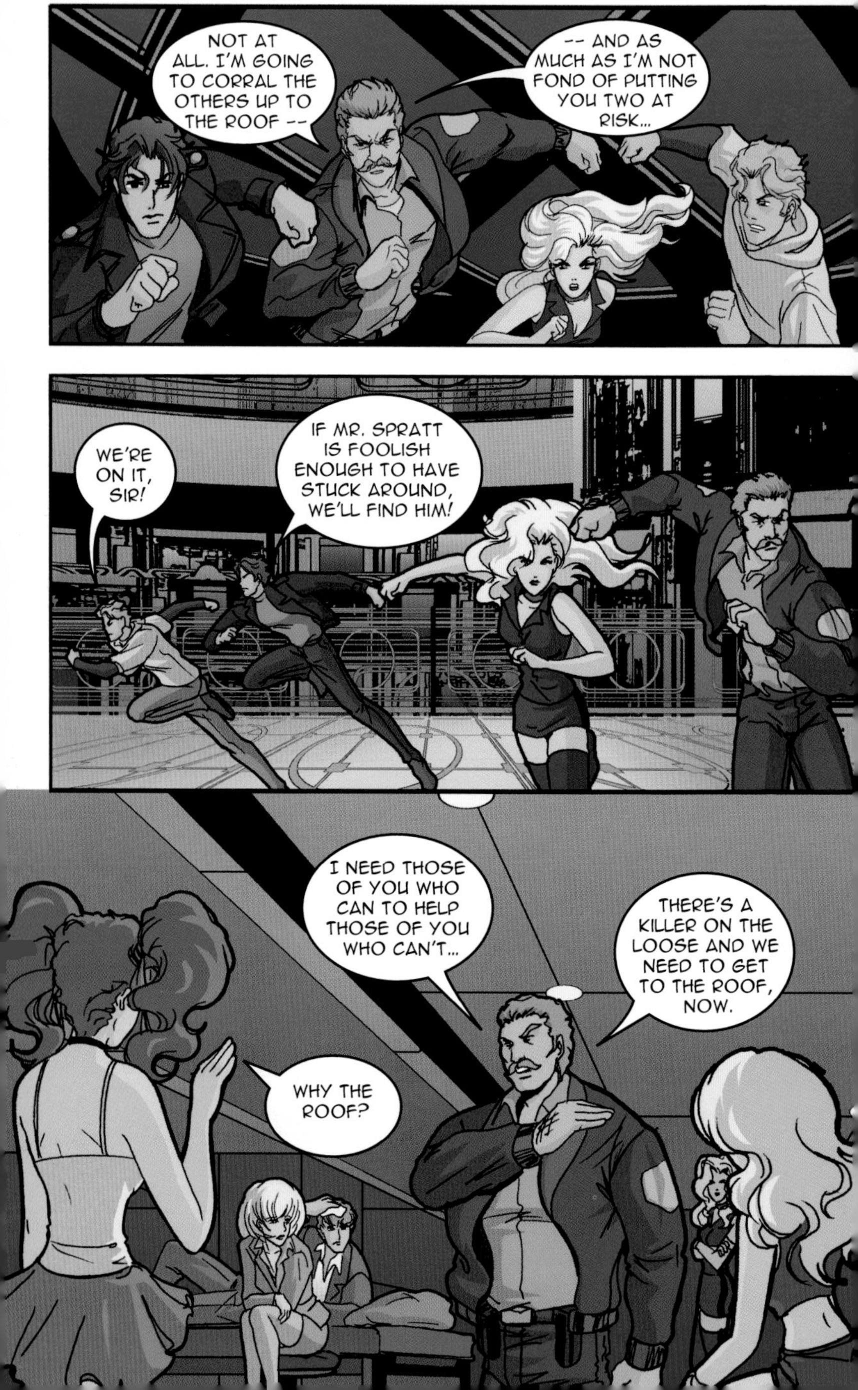
NOT AT ALL. I'M GOING TO CORRAL THE OTHERS UP TO THE ROOF --
-- AND AS MUCH AS I'M NOT FOND OF PUTTING YOU TWO AT RISK...
WE'RE ON IT, SIR!
IF MR. SPRATT IS FOOLISH ENOUGH TO HAVE STUCK AROUND, WE'LL FIND HIM!
I NEED THOSE OF YOU WHO CAN TO HELP THOSE OF YOU WHO CAN'T...
THERE'S A KILLER ON THE LOOSE AND WE NEED TO GET TO THE ROOF, NOW.
WHY THE ROOF?

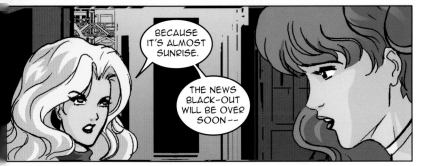

BECAUSE IT'S ALMOST SUNRISE.

THE NEWS BLACK-OUT WILL BE OVER SOON--

--AND THE REPORTERS AND THE REST OF THE POLICE WILL BE RETURNING TO THE LOT WHERE WE CAN CONTACT THEM VISUALLY.

EXACTLY.

TH-THANK YOU.

WHY ARE WE LOOKING HERE? THE BASEMENT MUST BE HUGE.

SWEEP OF THE BUILDING, TOP TO BOTTOM.

JUST LIKE DAD TRAINED US AND ATAC REINFORCED.

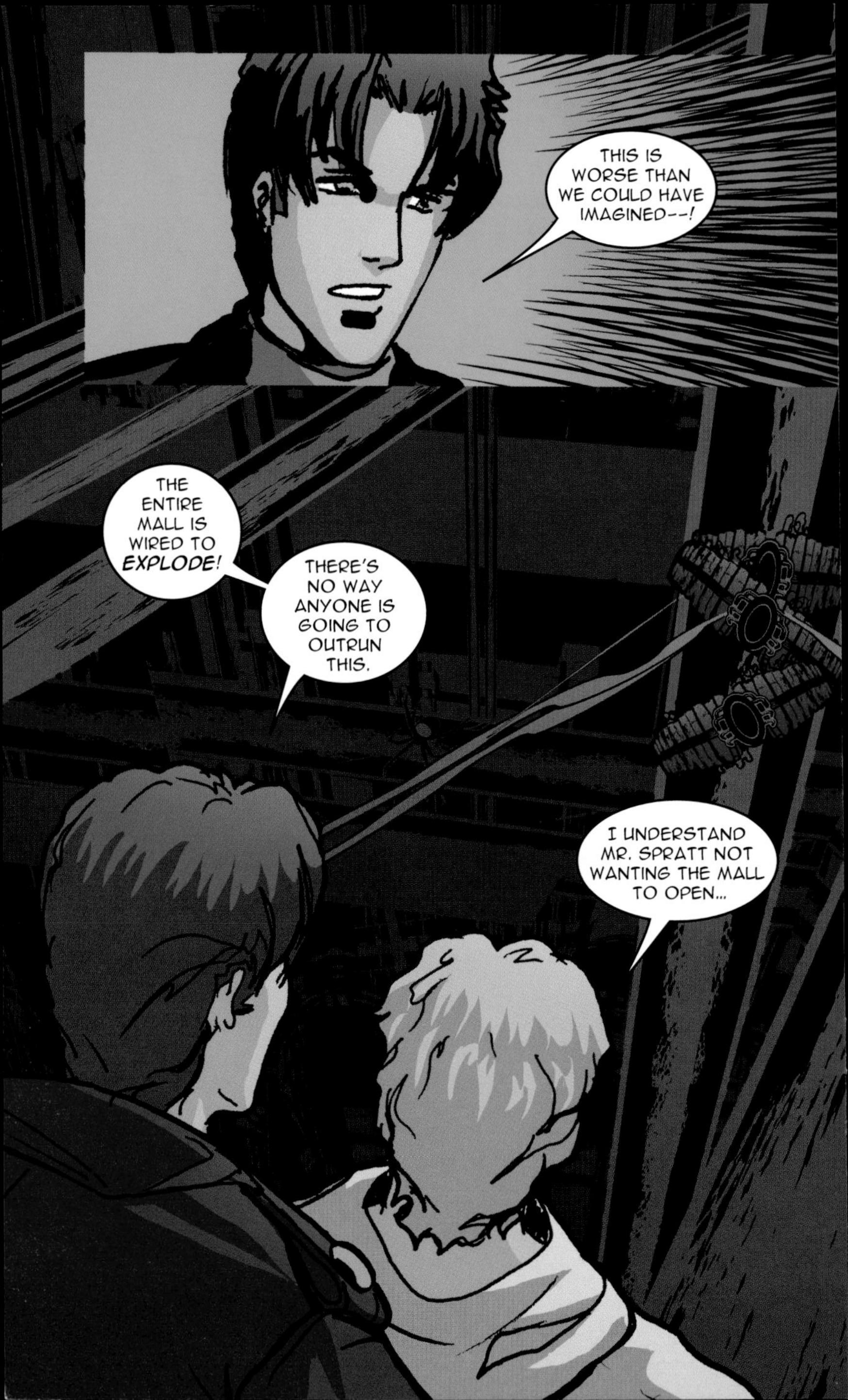
THIS IS WORSE THAN WE COULD HAVE IMAGINED--!
THE ENTIRE MALL IS WIRED TO *EXPLODE*!
THERE'S NO WAY ANYONE IS GOING TO OUTRUN THIS.
I UNDERSTAND MR. SPRATT NOT WANTING THE MALL TO OPEN...

CHAPTER ELEVEN

"...The Mall Will Be Exploding In Five Minutes!"

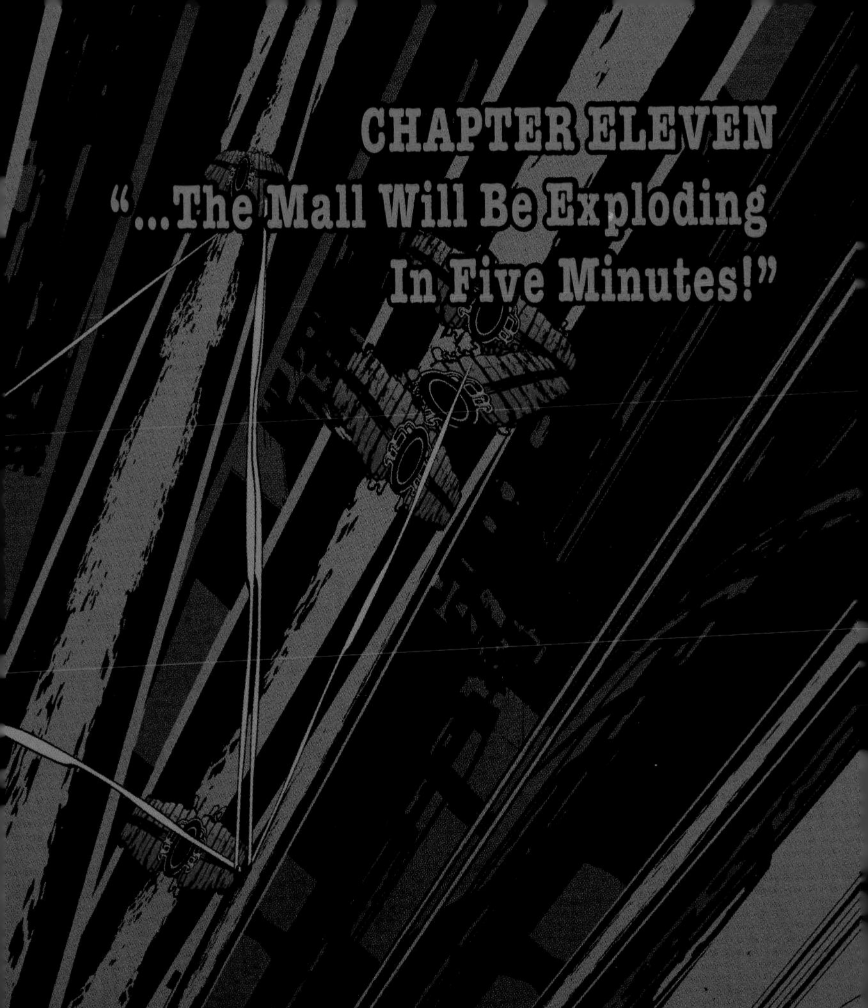

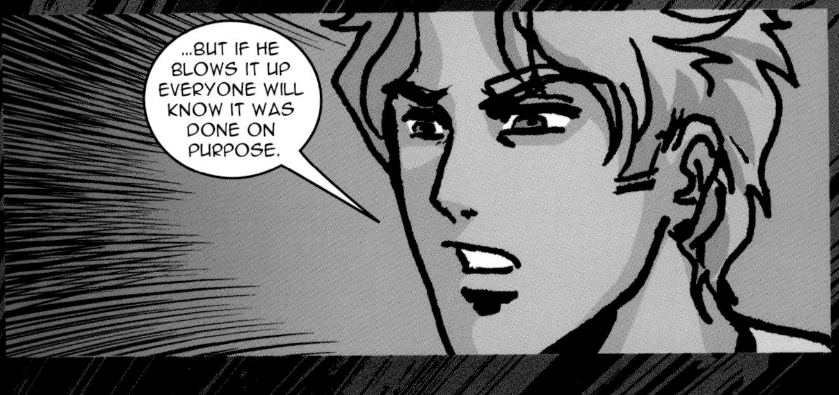
...BUT IF HE BLOWS IT UP EVERYONE WILL KNOW IT WAS DONE ON PURPOSE.

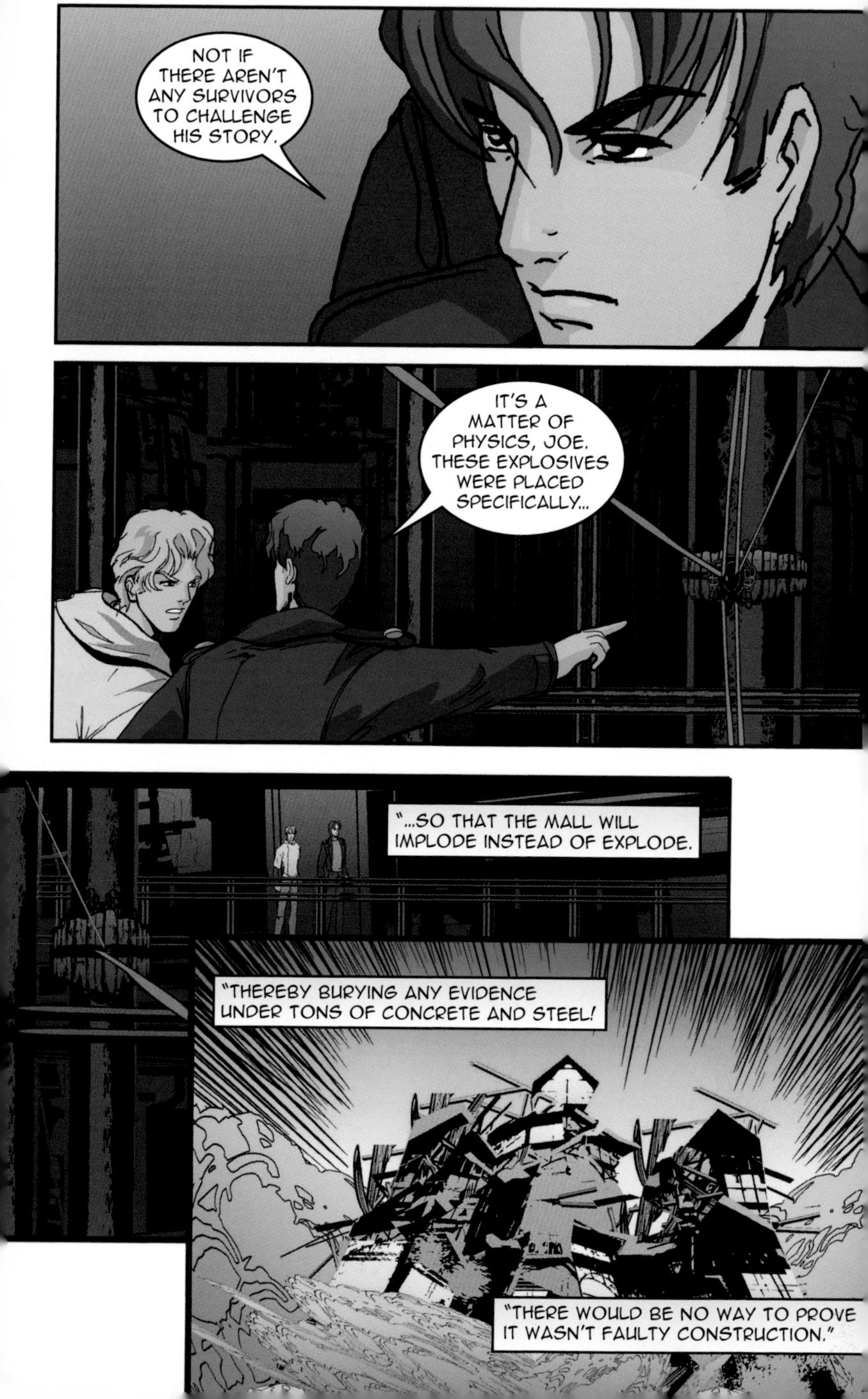
NOT IF THERE AREN'T ANY SURVIVORS TO CHALLENGE HIS STORY.
IT'S A MATTER OF PHYSICS, JOE. THESE EXPLOSIVES WERE PLACED SPECIFICALLY...
"...SO THAT THE MALL WILL IMPLODE INSTEAD OF EXPLODE.
"THEREBY BURYING ANY EVIDENCE UNDER TONS OF CONCRETE AND STEEL!
"THERE WOULD BE NO WAY TO PROVE IT WASN'T FAULTY CONSTRUCTION."

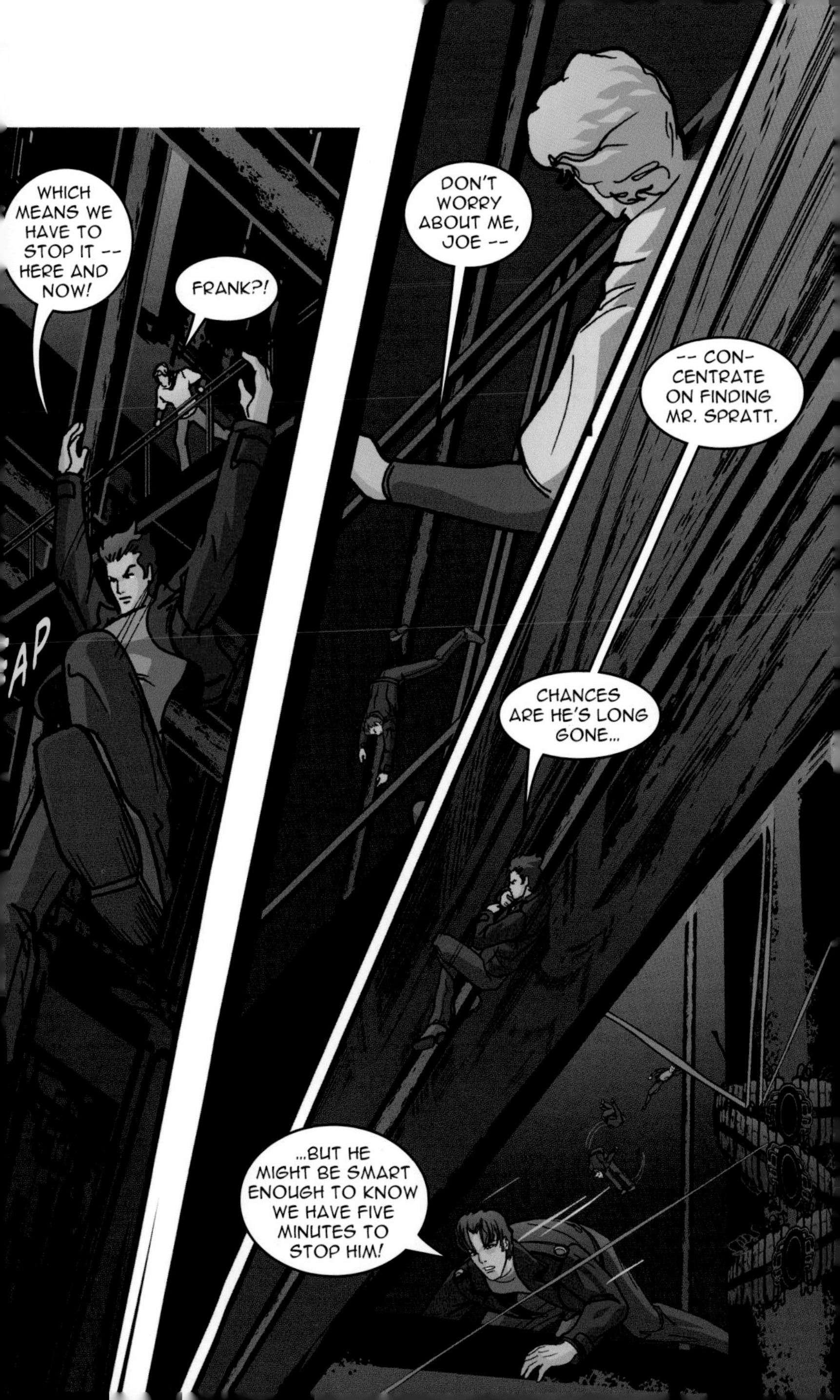
WHICH MEANS WE HAVE TO STOP IT -- HERE AND NOW!
FRANK?!
AP
DON'T WORRY ABOUT ME, JOE --
-- CON-CENTRATE ON FINDING MR. SPRATT.
CHANCES ARE HE'S LONG GONE...
...BUT HE MIGHT BE SMART ENOUGH TO KNOW WE HAVE FIVE MINUTES TO STOP HIM!

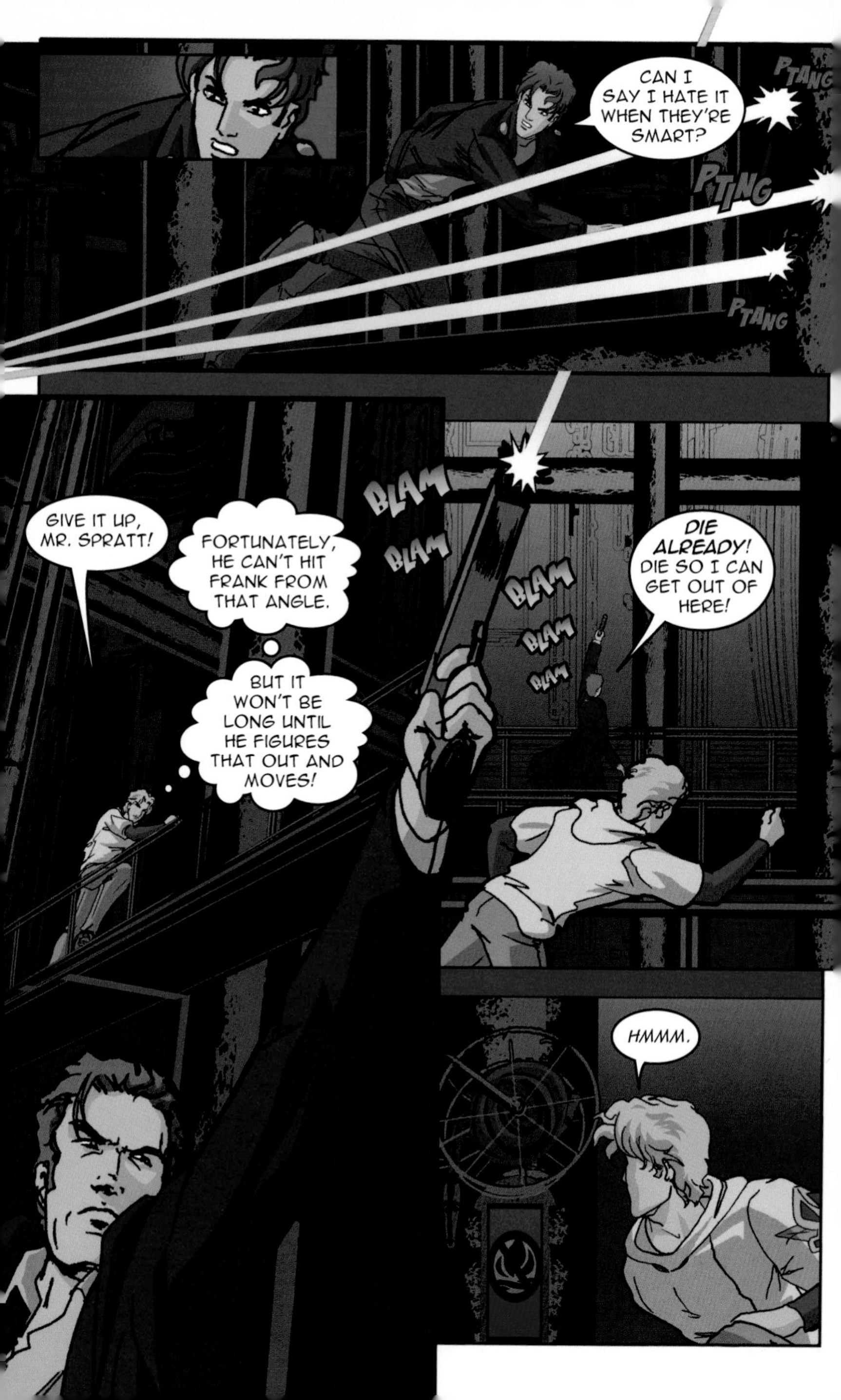
CAN I SAY I HATE IT WHEN THEY'RE SMART?
PTANG
PTING
PTANG
BLAM
BLAM
BLAM
BLAM
BLAM
GIVE IT UP, MR. SPRATT!
FORTUNATELY, HE CAN'T HIT FRANK FROM THAT ANGLE.
BUT IT WON'T BE LONG UNTIL HE FIGURES THAT OUT AND MOVES!
DIE ALREADY! DIE SO I CAN GET OUT OF HERE!
HMMM.

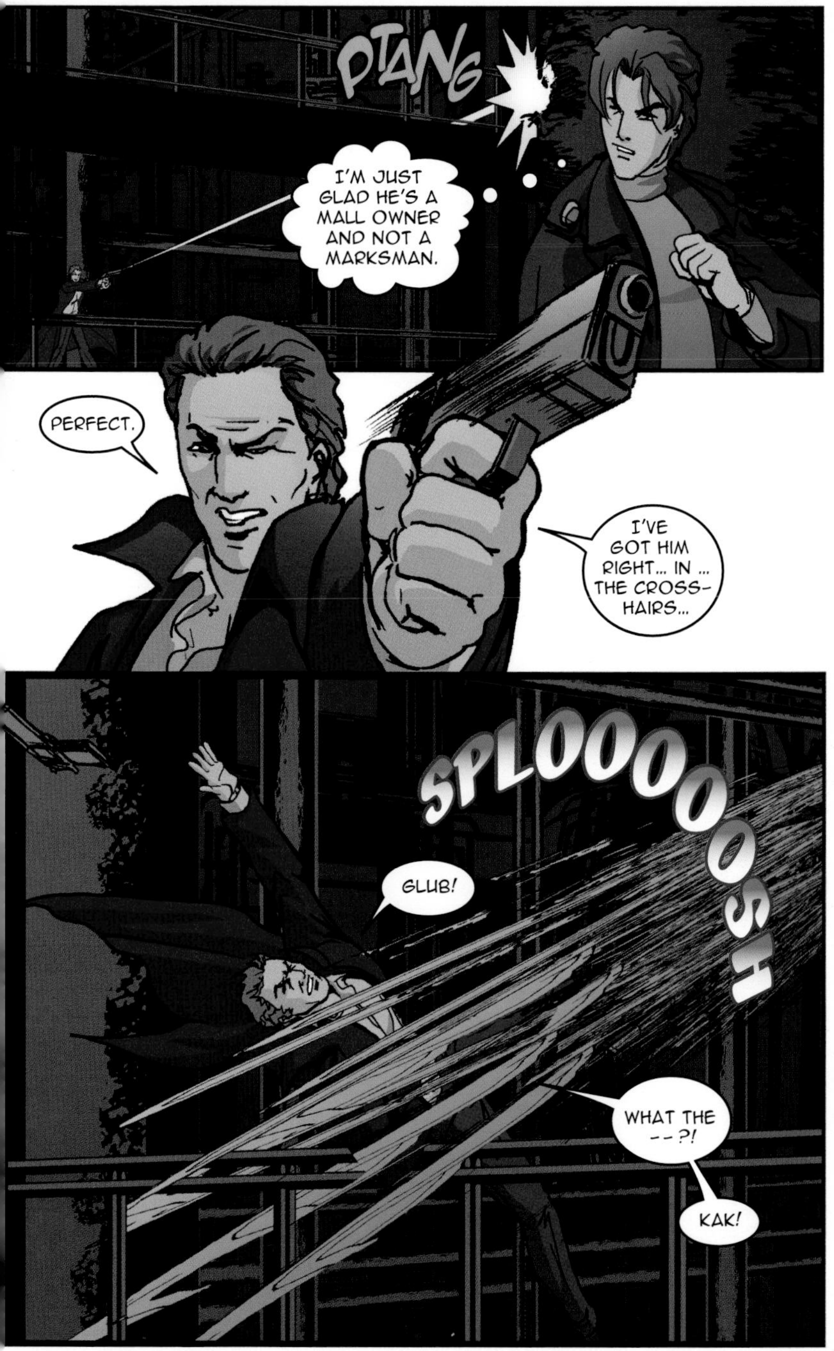
PTANG
I'M JUST GLAD HE'S A MALL OWNER AND NOT A MARKSMAN.
PERFECT.
I'VE GOT HIM RIGHT... IN ... THE CROSS-HAIRS...
SPLOOOOOOSH
GLUB!
WHAT THE --?!
KAK!

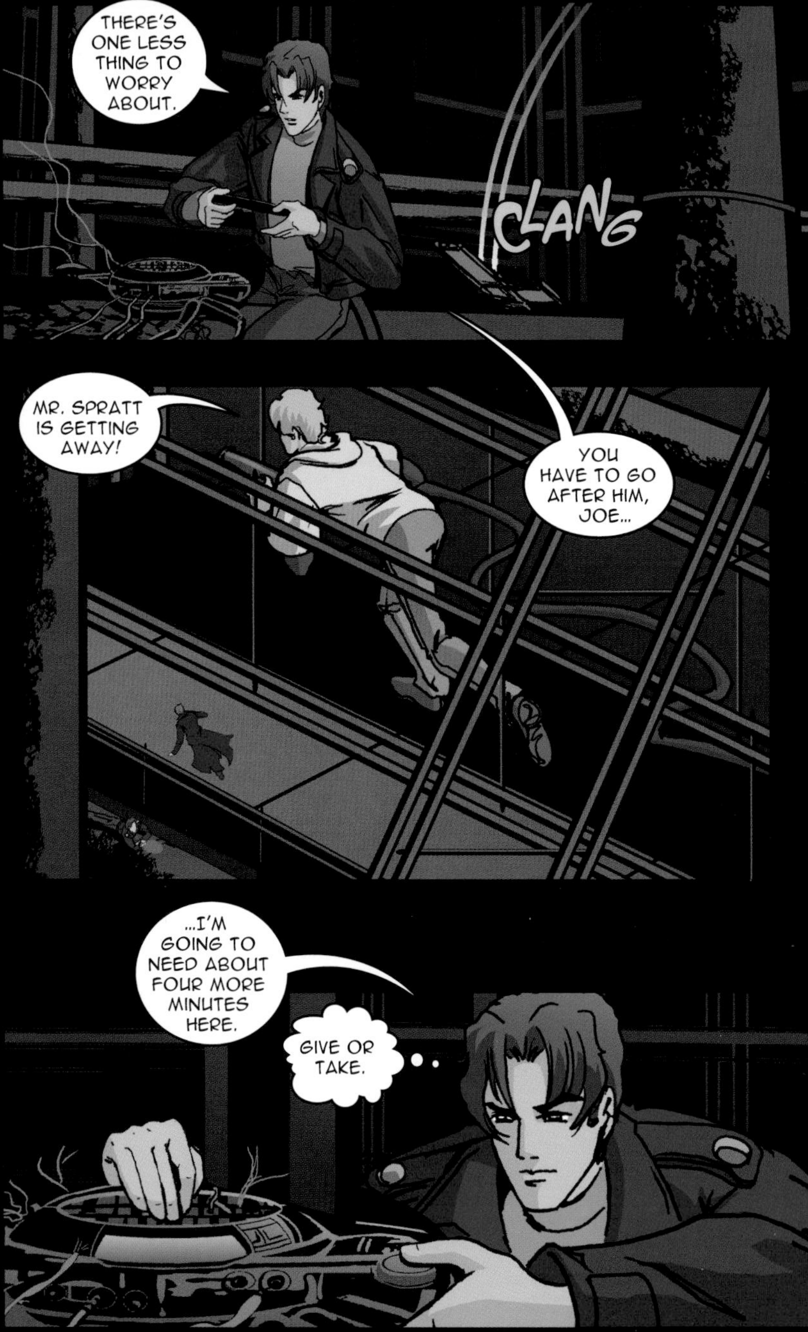
THERE'S ONE LESS THING TO WORRY ABOUT.
CLANG
MR. SPRATT IS GETTING AWAY!
YOU HAVE TO GO AFTER HIM, JOE...
...I'M GOING TO NEED ABOUT FOUR MORE MINUTES HERE.
GIVE OR TAKE.

CHAPTER TWELVE:
"Up on the roof..."

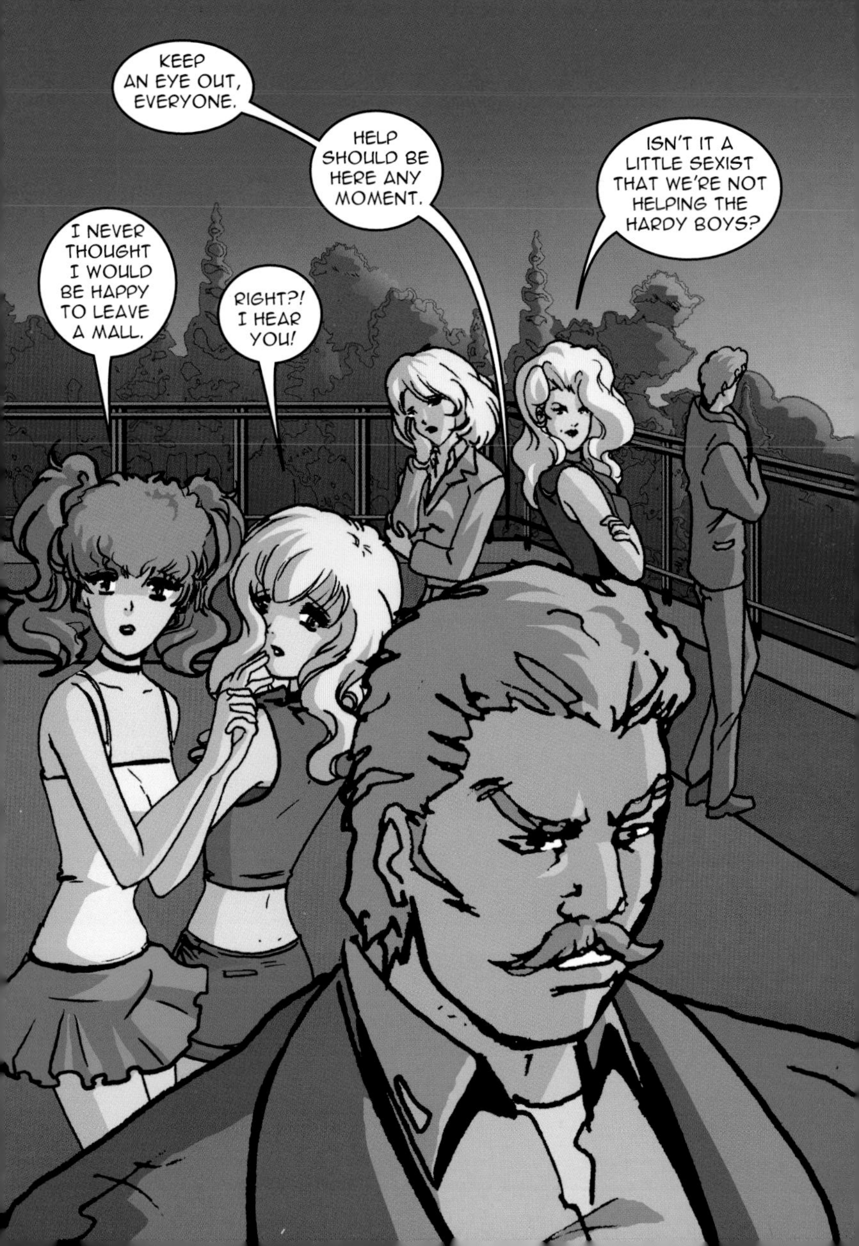
KEEP AN EYE OUT, EVERYONE.
HELP SHOULD BE HERE ANY MOMENT.
ISN'T IT A LITTLE SEXIST THAT WE'RE NOT HELPING THE HARDY BOYS?
I NEVER THOUGHT I WOULD BE HAPPY TO LEAVE A MALL.
RIGHT?! I HEAR YOU!

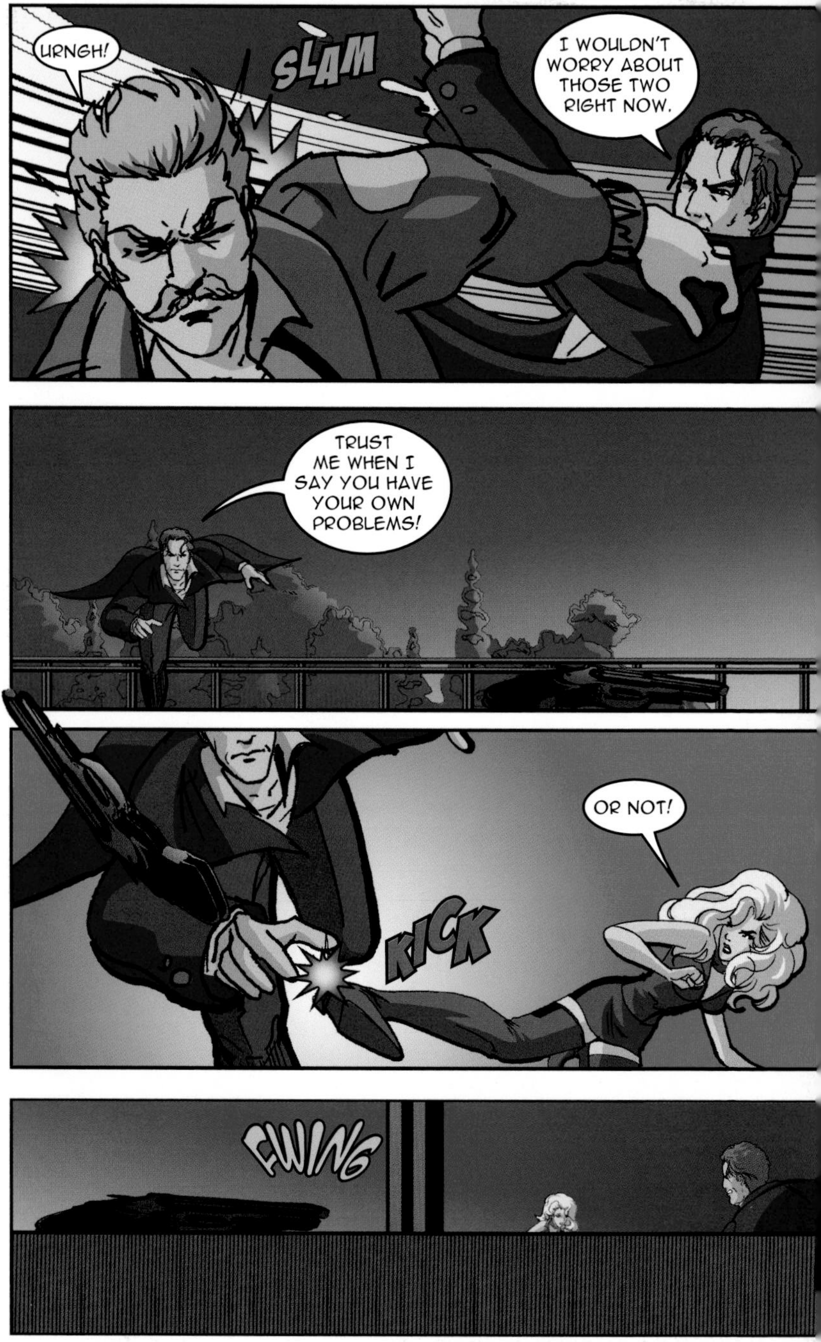
URNGH!
SLAM
I WOULDN'T WORRY ABOUT THOSE TWO RIGHT NOW.
TRUST ME WHEN I SAY YOU HAVE YOUR OWN PROBLEMS!
OR NOT!
KICK
FWING

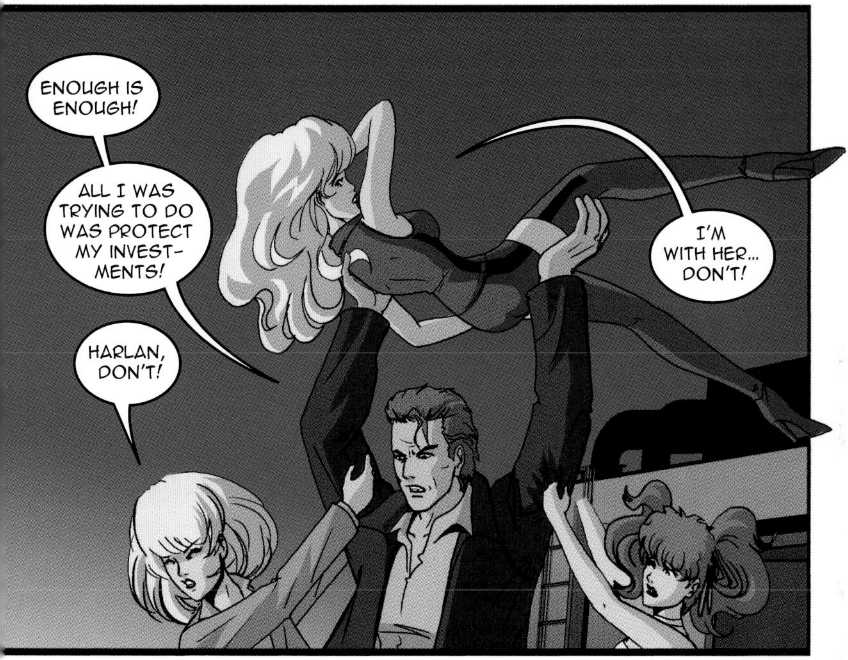
ENOUGH IS ENOUGH!
ALL I WAS TRYING TO DO WAS PROTECT MY INVEST-MENTS!
HARLAN, DON'T!
I'M WITH HER... DON'T!

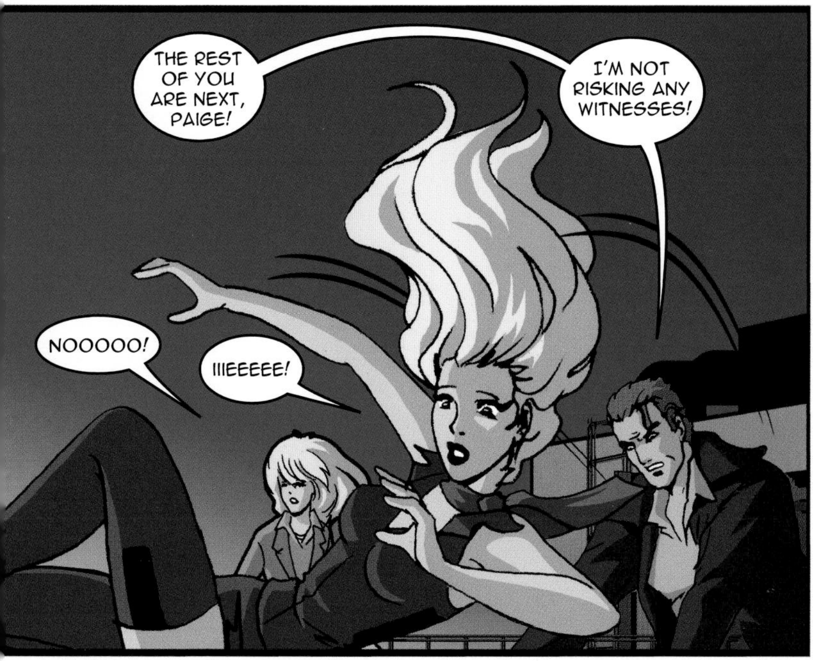
THE REST OF YOU ARE NEXT, PAIGE!
I'M NOT RISKING ANY WITNESSES!
NOOOOO!
IIIEEEEE!

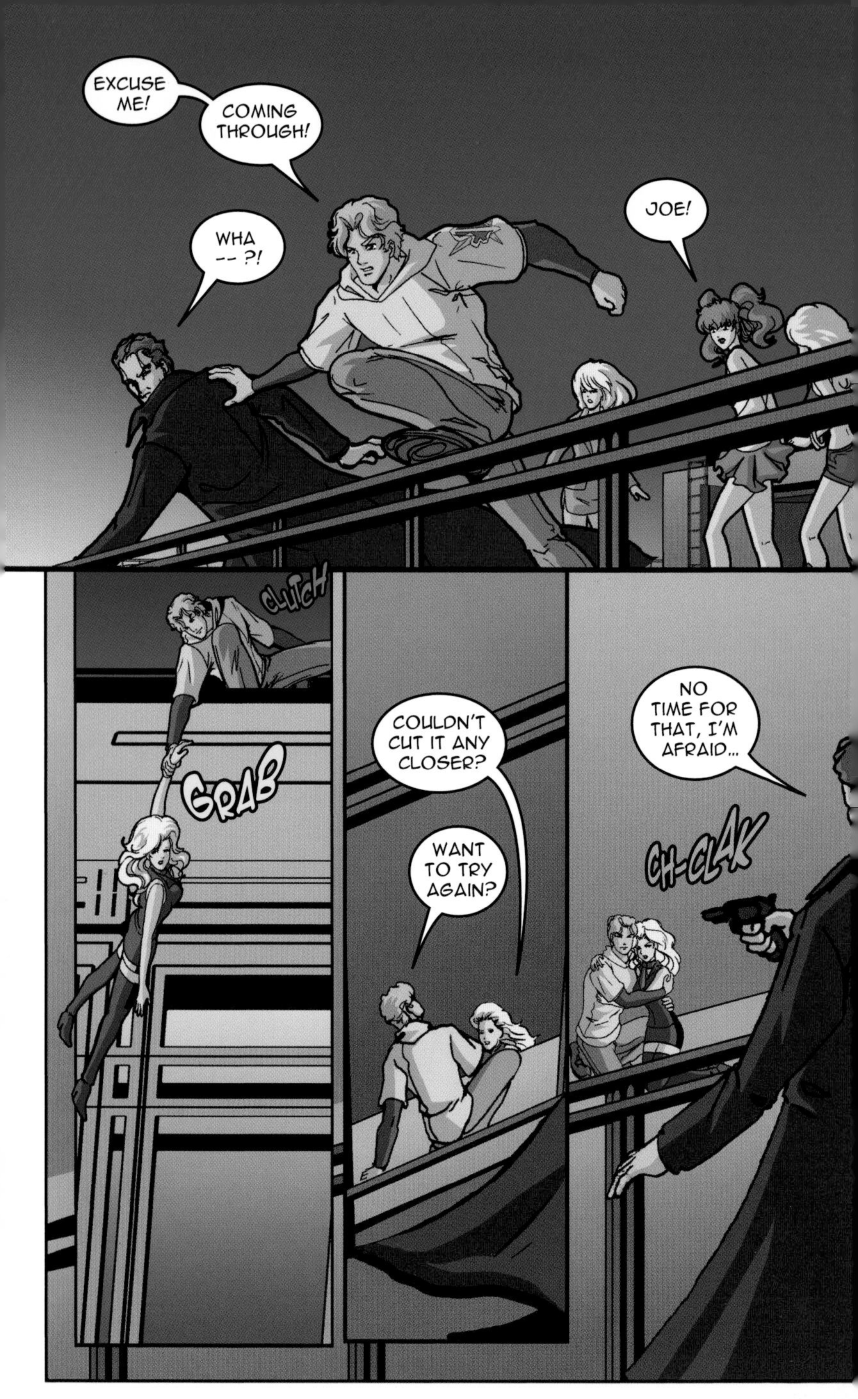

EXCUSE ME!
COMING THROUGH!
WHA -- ?!
JOE!
CLUTCH
GRAB
COULDN'T CUT IT ANY CLOSER?
WANT TO TRY AGAIN?
NO TIME FOR THAT, I'M AFRAID...
CH-CLAK

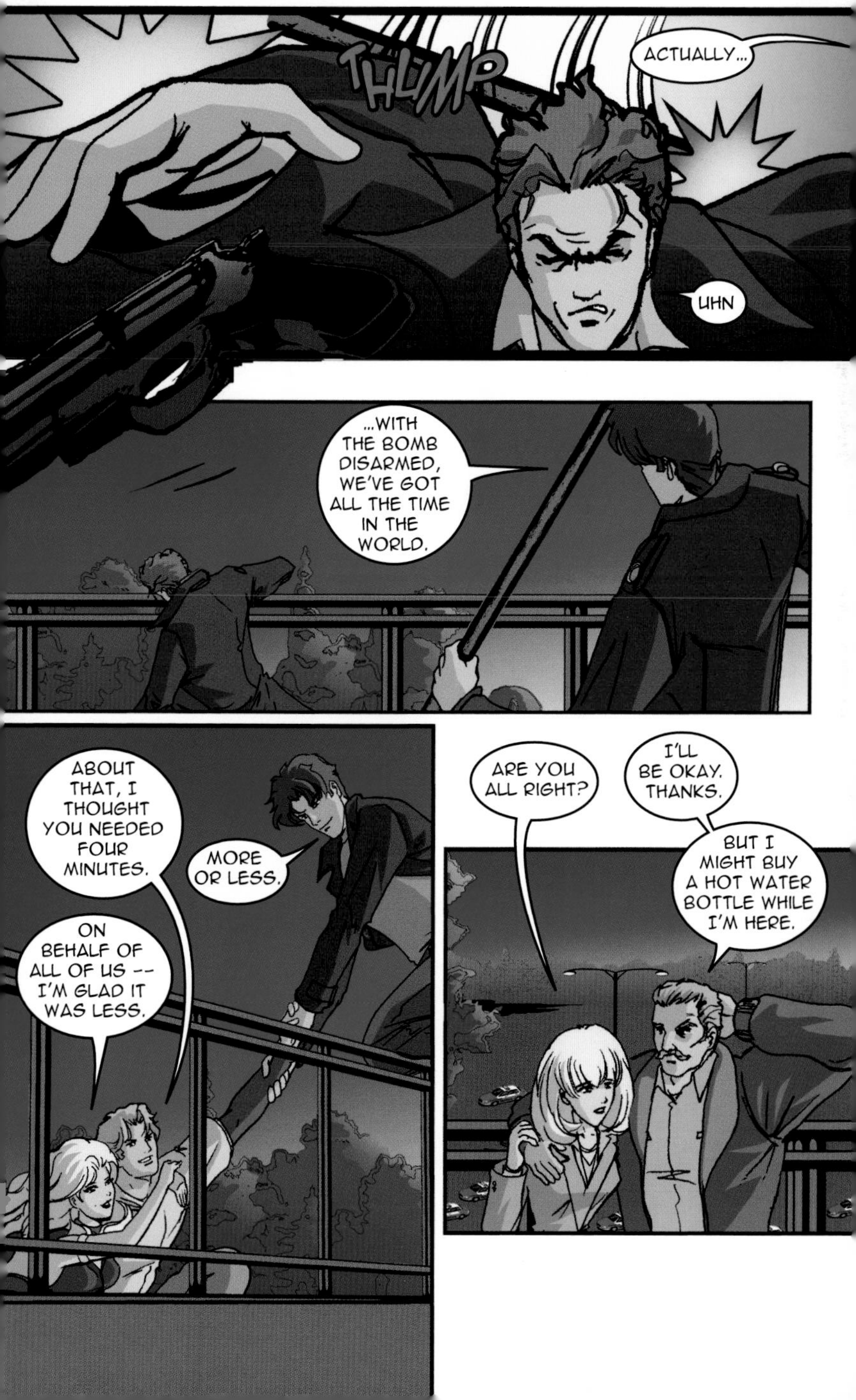
THUMP
ACTUALLY...
UHN
...WITH THE BOMB DISARMED, WE'VE GOT ALL THE TIME IN THE WORLD.
ABOUT THAT, I THOUGHT YOU NEEDED FOUR MINUTES.
MORE OR LESS.
ON BEHALF OF ALL OF US -- I'M GLAD IT WAS LESS.
ARE YOU ALL RIGHT?
I'LL BE OKAY. THANKS.
BUT I MIGHT BUY A HOT WATER BOTTLE WHILE I'M HERE.

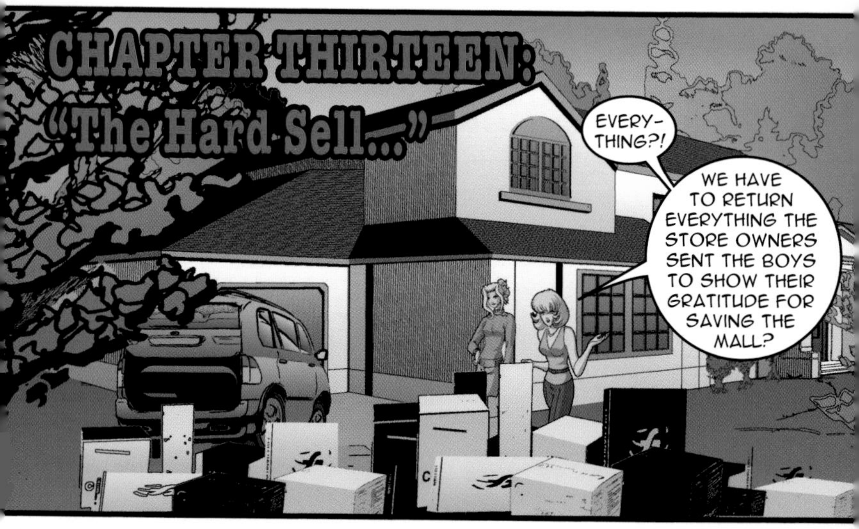
CHAPTER THIRTEEN:
"The Hard Sell..."
EVERY-THING?!
WE HAVE TO RETURN EVERYTHING THE STORE OWNERS SENT THE BOYS TO SHOW THEIR GRATITUDE FOR SAVING THE MALL?

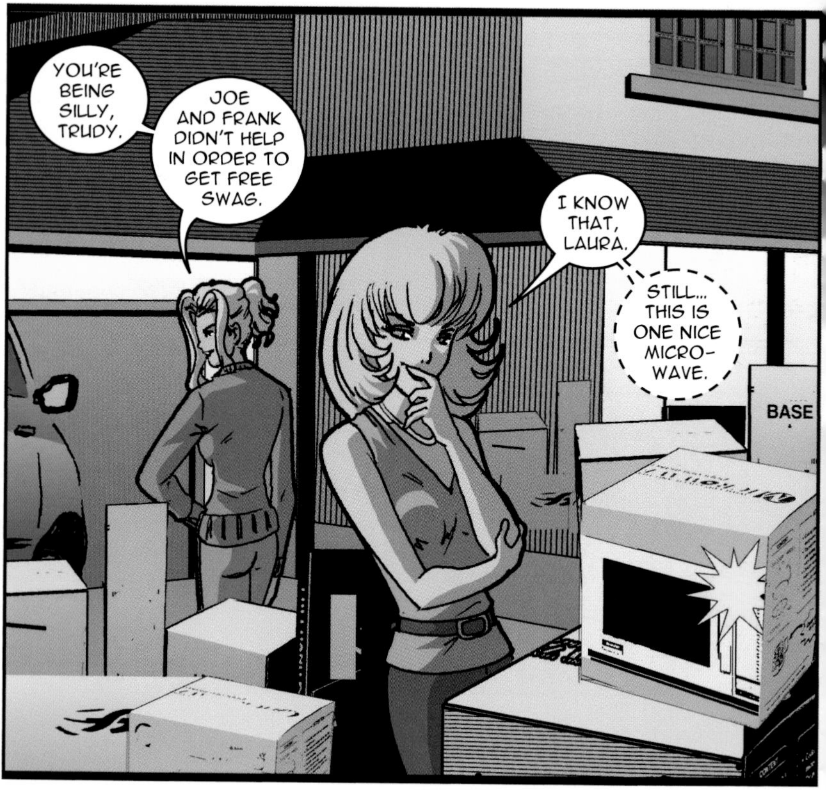
YOU'RE BEING SILLY, TRUDY.
JOE AND FRANK DIDN'T HELP IN ORDER TO GET FREE SWAG.
I KNOW THAT, LAURA.
STILL... THIS IS ONE NICE MICRO-WAVE.
BASE

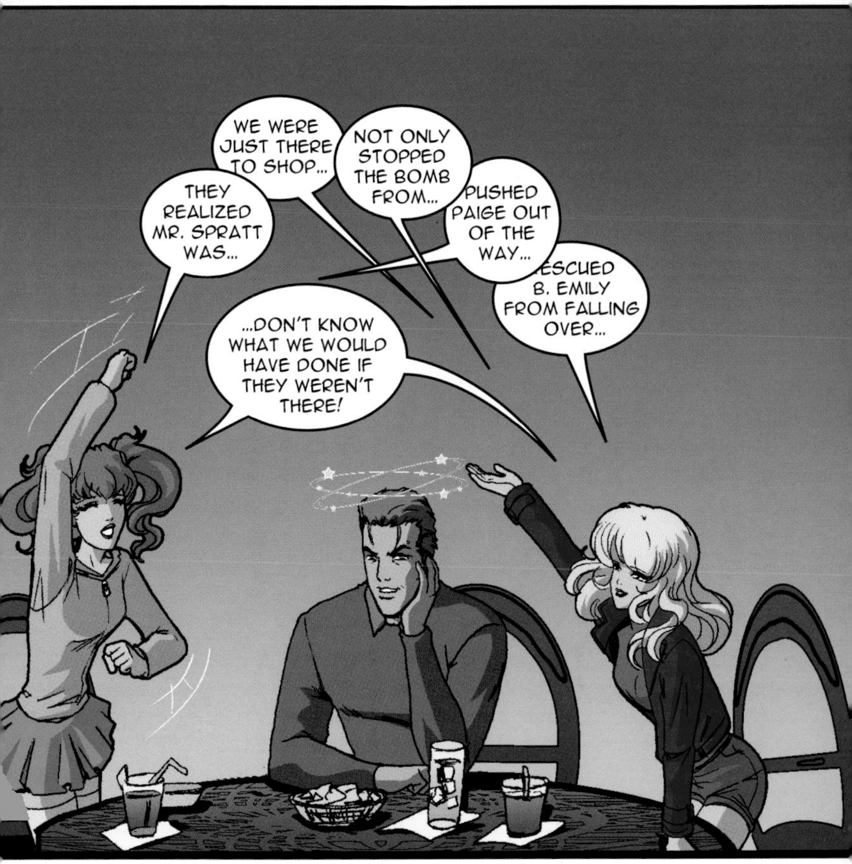

THEY REALIZED MR. SPRATT WAS...
WE WERE JUST THERE TO SHOP...
NOT ONLY STOPPED THE BOMB FROM...
PUSHED PAIGE OUT OF THE WAY...
ESCUED B. EMILY FROM FALLING OVER...
...DON'T KNOW WHAT WE WOULD HAVE DONE IF THEY WEREN'T THERE!

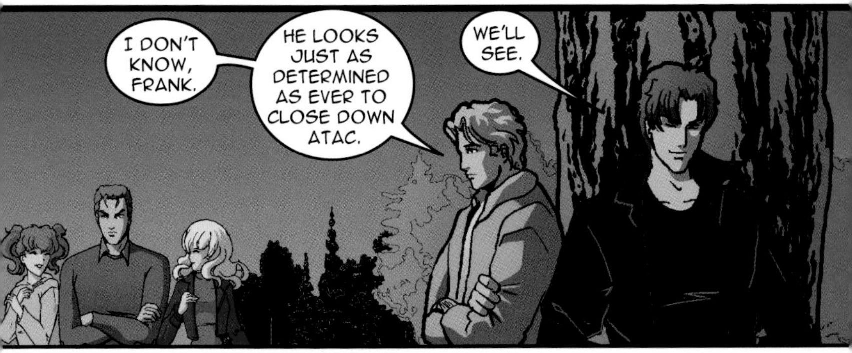

I DON'T KNOW, FRANK.
HE LOOKS JUST AS DETERMINED AS EVER TO CLOSE DOWN ATAC.
WE'LL SEE.

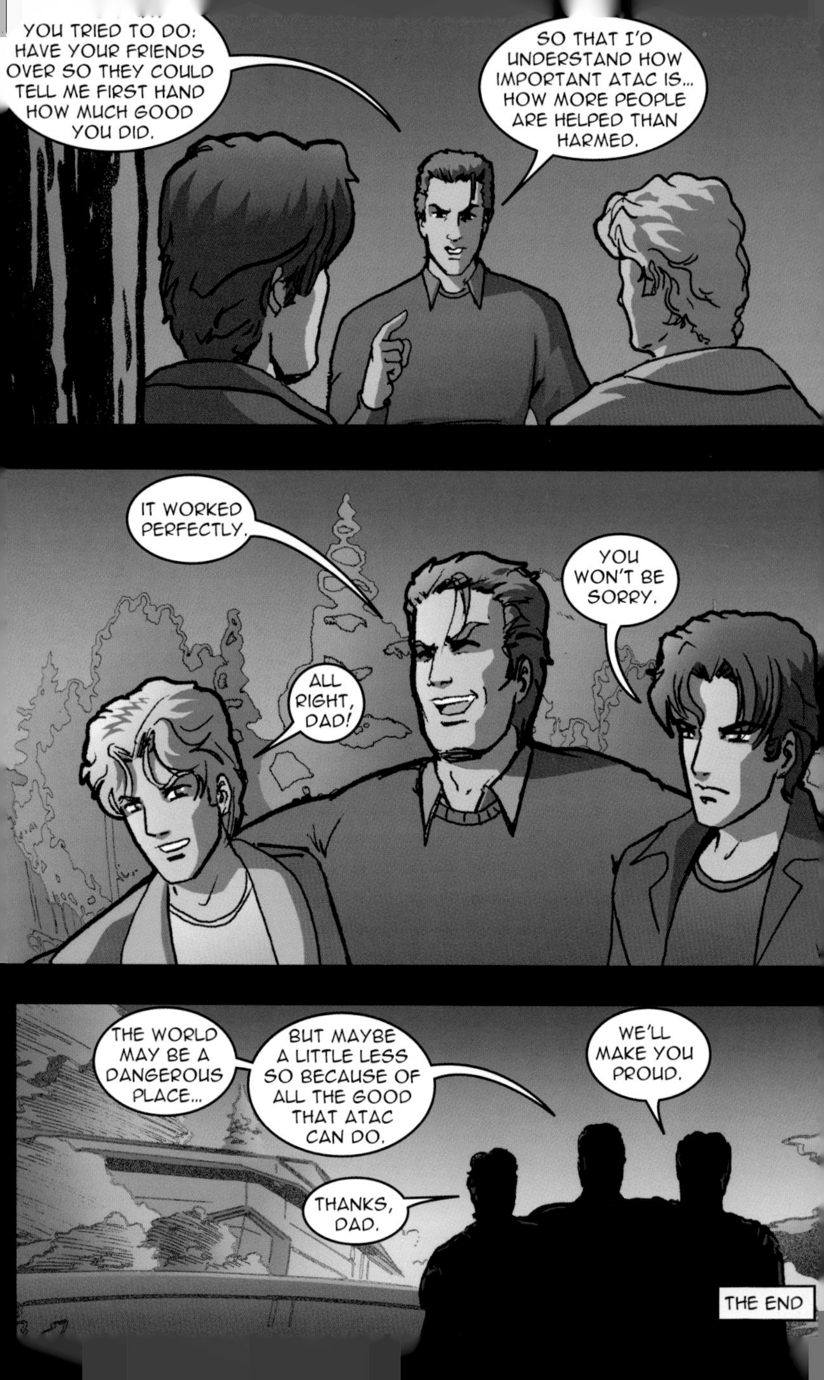
YOU TRIED TO DO: HAVE YOUR FRIENDS OVER SO THEY COULD TELL ME FIRST HAND HOW MUCH GOOD YOU DID.
SO THAT I'D UNDERSTAND HOW IMPORTANT ATAC IS... HOW MORE PEOPLE ARE HELPED THAN HARMED.
IT WORKED PERFECTLY.
YOU WON'T BE SORRY.
ALL RIGHT, DAD!
THE WORLD MAY BE A DANGEROUS PLACE...
BUT MAYBE A LITTLE LESS SO BECAUSE OF ALL THE GOOD THAT ATAC CAN DO.
WE'LL MAKE YOU PROUD.
THANKS, DAD.
THE END

Chapter One: "En Garde!"

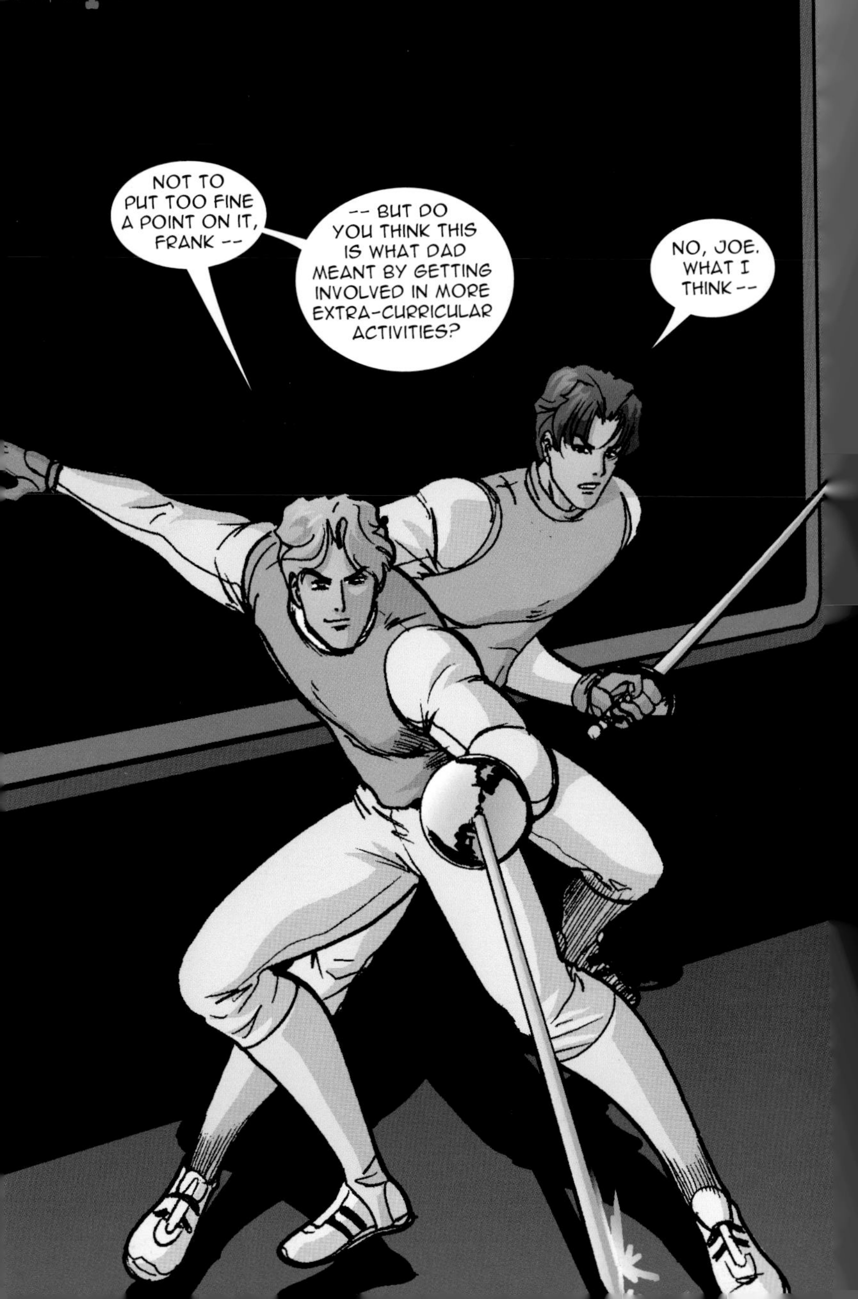

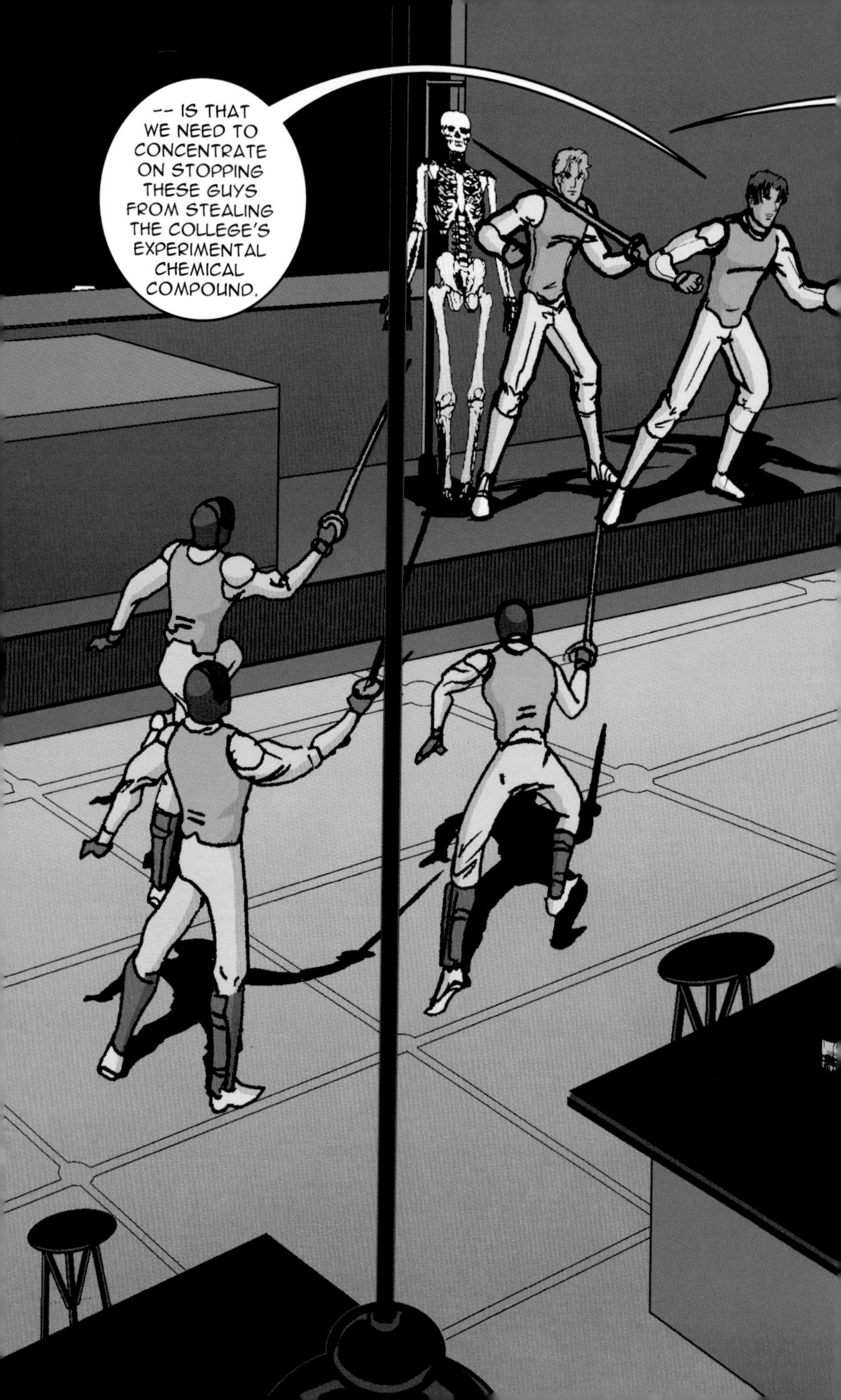
-- IS THAT WE NEED TO CONCENTRATE ON STOPPING THESE GUYS FROM STEALING THE COLLEGE'S EXPERIMENTAL CHEMICAL COMPOUND.

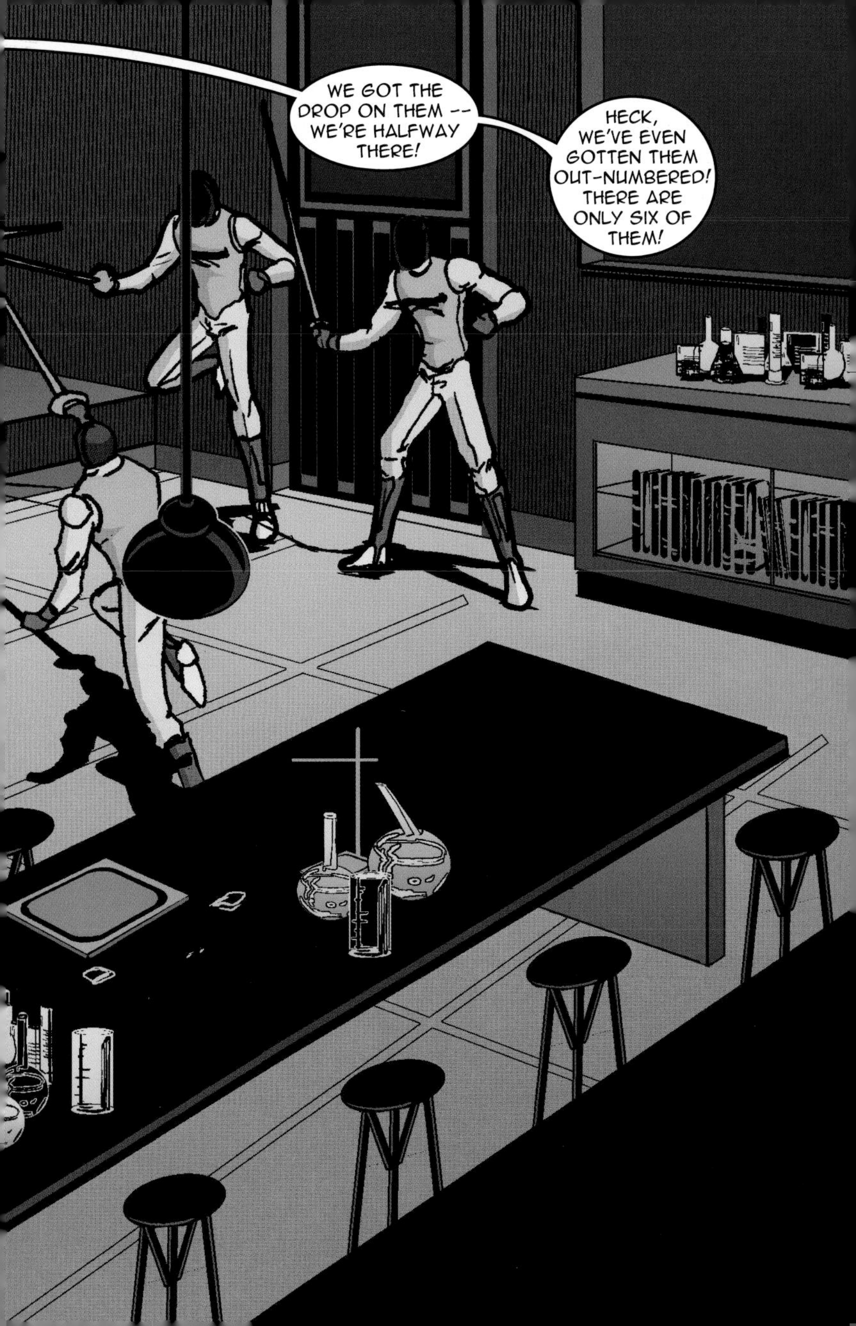
WE GOT THE DROP ON THEM -- WE'RE HALFWAY THERE!
HECK, WE'VE EVEN GOTTEN THEM OUT-NUMBERED! THERE ARE ONLY SIX OF THEM!

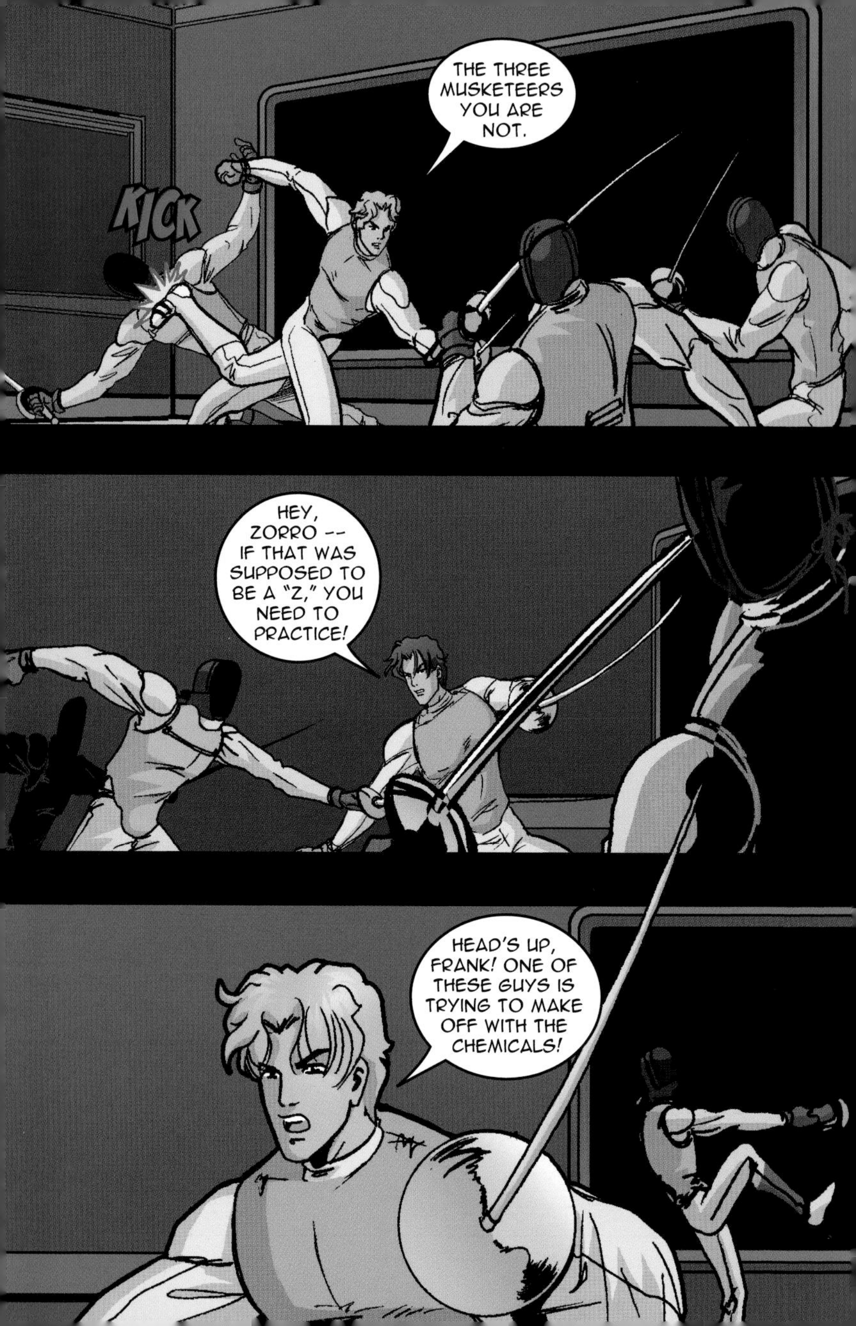
THE THREE MUSKETEERS YOU ARE NOT.
KICK
HEY, ZORRO -- IF THAT WAS SUPPOSED TO BE A "Z," YOU NEED TO PRACTICE!
HEAD'S UP, FRANK! ONE OF THESE GUYS IS TRYING TO MAKE OFF WITH THE CHEMICALS!

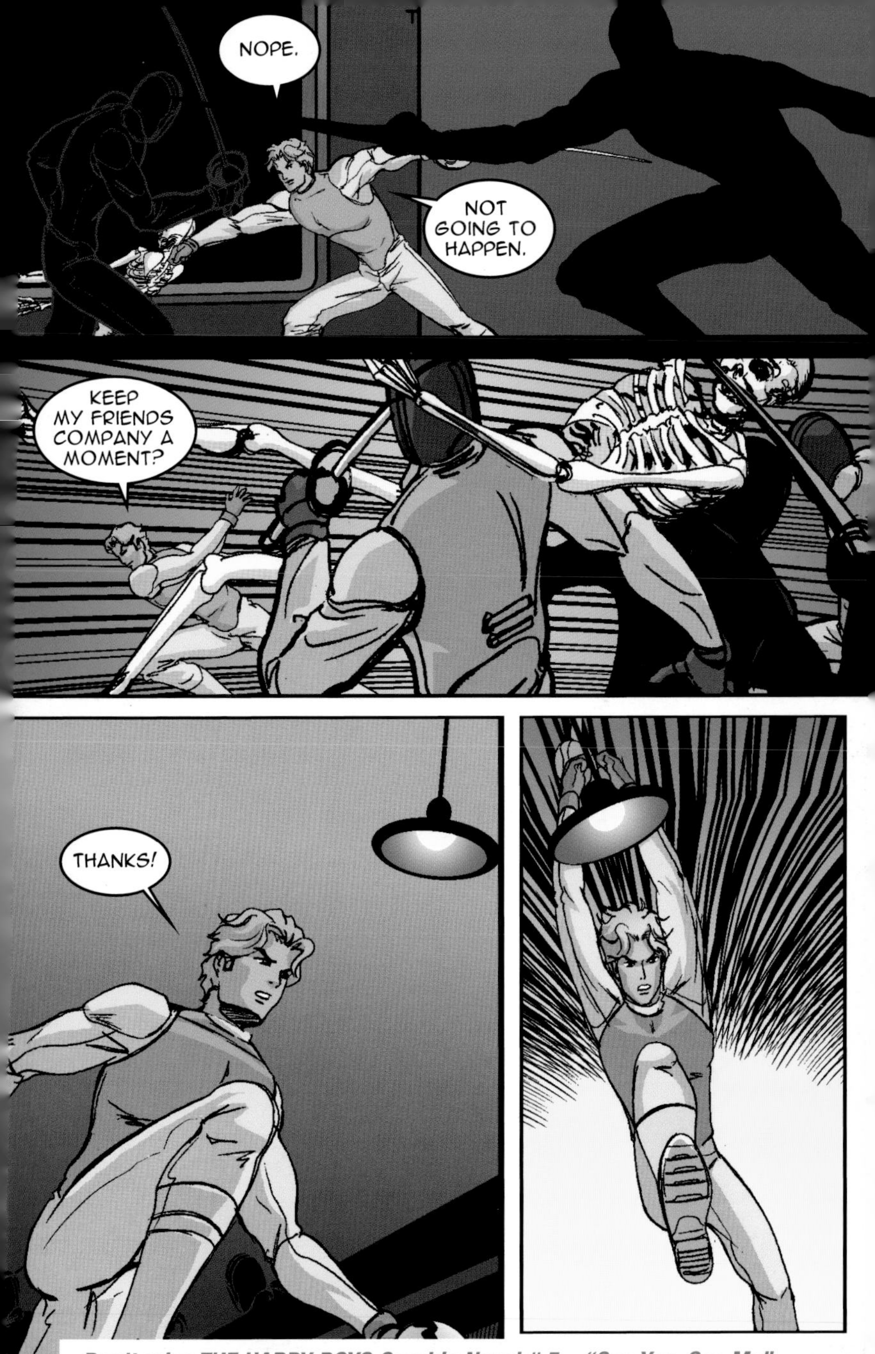
NOPE.
NOT GOING TO HAPPEN.
KEEP MY FRIENDS COMPANY A MOMENT?
THANKS!

Don't miss THE HARDY BOYS Graphic Novel # 5 – "See You, Sea Me"

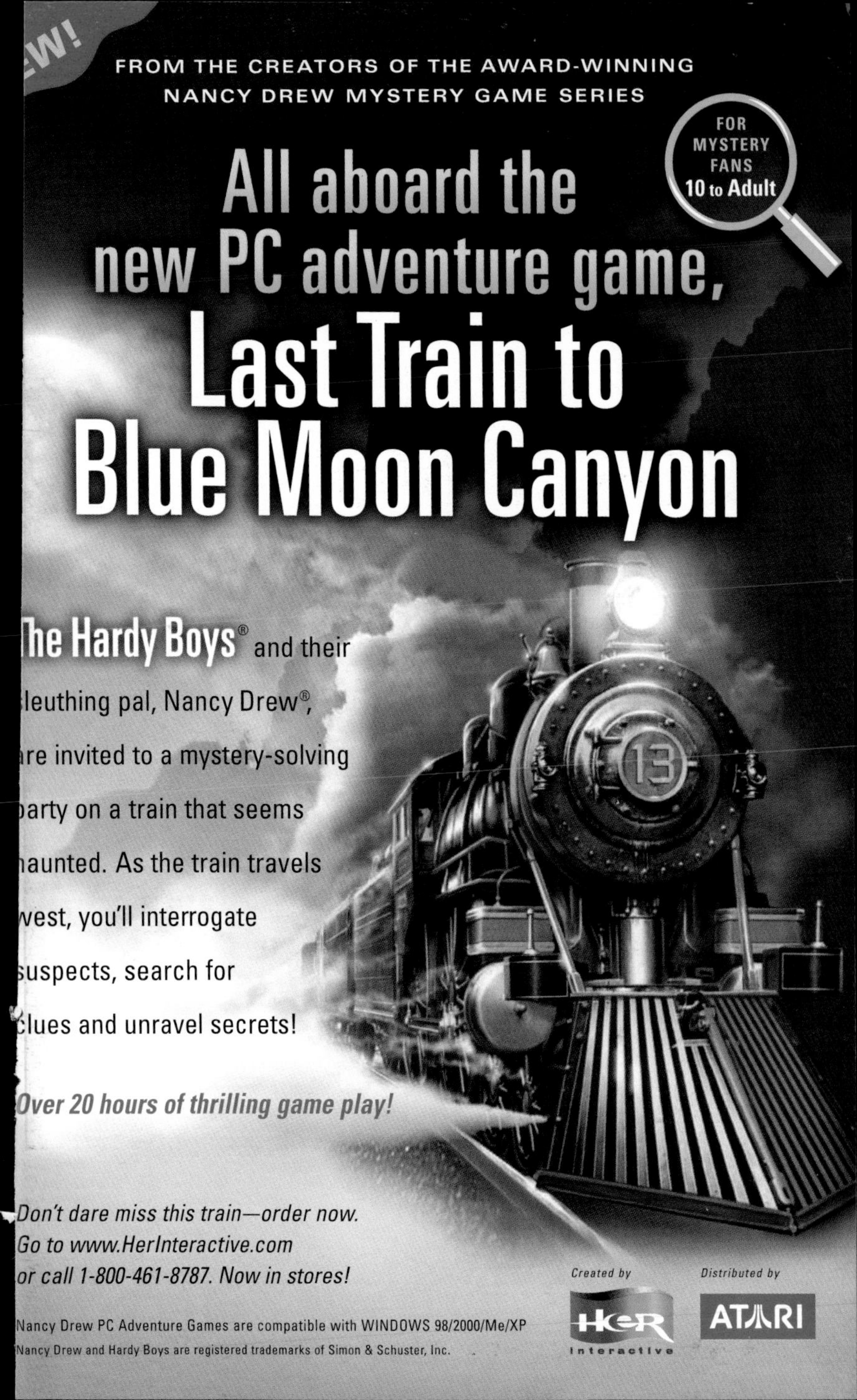
NEW!
FROM THE CREATORS OF THE AWARD-WINNING
NANCY DREW MYSTERY GAME SERIES
FOR MYSTERY FANS 10 to Adult
All aboard the new PC adventure game,
Last Train to Blue Moon Canyon
The Hardy Boys® and their sleuthing pal, Nancy Drew®, are invited to a mystery-solving party on a train that seems haunted. As the train travels west, you'll interrogate suspects, search for clues and unravel secrets!
Over 20 hours of thrilling game play!
13
Don't dare miss this train—order now.
Go to www.HerInteractive.com
or call 1-800-461-8787. Now in stores!
Created by
HER Interactive
Distributed by
ATARI
Nancy Drew PC Adventure Games are compatible with WINDOWS 98/2000/Me/XP
Nancy Drew and Hardy Boys are registered trademarks of Simon & Schuster, Inc.

CRIMINALS BEWARE!

THE HARDY BOYS®

UNDERCOVER BROTHERS

ARE ON YOUR TRAIL.

Read the paperback series that started it all

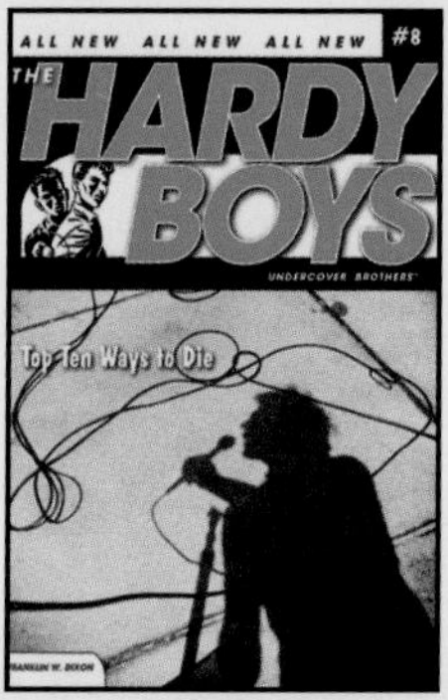

ALL NEW ALL NEW ALL NEW #8
THE HARDY BOYS
UNDERCOVER BROTHERS
Top Ten Ways to Die

Top Ten Ways to Die

Available February 2006

Madison Vee is the biggest thing to hit pop music since Britney—and someone is trying to kill her. To protect the young star, Frank and Joe join the tech crew of Madison's latest music video shoot. But a bunch of threatening notes and technical accidents make them realize that the wanna-be-pop-star-killer is right there, waiting in the wings—and ready to make Madison's next hit her last.

Have you read Frank and Joe's latest stories of crime, danger, mystery, and death-defying stunts?

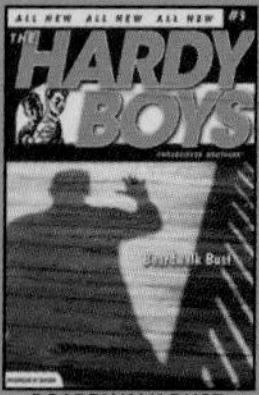

ALL NEW ALL NEW ALL NEW #3
THE HARDY BOYS

BOARDWALK BUST

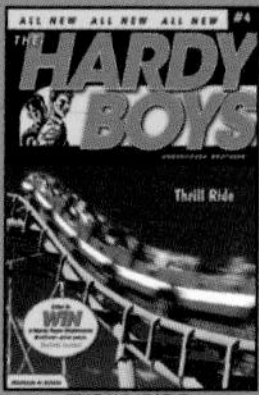

ALL NEW ALL NEW ALL NEW #4
THE HARDY BOYS
Thrill Ride
WIN

THRILL RIDE

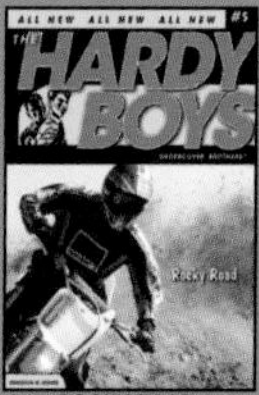

ALL NEW ALL NEW ALL NEW #5
THE HARDY BOYS
Rocky Road

ROCKY ROAD

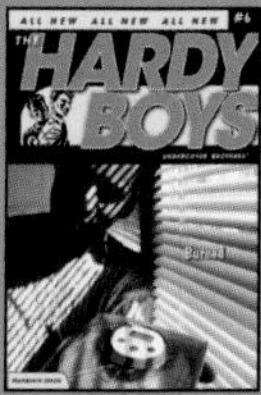

ALL NEW ALL NEW ALL NEW #6
THE HARDY BOYS
Burned

BURNED

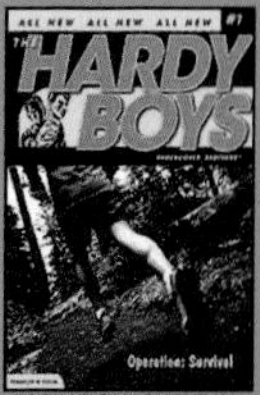

ALL NEW ALL NEW ALL NEW #7
THE HARDY BOYS
Operation: Survival

OPERATION: SURVIVAL

Look for a new book every other month, and collect them all!
Visit www.SimonSaysSleuth.com for more Hardy Boys adventures.

ALADDIN PAPERBACKS • SIMON & SCHUSTER CHILDREN'S PUBLISHING • WWW.SIMONSAYSKIDS.COM